Praise for *Anna's Crossing*

"Based on true events, this novel is a winner, especially for Amish-fiction enthusiasts."

—*Publishers Weekly*

"Those who summon the courage to read about the raw immigrant experience on this treacherous crossing will find a deeply satisfying story of conviction and hope."

—*Booklist*

"The touch of romance and many plot twists in *Anna's Crossing* keep Fisher's story entertaining."

—*BookPage*

"Anna and Bairn's sweet romance will satisfy readers with an interest in Amish history, as Fisher offers a look at the inhumane suffering they endured in their search for religious freedom."

—*RT Book Reviews*

"Unexpected twists and turns; themes of trust, faith, and letting go of the past; and a surprise ending add up to a thoroughly enjoyable read for Amish fiction fans."

—*CBA Retailers + Resources*

Praise for *The Newcomer*

"Full of adventure, suspense, an air of mystery, and sweet romance, the plot holds all the elements of an engaging story."

—*Christian Library Journal*

"The sights and sounds of the developing colonies and Philadelphia in 1737 complement Fisher's delightful rendering of such historical figures as Benjamin Franklin and enrich a more emotional, character-driven tale about identity, doubt, and belonging."

—*Booklist*

The Return

Books by Suzanne Woods Fisher

Amish Peace: Simple Wisdom for a Complicated World
Amish Proverbs: Words of Wisdom from the Simple Life
Amish Values for Your Family:
What We Can Learn from the Simple Life
A Lancaster County Christmas
Christmas at Rose Hill Farm
The Heart of the Amish

LANCASTER COUNTY SECRETS
The Choice
The Waiting
The Search

SEASONS OF STONEY RIDGE
The Keeper
The Haven
The Lesson

THE INN AT EAGLE HILL
The Letters
The Calling
The Revealing

THE BISHOP'S FAMILY
The Imposter
The Quieting
The Devoted

AMISH BEGINNINGS
Anna's Crossing
The Newcomer
The Return

AN AMISH BEGINNINGS NOVEL

The Return

SUZANNE
WOODS
FISHER

Revell

a division of Baker Publishing Group
Grand Rapids, Michigan

© 2017 by Suzanne Woods Fisher

Published by Revell
a division of Baker Publishing Group
P.O. Box 6287, Grand Rapids, MI 49516-6287
www.revellbooks.com

Printed in the United States of America

Library of Congress Cataloging-in-Publication Data
Names: Fisher, Suzanne Woods, author.
Title: The return / Suzanne Woods Fisher.
Description: Grand Rapids, MI : Revell, a division of Baker Publishing Group,
    [2017] | Series: Amish beginnings ; 3
Identifiers: LCCN 2017012176| ISBN 9780800727505 (pbk.) | ISBN 9780800728908
    (print on demand)
Subjects: LCSH: Amish—Fiction. | United States—History—18th century—Fiction.
    | GSAFD: Historical fiction. | Love stories. | Christian fiction.
Classification: LCC PS3606.I78 R47 2017 | DDC 813/.6—dc23
LC record available at https://lccn.loc.gov/2017012176

Most Scripture used in this book, whether quoted or paraphrased by the characters, is taken from the King James Version of the Bible.

Published in association with Joyce Hart of the Hartline Literary Agency, LLC

17 18 19 20 21 22 23   7 6 5 4 3 2 1

To the Benedicts,
my German Baptist family,
who first came to the New World at the invitation
of William Penn and settled in a corner of Penn's Woods.
Benedict means "good word." You're all that and more.

I take literally the statement in the Gospel of John that God loves the world. I believe that the world was created and approved by love, that it subsists, coheres, and endures by love, and that, insofar as it is redeemable, it can be redeemed only by love. I believe that divine love, incarnate and indwelling in the world, summons the world always toward wholeness, which ultimately is reconciliation and atonement before God.

—Wendell Berry

Cast of Characters

Note to readers: Many of these characters were first introduced in *Anna's Crossing*, and their stories were further explored in *The Newcomer*. Twenty-five years have passed since the little church of Ixheim stepped off the *Charming Nancy* ship in Port Philadelphia and settled into the New World. In *The Return*, you'll meet some new faces and get reacquainted with some familiar ones, though time might have weathered and grayed them a bit.

Tessa Bauer—fifteen-year-old daughter of Anna and Bairn Bauer, their only child.

Anna König Bauer—midforties, wife of Bairn, mother of Tessa. To quote Bairn, "She's the true minister in the family."

Bairn Bauer—midforties, minister to the Stoney Ridge Amish church. Husband to Anna, father to Tessa, brother to Felix. Highly skilled carpenter. Considered by many to be too lenient a minister, which suits him just fine.

Felix Bauer—midthirties, Bairn's younger brother, a

The Return

widowed father of twin boys, breeder of horses, a deacon in the Stoney Ridge Amish church. Convinced that Bairn gives him all the worst of the ministry jobs.

Hans Johann Bauer—early twenties, foster brother to Felix and Bairn, raised by their mother, Dorothea. Regarded as a talented blacksmith, one of the most important jobs in colonial America.

Dorothea Bauer—elderly and frail, widowed, mother to Bairn and Felix, foster mother to Hans.

Catrina Müller—midthirties, twice widowed, tutor to Felix's sons.

Maria Müller—elderly, widowed, mother to Catrina. The self-appointed busybody of the church.

Betsy Zook—seventeen years old, a fairly recent immigrant from Germany, lived on the frontier with her family.

Willie and Johnny Zook—Betsy's younger brothers, ages seven and nine, respectively.

Caleb—half-Mennonite, half Indian; his mother had been taken captive by the Indians; he became a slave to a Shawnee tribe.

John Elder—a Scots-Irish Presbyterian minister known as "the fighting parson." Lives in nearby Paxton.

Faxon Gingerich—German Mennonite neighbor to Bairn and Anna Bauer. Ordered the building of the Conestoga wagon. Tessa calls him Faxon the Saxon.

Martin Gingerich—Faxon's son, seventeen years old, sweet on Tessa. She calls him rumpled Martin.

10

Prologue

Up the Schuylkill River
November 16, 1762

As Betsy climbed up from the creek carrying two buckets of water, she heard the sound of her brothers' laughter, and then a man's deeper laugh. She stopped abruptly to listen, and cold water sloshed out of the buckets, spilling over her feet. She cocked her head, straining to listen; sound traveled downhill. Surely, the voice didn't belong to her father. He'd gone to Germantown early this morning to buy a new horse and wasn't expected until long after dark. And, of course, her father believed laughter and gaiety were the devil's handiwork. She heard the deep laugh again. Then she smiled.

Hans. He had come.

She quickened her step, moving as fast as the two heavy buckets allowed. Hans or no Hans, she had no desire to return to the soggy creek bank because her mother would need more water for the day's chores.

As she climbed the hill, her heart started to race and only partially because of exertion. Hans had *come*! He'd been to the Zook farm just a fortnight ago. He'd sent a letter to Betsy in the meantime, full of tender words and loving promises.

Six months ago, as her family had boarded that awful ship to sail to the New World, she never imagined that a man like Hans Bauer would be on the other side of the ocean, just waiting to meet her, waiting to fall in love with her. She had dreaded the journey—and it was every bit as horrific as she had heard about and feared and even worse—yet what she hadn't considered was that God's goodness would prevail.

Betsy stopped at the top of the hill to catch her breath. From where she stood on the crest, she could see Hans and her two brothers, Johnny and Willie, toss a pinecone back and forth to each other. Her mother leaned on the doorjamb of the open door to their crudely built log home, watertight for the coming winter but still so raw and unfinished. She was smiling, her mother, and Betsy was touched by the sight. There'd been little to smile over since little Marie had died on the ship. Hans had brought much to Betsy's family—joy, love, hope for the future.

She heard the jingle of a harness and turned to find a peddler and a donkey-pulled cart slowly making their way along the narrow Indian trail. She'd seen this man before. Her mother had bought an iron kettle from him a few weeks back. He waved to her and she set her buckets down. They didn't speak each other's languages, but a smile always worked. She pointed to the bucket of water and cupped her hands, mimicking that he should help himself to a drink.

The peddler eased himself off the cart. "Thank y', lassie. I'm a wee bit parched." He drank and drank, then let his donkey drink from the bucket. *Oh dear. Another trip to the creek.* She glanced down at the farmhouse. Mayhap Hans would go with her, and they could have time alone, without Johnny and Willie and their silly teasing.

The peddler wiped his mouth on his shirtsleeve. He peered at Betsy's prayer cap, barely covering her thick blonde hair, then took a few steps to the back of his cart. In it were two old battered trunks, tied with rope. He undid one knot and lifted the lid, rummaged through the trunk, all the while mumbling to himself. With an "Aha!" he found what he was looking for. He spun around and reached an open palm out to Betsy. In his hand was a hair clip. "A bonny lass deserves somethin' pretty."

She shouldn't accept such a fancy thing. Her father would be furious if he knew she took a gift from a peddler—even Hans would frown. But the clip was lovely, and it would be a sweet surprise for her mother on this beautiful autumn day while her father was away in Germantown. A secret between them to remind each other that it was always darkest just before dawn.

She reached out and took the clip from the peddler. "Denki," she said, and gave him a smile. "Viel denki." *Many thanks.*

He smiled, pleased, and re-tied the rope on the old trunk before climbing back on his cart. Clucking to his donkey, he went along his way. Betsy tucked the hair clip in her prayer cap, a hidden touch of fancy, and saw something off in the distance. Her skin prickled. A man, an Indian, was watching her from the far edges of the forest. She froze, held her breath. When she looked again, he had disappeared. Here and then gone.

Were the tree shadows playing tricks on her? Her brothers claimed they were always seeing Indians. Pure foolishness, their father insisted. She heard the fading jingles from the donkey's harness. Surely a peddler wouldn't be casually making his rounds if he'd heard word of restless warriors, and he'd be the first to hear. She shook off her dread. There was nothing to fear! She picked up the buckets and hurried down the hill to greet Hans.

1

Beacon Hollow
Lancaster County, Pennsylvania
April 20, 1763

Tessa Bauer stopped in her tracks when she heard the horse's huffing sound. Moving slowly, she hid behind a large tree and watched the stallion slide gracefully through the forest. It was the fifth time she'd seen the legendary horse. The phantom stallion, he was called. No one believed she'd actually ever seen him, no one except Felix, who believed everything she told him. He was sweet like that, her uncle Felix.

She'd grown up hearing all kinds of tales and rumors about this magnificent horse. The story had spun that he was a spirited Flemish stallion brought to Pennsylvania shortly after William Penn's arrival. The horse was meant for the Penn stables, but as the stallion was brought ashore, he managed to break loose and vanish into the deep wilderness. Over the years, rumors of sightings floated from Philadelphia to Lancaster Town, and greedy men would rally together to attempt a capture. All efforts proved futile, of course, because this was no ordinary horse and they were quite ordinary men.

And then five years ago, in late spring, a wild horse broke down Felix's pasture fence to mate with his broodmares just as they came into season. Felix was outraged at the intrusion and rebuilt the pasture into a near-fortress. Alas! Too late. The broodmares had been compromised.

Eleven months later, Felix was grinning ear to ear. There was no doubt in his mind, nor in Tessa's, that the newborn foals had been sired by the mighty and mysterious stallion. Even at birth, the foals were enormous. As quickly as Felix could, before his mares went into season, he lowered the pasture railing and prayed the stallion would return.

And so he did. For the last five springs, in the cover of night, the stallion returned to Felix's broodmare pasture. Felix had never seen him, not once, not like Tessa. He had tried—once he had accompanied Tessa into the woods to look for him. To wait and watch, but he wasn't patient, her uncle Felix, and stallion hunting required patience. The first time Felix's stomach rumbled for dinner, he gave up and set out for home. But he was grateful to the Flemish stallion, or more likely its son or grandson—whichever one it was that paid calls on his beguiling broodmares. He prayed it would continue. He dubbed this new breed of horses the Conestoga horse, named for the valley the wild stallion roamed.

Tessa stilled. She heard crunching. Slowly, so slowly, she peeked her head around the tree and saw the stallion had discovered the carrots she had left him, dug out of a storage barrel from her family's root cellar.

Oh my. He was a stunning animal, truly breathtaking.

If she reached out a hand, she could touch him, stroke his glossy black coat. He must know she was close by. His ability to smell her, to sense her nearness . . . he must know.

Dare she try? She leaned forward, reaching a hand out, when suddenly an eagle let out a shriek overhead and the wild horse startled, then bolted. He stopped, turned, and looked at Tessa—right at her, as if he recognized her!—before he trotted away and disappeared into the dense woods.

Wait, just wait, until Tessa told Uncle Felix the news. Spring had come, the wild stallion had returned. And she had made some headway in drawing close to him, at least enough headway that he looked less as if he was preparing to bolt. That was an improvement from last year's brief and unsuccessful encounters.

She hurried through the woods to get home. In one large jump, her long legs crested the rushing creek that ribboned her family's farm. As she climbed up the creek bank, she felt a rare, fleeting moment of gratefulness to have inherited her father's height. Bairn Bauer stood six foot six inches, and Tessa, at age fifteen, was five foot ten inches tall and still growing. But the moment of gratitude faded as suddenly as it had come, just as it always did. She hated towering over others, especially men and boys.

As she passed the sheep's pond, she slowed to a stop and bent over to study her reflection in the still water. The face she saw there was disappointing. A high forehead, short nose, cheeks sprinkled with freckles, deep-set eyes, a too-wide mouth. So plain, so very plain. Too plain to attract a man's notice, especially a man like Hans, who had won her heart over, for he was her hero.

Hans Bauer was a foster brother to Tessa's father, Bairn, and to her uncle Felix. He had been raised from birth by Tessa's grandmother, Dorothea, and shared her interest in horses. He was the blacksmith for the church, as well as many farming neighbors, as his skills at the forge were unsurpassed. Best of all, he was slightly taller than Tessa and handsome— more handsome than any man in Pennsylvania bar none— with a chiseled face, snapping brown eyes, a splendid chin, and wavy auburn hair that fell to his shoulders. Handsome Hans. She knew that giving such significance to a person's physical beauty was the way of the world and not *their* way, not the way of the straight and narrow, but she couldn't help herself. Tessa could never remember a time when her heart wasn't utterly devoted to Hans.

Sadly, he hardly noticed her.

She looked again at her reflection in the sheep pond. So grave, so serious. Perhaps if she smiled more. Her mother often said that a woman's beauty rested in her smile. She practiced a few smiles and thought she looked rather ridiculous. She could hear her mother's voice as clearly as if she were seated beside her: "Tessa, beauty is of very small consequence compared with good principles, good feelings, and good understanding."

Tommyrot. Beauty was beauty.

She jumped to her feet and ran toward Beacon Hollow, her home. As soon as she reached the lane that led to the large stone house, she slowed. There was Faxon Gingerich, their Mennonite neighbor across the way, bearing down on her atop his plow horse. Faxon the Saxon, she called him, though not in shot of his hearing. Beside him was his son, Martin, whom Tessa considered to be a boy of low character. She hadn't seen Martin in months and months, which suited her nicely. They were nearly the same age; he was a year or two older, though she was always head and shoulders taller than him. Tessa's father, who disliked farming but

18

loved carpentry, had hired Martin for the past few autumns to harvest the corn. The first year Martin was hired on, he started a vicious rumor that giants ran in Tessa's family, and given that she was a tiny bit sensitive about her height, she still hadn't forgiven him.

They halted their horses when they met up with her; she stood before them with her hands linked behind her back. Faxon the Saxon barely acknowledged her, but she expected as much. She was young, she was female, and she was not Mennonite. Three strikes, to his way of thinking. His gaze swept over the large yard, from the carpentry shop over to the sawmill down by the creek, seeking out evidence of her father's presence.

Martin sat awkwardly on his horse, his ill-fitting clothes dangling on him as if he hung on a hook. His pants were too short and his coatsleeves were too long. He wore no hat and his hair was unruly and wind-tossed, flying off in all directions. He was a rumpled mess. Rumpled Martin.

"Is he in the shop?" Faxon Gingerich said, not bothering to look at Tessa as he spoke.

"No. My father hasn't returned from the frontier yet," Tessa said. "My mother's expecting him back any day."

After bishop Jacob Hertzler had been injured in a fall two years ago—the only Amish bishop in all the New World—her father had traveled by horseback to the frontier twice a year to act on his behalf: marrying, burying, baptizing. The trip usually took him two weeks, but he'd been gone for three.

Faxon's glance shifted to the stone house before resting on Tessa, the wind tugging at his beard. "Do you know which direction your father headed?"

"Up the Schuylkill River."

Faxon stared at her, his face settling into deep lines.

Tessa felt the first ominous tickle start up her spine. "Have you news? Has something happened?"

Faxon's bushy eyebrows promptly descended in a frown, no doubt thinking she didn't know her place. It was a common complaint fired at Tessa. Who did she think she was, asking bold questions of an elder?

Worried about her father, that's what she was. Tessa stared back at him, her head held high, erect. "Is my father in danger?" Tessa looked from Faxon the Saxon to rumpled Martin and caught their concern. Something *had* happened.

Faxon ignored her question. "Where's your mother?"

"She's gone to a neighbor's to take a meal. They had a new baby. You know how she loves babies." Everybody knew that, everybody except for Faxon the Saxon. He wouldn't know that about Anna Bauer because he wouldn't care. He did not hold much regard for any Amish person apart from Bairn Bauer, for whom he had a grudging admiration.

Faxon swung a leg over his horse to dismount. "Has he made progress on the wagon?"

"Some. It's not finished though."

He stood, feet planted, and she knew exactly what he wanted. To see the wagon. Faxon Gingerich had come to her father last summer with a request for him to build a better hauling wagon. Faxon made frequent trips to Philadelphia to sell and trade products and was fed up with wagon wheels stuck in mud. The provincial government was abysmally slow to cobble roads, so he had decided there must be a better design for a wagon. He just couldn't figure one out.

Tessa wasn't sure her father would want her to show the unfinished project, but she was proud of his ingenuity, and she could tell Faxon would not be dissuaded from seeing it. "I'll show it to you if you like. I'll try to explain the design."

Rumpled Martin jumped off his horse, and she was startled to see that they were now about the same height. He noticed that she had noticed and gave her a big goofy grin. Appalling.

She led the way to her father's carpentry shop in silence. Hand tools hung neatly along the walls, but most of the shop was taken up with the enormous wooden wagon, eighteen feet from stern to bow. She opened the door and held it for Faxon, enjoying the sight of seeing his bearded jaw drop so low it hit his chest. It was not a common sight to see Faxon the Saxon look nonplussed, and Tessa relished the moment. Savored it.

She inhaled the scent of wood shavings, linseed oil, and wax. Smells associated with her father. Worry circled her mind like bees around flowers. Where *was* he?

Faxon's gaze roamed slowly over the wagon; he peered into it, then below it. Its base sat on wooden blocks, as her father hadn't made wheels yet. "A rounded base? What could he be thinking?"

He had immediately honed in on the most noteworthy improvement that Tessa's father had made—the one that set it apart from all other wagons. "It's like the keel of a ship. My father used to be a sailor. He said that the curved bottom would keep barrels and goods from shifting and tipping and rolling around."

"If he can pull that off, it will be a miracle," Faxon muttered. He and his awful son walked around the wagon, crawled under it, bent low to examine each part of it, murmuring to each other in maddeningly low voices.

"My father said this wagon will be able to haul as much as six tons of freight."

Faxon Gingerich shot up from a bent position so fast that his long, wiry beard bounced against his round belly. "*How* much?"

"Six tons. Assuming, of course, that you've plenty of horsepower to pull that kind of weight."

With that piece of information, everything changed. Faxon's countenance lightened, he continued inspecting the wagon but without the constant frown.

"It's not meant for people to ride in it," Tessa said. "Strictly a freight wagon. The teamster walks along the left side."

The frown was back. "No place for a teamster to sit?"

"There's a board for him to sit if he grows weary." Tessa bent down and slid out a wooden board.

"How many oxen would be needed to pull six tons of freight?"

"Quite a few. At least six."

Faxon's forehead puckered.

"Or horses could be used too."

"Not possible," Faxon said. "They're not strong enough. Has to be oxen."

"My uncle Felix has bred a type of horse that can pull the kind of heavy freight that the Conestoga wagon can carry."

Now Faxon's bushy eyebrows shot up to his hairline. "The Conestoga wagon?"

"That's what my father calls it. To honor your valley. He said you gave him the idea for it. Credit goes to you."

Faxon the Saxon's chest puffed out and he very nearly smiled. It often puzzled Tessa how personal significance was needed for men to see things clearly. Their secret pride.

"Looks nearly finished to me. Just missing wheels."

"Wheels, yes, but there's still quite a bit of hardware to be made," Tessa said. "Plus pitch will be needed make the seams watertight. And my mother and Maria Müller will sew canvas cloth to cover the wagon bows, front to back."

Rumpled Martin regarded her thoughtfully. "You seem to know a lot about it."

Sarcasm. He may be taller now but he was just as rude. She ignored him and spoke only to his father. "You can find out more about it after my father returns."

Faxon's pleased look instantly faded. He exchanged a look with rumpled Martin, whose misgiving showed plain on his face. A dark cloud descended in the carpentry shop. Something *had* happened along the frontier. "Tell me what's happened."

Faxon's face flattened and he went stone still for a full minute. "Trouble has come to our brethren in the north. There's been another Indian attack on families who settled along the Schuylkill River."

Tessa felt an unsettling weakness in the base of her stomach. These stories had become too common. "Did you recognize any names?"

"Just one. Zook. William and Martha Zook. The parents were found dead, the children were taken captive."

Tessa's heart started to pound. "Betsy Zook?"

"A girl said to be about your age. Smaller than you, though." His eyes skimmed her from head to toe. "Much, much shorter. Blonde hair."

Tessa gave a slight jerk of her chin. *That's her, that's Betsy.* The Zooks had immigrated to Berks County from Germany just about a year and a half ago. Tessa had met Betsy when the Amish churches gathered for spring and fall communion.

Betsy was a beautiful girl, beloved by all, kind to the core. Tessa disliked her.

Betsy was everything Tessa wasn't. She was petite while Tessa was tall. She was curvy while Tessa was a table—flat with long thin arms and legs. She was perpetually kind while Tessa had touchy feelings.

But Tessa's dislike had nothing to do with Betsy. It had to do with Hans Bauer. From the moment they met, Hans fancied Betsy Zook.

A sick feeling roiled in Tessa's middle. So often, she had wished Betsy's family would just move away, go west. Go east. Go somewhere. She had even prayed for it! Especially so, after she learned that Hans had gone to visit Betsy, numerous times.

But she had never wished for Betsy to be a victim of an Indian attack, to be taken captive.

Faxon Gingerich swept a glance over the large stone house her father had built, strong and sturdy. "Your father did well to bring you all down here, so many years ago, although your grandfather wanted to stay north. The frontier has become a devil's playground."

Faxon and Martin walked back to the horses and mounted them.

"I will pray your father returns safely and soundly," Faxon said, before turning his horse around and starting down the lane.

"Don't worry, Tessa," rumpled Martin said. "I'm sure he'll be home soon." He gave her a reassuring smile before cantering off to join his father.

Until that moment, it had never occurred to Tessa that her father might not return at all.

❧

Lancaster Town, Pennsylvania

The news of the Indian attacks had spread all over Lancaster Town. Felix Bauer had finished his business at the trading post, pleased that he had been able to trade his brother Hans's newly forged iron tools for a winter's pile of skins from Will Sock, a Conestoga Indian. He could use those skins to make harnesses for this new breed of horses. The size of that young colt in his pasture—sixteen hands? Seventeen? And still growing. It was a freak of nature.

And that put it right up Felix's alley. He was fascinated by anything and everything that jolted a person's staid expectations. Just last month, he'd found a three-legged bear hiding in a cave. Most folks would have turned tail and run, but not Felix Bauer. He set a trap, caught the three-legged bear, brought it to a frolic to show everyone because there was often doubt and speculation about his weird sightings, rumors to squelch that he was prone to exaggeration. Then he carried it, caged, in a wagon up into the mountains and let it go. Hans said he was crazy. He should've shot the three-legged bear for its pelt, but Felix saw it differently. He'd thought the bear'd had a hard enough life, and if it could survive on three legs, it deserved a chance to live.

Anyway, there Felix was, pleased as could be over his last trade of the day, ready to head home with a wagon full of deerskins, but he couldn't find Hans, which meant he couldn't find his nine-year-old twin boys, either. They followed Hans like two puppies, but Felix wasn't confident of his ability to mind children. A few weeks ago, after the last visit to Lancaster Town, he found the three of them in the front of a

crowd, examining the heads of two renegade Indians stuck
on a pole. It was not uncommon to display gruesome sights
in the center of town to warn others of misdeeds, but Felix
couldn't believe that Hans would allow his boys to gawk at
two human heads, so recently killed.

Felix heard the boys before he saw them. Rifle shots, then
a loud cheer. He shook his head. Hans must be involved in
a shooting match.

Shooting matches were often held for a prize: a fat turkey,
a jug of whisky, or a rifle. The target was usually the fairly
large head of a handmade nail, and the range was about
sixty yards. There were tales of men who could hit the nail
head squarely with two bullets out of three. It dawned on
him that was probably where the expression came from: to
hit the nail on the head.

Well, Felix sighed, at least he knew where they were.

He stopped at the town well to fill a water bucket for his
horse and listened to the excited talk about a recent Indian
attack coming from a clump of men.

Felix drew water up from the well and filled his bucket.
Half listening, half preoccupied with how hungry he was—
the scent of baking bread floated over from a nearby oven—
and then he wondered if he should buy the boys something
to eat now or wait until they reached home. These Indian
attacks were usually half rumor, half truth, and he didn't
want to bother ferreting out the difference.

All eyes were fixed on one man who seemed to be the
source of information, a stout fellow with a head too small
for his round middle. "On Monday," this news bearer said,
"an unsuspecting farmer was tomahawked right in his cornfield. It was a warning sign, so the neighbors all forted to-

gether. They figured they'd be safer that way, but it must have acted like a honey pot for the Indians. Back they came in the dead of night. They surrounded the farmhouse, howling their eerie death halloos."

The gathered men exchanged anxious looks. The death halloo was a horrifying shriek, a sound that filled the air and lingered. It was the sound made by a warrior, a scalp yell, after killing his victim.

"Where'd you hear this?" one fellow asked.

"I just come from there. One boy escaped the raid by hiding in a hollow tree. He waited in the tree until daybreak until he was sure no Indian was left. Then he ran for help." The news bearer shook his head. "Poor little bugger. Only six or seven years old and he saw his parents killed. He said his brother and sister were taken away."

Felix winced at the news. It was a troubling time for the frontier settlers, stirred up by seven years of war between the French and the British. Indian attacks came unexpectedly and created great fear among the vulnerable farming families. The raids were increasing as squatters moved onto Indian hunting grounds—land reserved for their use by William Penn himself—yet the squatters refused to leave. In retaliation, the Indians burned houses, brutally killed men, women, and children, scalping them, leaving their bodies for wild animals to feast on.

Felix pushed himself into the circle of men. "Where did this happen?"

"Up the Schuylkill River."

A chill danced up his spine. That's where his brother Bairn had been traveling. Felix was suddenly aware that his two boys had eased up beside him. From the corner of his eye, he saw Hans slip next to him, a questioning look on his face.

"What's happened, Felix?" Hans said.

Felix glanced at his sons. Switching from their dialect to English so his sons would not understand, he said, "There was another Indian attack up north."

"Anywhere close to where Bairn went?" Hans asked.

Felix looked into Hans's face and saw that he was as shocked as he was by the gravity of the situation. He gave a brief nod and turned to the news bearer. "Do you know any names of the families? Or what church they were part of?"

"No. All I know is it was their own fault. They were pacifists. Pathetic." The news bearer appraised Felix's garb curiously, his large-brimmed felt hat, his handwoven brown overcoat, his moustacheless beard, and realized he must be one of those pathetic pacifists. "They wouldn't fight back. Just stayed frightened to death in their house until the savages put them to death and stole their children. It's their own fault."

Felix reached for his sons' hands and gripped them tightly, as if he could protect them from all the troubles of the world.

Hans jabbed him in the ribs with his elbow. "This is just what John Elder warns us about, Felix."

Felix didn't raise his head to look at Hans. John Elder, a neighbor in nearby Paxton, was a Scots-Irish preacher known as the Fighting Parson because he kept a rifle in his pulpit and encouraged his parishioners to bring their rifles to church. John Elder was an avowed Indian hater and stirred up trouble even when there was none. Felix considered John Elder to be a fool; Hans considered him a prophet.

The news bearer opened his saddlebag and pulled out a large family Bible, a Froschauer Bible. He held it out to Felix. "You're one of 'em, ain't you? I found it in the cellar."

"You were looting?" Hans said, bitterness in his voice. "Plundering the homes of those poor beleaguered people?"

The man scowled. "I was burying the dead."

And afterward, Felix thought, helped himself to what was left from the raid.

"Take it. I don't want it. It's giving me nothin' but bad luck."

"You stole a Bible," Hans said. "The most cherished possession a family had in their keeping. They brought it all the way over from Europe. And you stole it."

"You'd rather it be left for the Indians to desecrate?" The stout man jammed it in Hans's hands. "I don't want it. I can't understand a word in it. Take it."

Still gripping his boys' hands, Felix started toward the horse and wagon. After the boys scrambled in the back and found a spot to settle on top of the skins, he untied the reins, expecting Hans to have already climbed on the wagon seat. But Hans hadn't budged from the water well.

Felix retied the reins to the hitching post and walked over to him. "We'd best get home."

Hans looked as if he'd been struck by lightning. "I know this Bible. I've held this Bible in my hands. I've heard Betsy's father read from it."

"It can't be, Hans. Bibles look alike." Felix took it out of Hans's hands and opened it to the center. There was the family history, recorded in a spidery handwriting. He ran a finger down the page until he came to Betsy Zook's name, entered on the day of her birth: *Elizabeth Ann Zook, b. July 28, 1746.*

Hans saw it, bent over, and wretched, right on the well.

2

Beacon Hollow

For two nights in a row, Anna Bauer had startled awake, woken from a disturbing nightmare. In her dream, she saw her husband, Bairn, tied between two trees while savage warriors built a fire at his feet. She could do nothing to save him, but stood watching while he begged for mercy. She bolted up in bed, heart beating like a drum, praying that God had not sent the dream to prepare her, to fortify her for what was to come, so it was not entirely a surprise to her when Maria Müller first arrived to relay the news of the attack on the Schuylkill settlers.

One by one, neighboring women arrived at Beacon Hollow to gather in Anna's kitchen, intending to bring succor. Instead, they heightened the drama with a mixture of facts and fears. They sat at the large wooden table that Bairn had built, sharing news that had trickled in from Lancaster Town.

April sunshine fell through the window and illuminated Anna's hands. The beauty of it should have calmed her, but it served as a stark reminder of how far from peace she felt.

She hooked the teakettle on the trammel in the fireplace and noticed that her hands were shaking. Her last words to Bairn, before he'd left to go on the circuit, were a warning. *Be careful*, she had said, grasping on to him as if she could hold him back. She knew Bairn's life was in God's hands, that he was as safe on the frontier as he was in his carpenter's shop. She *knew* that, but she had felt an uncommon anxiety as he set off to go north. He would be utterly vulnerable.

It wouldn't take much to provoke warring Indians to attack a white man alone on horseback. The frontier had quieted after seven years of war between the French and the British, but as more settlers arrived, absorbing hunting grounds into farms, skirmishes with the Indian had started up again.

Anna was aware that the Amish of Berks County did all they could to remain on good terms with the Indians, offering friendship and hospitality, sharing bounty from their fields. Whenever Bairn went north, he brought gifts of food with him to give to any Indians he encountered. He encouraged the Berks County settlers to do the same, especially after the Jacob Hochstetler tragedy. Jacob's wife had refused food to an Indian who had appeared in her kitchen one day. Whether truth or rumor, it was thought to be the reason the Hochstetler family was targeted for an attack when other settlers were left alone. Jacob and two sons were taken captive, his wife and their other children were killed.

For the longest time after the Hochstetler attack, the women in Anna's church worried the story over and over. They repeated gruesome details as if the event had just transpired: the mutilated bodies, the charred timbers of the house, the missing sons.

And then they added the bits and pieces of what they

claimed to know about those ruthless Indians: they delighted in torture, they ate white babies, they took pleasure in unhinging the white man's mind.

On this afternoon, waiting for the water to heat in the kettle, Anna let the women talk amongst themselves as she spooned tea leaves into cheesecloth and twisted the bundle tight. She took her time letting it steep in the steaming water. She knew the women were tiptoeing around the subject that was on everyone's mind: Where was Bairn? Had he been hurt in the attack? He should have returned days ago.

Everyone stilled when a noise was heard outside. Anna rushed to the door and opened it wide to peer down the lane. A farmer in an ox-drawn wagon passed slowly on the road beyond the garden fence. The clatter of his iron-rimmed wheels raised a trail of dust. She closed the door and managed a shaky smile at her friends. She poured each woman a mug of tea and set it before them.

Maria Müller sipped her tea, then puckered her lips. "Those Iroquois do not govern themselves by reason, let alone good sense."

"I've heard that they chop off their victims' hands and feet and flaunt scalps as trophies," added Barbara Gerber.

Others quickly chimed in.

"They're savage pagans who need to be civilized and converted."

"I've heard that once they've exhausted their cruelties, they kill the men with a blow to their head. And before they kill the women, they defile them."

Anna felt the hair on the back of her neck rise, though it was safely pinned beneath her prayer cap. Stunned and sickened, she listened to it all without a word, grateful that

Tessa wasn't in the kitchen to overhear. Her daughter had a vivid enough imagination as it was.

Earlier this afternoon, after Anna had returned from a visit to welcome a neighbor's new baby, she had sat by the fire to sew the hem of Tessa's favorite dress. Her daughter grew like a weed; she had hardly finished hemming a dress when it needed to be let down. She had set the task down when Maria arrived at the door. Now, she reached over to her sewing basket and picked up the dress to finish the hemming, to avoid listening to the women's recycled terrors. She examined her stitches, trying to settle her mind by finding comfort in a common household chore. An ordinary dress for an ordinary day.

Or were ordinary days a thing of the past?

If this were an ordinary day, Bairn would be walking through the door soon after spending hours either at the sawmill beside the creek that wove along their property or in his beloved carpentry shop, hungry as a bear.

She squeezed her eyes shut. Where could Bairn be? Why hadn't there been some word about him? How could word travel of the attack so quickly down from the top of the Schuylkill, and yet nothing of her husband's whereabouts?

Anna rebuked herself for her worrisome thoughts. Those poor families up the Schuylkill would never again have an ordinary day, and here she was fretting about her husband, strong and capable and savvy to the ways of the wilderness. She picked up her sewing and went back to her work.

Still, she could not keep her mind from returning to the same question: where was Bairn?

It was nearly twilight by the time the women finally left Beacon Hollow. Tessa walked toward the house with a rock in her heart. Her mother sat by the giant stone fireplace, staring at the smoldering fire, a worried look on her face. She hadn't even heard Tessa come in.

"Mem? Mem? Are you all right?"

Her mother jerked, startled. "Oh, Tessa. Yes, I'm fine." She rose, gave her a soft smile, and reached out her hand to her. "Where have you been? Maria was asking for you."

Which was exactly the reason Tessa stayed out in the barn, watching the sheep and her new twin lambs until they left. She was no fool. Maria Müller made her feel like a pecked chicken. She fussed over Tessa, talking about her as if she wasn't even there. "How tall is she now, Anna?" "Goodness, Bairn is going to have to raise the roof." "When will she stop growing?" "She's taller than every man in the county, barring her own father."

Early Monday morning, Maria had arrived at Beacon Hollow and settled herself by the hearth for what appeared to be a rather long visit. "I've come to keep you company, Anna, whilst Bairn is off on circuit," she announced, as if she were bestowing a great favor.

Tessa had started for the door, but her mother put a hand on her arm and gripped it tightly. She wasn't going to let her escape from chores that easily. Her mother turned to Maria with a sweet smile coating her firm words. "You're always welcome in our home, Maria. But in any case, it is Monday and there's work to be done to prepare for Sunday church. Don't mind us as we finish our chores." Then her countenance softened. "Bairn will be home any day now, and we want him to have a clean home to come to."

Tessa thought their home was plenty clean, but never-theless, she and her mother spent the morning in a frenzy of housecleaning, rousting dust and cobwebs from the corners of all three downstairs rooms. Maria remained cozy by the fire, chattering about anything that flittered through her mind, most of which was utterly trivial, complete nonsense, while Tessa and her mother waited on her hand and foot. Tessa was so eager to flee the kitchen that she even volunteered to load the woodbox—anything to get outside and away from Maria's endless stream of babble. Her mother said no.

By the time the house was cleaned and they gathered around the table for noon dinner, Tessa was ravenously hun-gry. Too hungry to notice that Maria's beady eyes were fixed on her. Too hungry to keep a check on her quick temper, which Maria had a way of tweaking.

Maria turned to Anna, seated next to her. "Has Tessa started her monthlies yet? She won't stop growing until the flows start, you know." In a gloomy tone, she added, "Oh, I do hope she won't have the trouble you've had bearing children, Anna."

Tessa was suddenly and fiercely angry. She rose to her feet. "My monthly flows are none of your concern! *None!*"

It was a bold and impulsive statement. As soon as Tessa spoke it, she regretted having done so. She pressed her hand over her mouth and stared at Maria, then at her mother, expecting shock to register on their faces.

It did. Shock combined with indignation.

Maria rose to her feet, nose wrinkled, mouth puckered, her bony shoulders pulled back and her chest lifted high, as if she'd just sucked in a deep breath and dared not let it go. Without another word, she scooped up her black bonnet and swept out the door. Tessa's mother followed Maria outside, soothing her ruffled feathers, trying to make amends. It must not have been successful because she was soon back in the kitchen and, through the window, Tessa could see Maria spanking her pony's rump with the reins to hurry her down the lane.

Tessa whispered a feeble apology. "I know you're angry."

"Not angry. But I am terribly disappointed in you for not holding your tongue."

That was worse, Tessa knew. At least when anger vented, it was over and done with. Disappointment lingered.

Anna picked up plates from the table and put them in a bucket to wash. "You're fifteen years old, Tessa. Nearly a woman. You must not let your frustrations boil to the surface."

"But Maria can be so vexing!"

Her mother's lips tightened. "She has known you since you were born. You're like a granddaughter to her. She worries about you."

"Why does she have to stay at our home for hours and hours?"

"Because she's lonely in that empty house." Her mother picked up a broom and handed it to Tessa. "She shouldn't have spoken so frankly about private matters. I know she vexes you. But it wasn't cruel, what she said. What you said to her—that was downright rude."

"It's how I felt. My monthlies are not her concern." Tessa was worried enough about her monthlies or, rather, the lack of them.

"She's lonely, Tessa. Loneliness can cause people to dwell on things. They have too much time to think."

Later that afternoon, Tessa took a loaf of freshly baked bread over to Maria's with a contrived apology, determined to sound heartfelt. She wrote the script in her mind all the way as she walked down the road.

To her shock, when she knocked on Maria's door, she was invited in and warmly welcomed. As Tessa stood in the middle of the little room, she got a sense of how lonely Maria's life was. One plate, one cup, one fork. Her husband, Christian, had passed, her daughter, Catrina, had moved away years ago. She'd closed off most of the rooms in the house and set her bed in the kitchen, near the fireplace. And it was only a small fire, barely warming the room.

Tessa felt the tiniest glimmer of compassion for Maria. Yet something seemed odd. Maria was pleasant looking; her face wasn't all pinched up and puckered the way it normally looked. And goose feathers littered the kitchen floor, spilling out of a sack by the hearth. There were even feathers on top of Maria's prayer cap. "You seem happy." It was an unusual sight.

A big smile filled Maria's thin face. "I am. I am uncommonly happy."

Tessa wondered if she might have partaken in strong drink. "Are you making new pillows?" she asked, gesturing to a neat pile of cotton fabric on the tabletop. Store-bought fabric! Not the coarse linen sheets Tessa slept on. She knew that Maria rarely spent a penny except for necessities.

"I am. I have cause for celebration." Maria pulled a letter from her apron pocket and a feather lifted from her shoulder and floated to the ground. "When I returned home today, I found a letter at my doorstep. My daughter, Catrina, is moving home. Within a few weeks' time, she said."

Oh, what a relief! Maria would have someone to fuss over and leave Tessa alone. After delivering her apology to Maria for being rude and receiving a pardon of forgiveness, she had practically skipped all the way home. That happiness had carried Tessa all the way from yesterday until this afternoon, when Faxon Gingerich gave her news about the Indian attack on the Zook family.

She watched her mother, who kept one eye peeled on the windows as if she expected to see her father riding in any minute. The last of the day's light slipped through two west-facing windows and made yellow stripes on the planked wooden floors. There were six windows in all, two each facing west, east, and south. Some church members had criticized Tessa's father for adding luxury and extravagance with those windows, as if flaunting his wealth.

While it was true that the Bauers were the wealthiest family in the church, it was not the reason he had built the house with so many windows. Having windows was something Tessa's parents felt was a necessity, not a luxury.

Tessa's father had lived on the open sea and did not like to feel confined to dark rooms. And her mother still shuddered whenever she spoke of the lower decks of the *Charming Nancy* that brought the church of Ixheim to the New World. The darkness had felt oppressive. Tessa set the table with two pewter plates and two spoons. Such a large table, flanked by solid and straight chairs. Her father had built it, planning for children to fill each chair, but it was not what God had in mind for them. Out in the family graveyard were three little graves alongside her father's father and her mother's grandparents. Tessa was their only daughter, and the only child to survive the first year of infancy.

Her mother took a kettle off a lug pole set across the inside of the chimney, hanging low over the fire. Potpie, her father's favorite. She made a point of fixing it on the day she expected him home. He said it made the journey home swift and sweet, to think of potpie waiting for him on the table.

Potpie was the first dish Tessa had learned to make, because it was simple to make and didn't require close attention from the cook. Almost any kind of meat sufficed for potpie, though her father's favorite was lamb. It was "spoon meat" and leftovers could be stretched with added ingredients and reheated to be just as good, sometimes even better, on the second day.

At the hearth, Tessa's mother opened the lid to her bake kettle to check on the corn pone. It was another of her father's favorites: soft and succulent in its center, a thick crust around it. The bake kettle was a Christmas gift from Tessa's father, designed by him and forged by Handsome Hans in his smithy shop. The pot had three legs so it could sit in the ashes. The lid was inside, resting on a ledge an inch below the rim. With such a kettle, Tessa's mother could brown her pone on top by covering the lid with hot coals. She often made it the night before and set it in the hot ashes on the hearth, ready for breakfast.

Clearly, her mother had been expecting her father home today.

Her mother set the bake kettle on a flat stone on the table to cool and looked up at Tessa. "So what else did Faxon Gingerich say about the attack?"

"He didn't call it an attack. He called it a massacre. And he said that Betsy Zook had been taken captive. Her brothers too."

Her mother stilled, then sank into a chair. In a trembling voice, she asked, "Are they sure it was the Zooks? Our Zooks? Could it be a rumor? Rumors have wings on them."

"Faxon Gingerich seemed to be sure." Tessa sat down at the table facing her mother. "Why would they steal children?"

"Different reasons," her mother said in a quiet voice. "Some are taken to be slaves."

"Slaves?"

"Meant for labor." Tessa must have had a horrified look on her face because her mother was quick to add, "It's not just the Indians who take captives. It's an age-old practice around the world. Even Europeans used to capture others to acquire laborers."

Tessa rubbed her finger along the smooth edge of the table. "Will they hurt Betsy?"

"I think . . ." Her mother hesitated, just slightly, but enough that Tessa knew she was carefully weighing her words. "I think that if they wanted to hurt her, they would have done so. Capture is rarely an act of caprice."

"Caprice?"

She lifted her eyes. "Whim. Rarely done on a whim."

"What will they do with Betsy? Will she be able to stay with her brothers?"

"I don't know. Captives are taken to avenge losses or to replace lost relatives. Sometimes it's for ransom." She turned to look into the fire. "Or perhaps for assimilation. As tribute." She glanced at Tessa. "Adoption."

"Betsy might be adopted as an Indian?"

"Among some tribes, it's a tradition to replace a dead brother or sister through adoption."

"Why? Why would they want someone who doesn't want to be with them?"

"They believe the spirit of their loved ones resides in those they adopt, including white captives."

"But it's more likely she would be ransomed, isn't it? The British soldiers will find where she's been taken and offer a ransom for her, wouldn't they?"

"I wish I could say yes, but I've always told you the truth, Tessa. And the truth in this case is that I just don't know. It's hard to predict what the British soldiers would do about ransoming child captives. Sometimes, captives never do return to their homes. They adjust to their new life, grow fond of their new families. I've even heard when some are offered liberty, they choose instead to stay with the Indians."

As she and her mother sat at supper, Tessa bowed her head for a silent prayer. The Bible taught to be thankful in all things. All things. But her heart wasn't feeling a bit thankful. Her old dog Zeeb, given to her as a pup by a Conestoga Indian named Will Sock, sensed her turmoil and put his head down on top of her feet.

She and her mother ate in silence, both lost in their thoughts. Tessa could barely eat, she just pushed her food around on the plate with her fork.

Her mother put her spoon down and said, "Papa will be home soon, Tessa. Don't overworry his absence."

Tessa nodded and managed to find her voice. "I'm not. I mean, I am, but it's not just Papa I'm worried about." She twisted a corner of her apron. "There were so many times I wished Betsy had never moved here. Times I prayed she would just go away."

From the moment Tessa had first met her, over a year ago,

she had resented Betsy. She recalled standing at the window, watching Betsy light from her wagon when her family came for a church gathering. Betsy was the smallest woman she'd ever seen, as small as a child. Tessa remembered being transfixed by her face, her rosebud mouth, smooth white skin, and those luminous eyes. They were astonishing eyes, pale blue and brimming with a mixture of innocence and wisdom. Her thick, curly blonde hair refused to be constrained by her prayer covering; tendrils of ringlets framed her face, floating on the slightest breeze.

But the vision that was seared in her mind was how Hans had reacted to Betsy. He watched her with the tenderest of care. Almost worshipfully. Tessa had hated Betsy from that very first moment. Hated her!

"You prayed for Betsy to leave because of Hans?"

Her mother's voice startled her, snapping her back to the present. Tessa nodded. A tear fell on her lap, one, then another. "Is it possible my prayer came true?"

"God doesn't answer our prayers because we wish Him to. And He doesn't dislike the people we dislike either. That would amount to making God in our own image. He answers prayers for our good, and for the good of others." She sighed. "It was a selfish desire—to want Hans's attention all to yourself. You can't control a person's heart. But I am sure you would not have wished this terrible thing upon Betsy."

That *was* true. Tessa might not be the most charitable person in her church, but she would not have wanted such a horror to be inflicted on anyone, even Betsy Zook. "Mem, do you think Papa has encountered the warriors?"

"Faxon Gingerich seemed to have specific details of who had been killed or taken captive, did he not?"

"Yes. Yes, he did."

"And your father's name was not mentioned."

"No."

"Fear and horror are terrible things, Tessa. They feed on each other. I caution you to guard your thoughts so that fear does not run away with them." She handed a mug of warm milk to her. "Go now, get some sleep. Tomorrow will come soon enough." She smiled. "You can take the dog upstairs with you tonight. And add Betsy Zook and her brothers to your prayers tonight."

"Of course." Tessa felt the sting of her words, for it had not occurred to her to pray for Betsy.

As she trudged up the stairs, she wished for the hundredth time that she were more like her mother. Somehow, Tessa's mother did not allow herself to let worries settle in. It was her great faith, her father always said. That's what gave Anna Bauer the ability to face life head-on.

What if her father had been hurt in an attack? What if no one knew he'd been killed? She could hear his voice in the rafters, imagine what he would say and do if he were with her. He would grab her shoulders and press her firmly into a chair, admonishing her with his thick Scottish brogue because he knew how she loved to hear it. "Yer imagination is far too active, Tessa darlin'. Y' must seek t' control its excesses."

She set her candle on the nightstand and sat on the sag in the middle of her rope bed—another thing suffering under her father's absence. Her bed ropes needed tightening and only her father was strong enough to do it just right. Tears filled her eyes and she dropped to her knees to pray for God's mercy. She resolved to strive more earnestly for a pure heart, an obedient heart, to please God with her thoughts and to disabuse Handsome Hans of any romantic thoughts. Before she rose to her feet, she asked God to watch over Betsy, to protect her. To bring her home.

But Betsy Zook no longer had a home.

Tessa unpinned her long hair and brushed out the day's tangles, then tucked it all back into a nightcap. Though it was late and she was exhausted, she couldn't sleep. She lay staring at the tree shadows that moved across the windows in the wind. She thought about Indians and their fierce pagan ways, their disquieting stealth. She tried a trick her father had taught her to aid sleep: to imagine she was on a ship, and her churning thoughts were only the sea, rocking her bed as it had rocked her father's ships.

Still, her mind refused to settle.

Old Zeeb lifted his head, ears pricked. Tessa lurched to her feet and moved to the window to peer down at the path that led to the house. She heard the sound of hooves pounding toward the house. Her father? Had he come home?

She ran down the steps and met her mother at the door, her hand on the latch. "Bairn?" her mother called through the thick wooden door.

"It's me, Anna. It's Felix. I have news about Bairn."

Her mother unlatched the door and flung it open.

3

Beacon Hollow

"He's safe, Bairn is."

Felix stepped in and walked to the large hearth fire. As he warmed his hands over the glowing coals, he looked over his shoulder at Anna. He saw Tessa sit down on the bottom step of the stairs and circle her knees with her arms. "He wanted you to know. He'll return in the morrow."

"Thank God," Anna breathed, sagging with relief. "Where is he? When did you cross paths with him?"

"He sent word by a messenger to Not Faxon's Farm. He wanted someone with you when you got the . . . when you heard the news."

"Because of the Indian attacks?"

Felix turned to face Anna. "So, you've heard, then."

She nodded. "Faxon Gingerich came by to see the wagon Bairn is building. He told Tessa that he heard Betsy Zook had been taken captive."

"I heard as much in Lancaster Town." Felix dropped his eyes to his hands. "The messenger said that Bairn had been lodging at Jacob Hertzler's when the attacks occurred."

"I was concerned he would be overtaken on a trail." Anna covered her face with her hands, and dropped her chin to her chest in relief.

Felix realized Anna had been far more worried about Bairn than she let on. She was like a second mother to him, always had been, and it startled him to see her shaken. She was never shaken. She was a rock.

"Where is he now?"

"He went to Lancaster Town to meet with the sheriff. A boy, one of the Zook boys, he hid in a hollow tree, waited out the attack, escaped and made it to the Hertzlers'. Smart boy, and young too. It was decided that Bairn would bring the boy to Lancaster with him, that it wasn't safe to keep him up north. The sheriff wanted to ask the boy about the attacks. He's the only living eyewitness." He waited a moment to let her take in the information. "Bairn wrote to tell you he'll be coming in tomorrow and bringing the boy with him, unless you'd rather he find another foster home."

"Of course I don't mind," Anna said. "Of course we don't, do we, Tessa?"

She turned to Felix's favorite niece, his only niece, who dipped her head in quick assent. "There's plenty of room upstairs."

"I wouldn't mind having him at Not Faxon's Farm. He could play with the boys." The name of Felix's land had evolved into Not Faxon's Farm because Mennonite neighbor Faxon Gingerich applied steady and persistent pressure to sell him the farm after a winter flood shifted the course of a stream bordering their properties. The stream no longer ran though Faxon's land but through Felix's, and he wanted that water to build a gristmill.

Felix considered the shifting stream as a sign of God's providence, a blessing on his horse farm, and refused to sell. Plus, he did not like Faxon Gingerich for many reasons, particularly so after he heard him refer to the Amish as second-class Mennonites. So Felix wouldn't budge, nor would he retaliate in verbal barbs. But he did start calling his land Not Faxon's Farm and the name stuck.

The fire was dying down and Anna, just noticing, rose to bank it. "Don't worry, Anna. I can't stay long."

Nonetheless, she added some kindling to warm the room. "How is Hans?"

Tessa's ears perked up. Felix noticed that kind of thing. "Well, that's one reason why it might be best not to have Betsy's brother at Not Faxon's Farm. There's no calming Hans. He's wild with worry. I wish I could assure him that Betsy will soon be found and restored." He shrugged. "But I don't know that. I don't have any idea what will become of her. There's no assurance that her captors will be kind."

Anna took some oatmeal cookies out of a tin, Bairn's favorites, and handed a few to him. As he chewed, he realized he was hungrier than he thought. Not so much for food, but for a woman's way with food.

"Hans wants to go after Betsy," Felix said, "but I told him no, to sit tight, to wait until more information is found out. Hans doesn't want to wait. He's like a caged animal. He has to keep moving, he can't be still. I fear that having Betsy's brother in our home would only stir up his distress."

"Mem says that they won't kill Betsy," Tessa said. "She thinks they would have killed her right there if they were going to."

Felix looked across the room at his niece. "I suppose so.

But it's hard to know what they might do. The situation is getting desperate. The Indians are fighting for survival." He rose to his feet. "Sounds like Hans and Betsy had talked about getting married soon. I can't blame him for feeling so anxious about his sweetheart."

Tessa's shoulders slumped. Felix noticed. He knew how she felt about Hans; she made it no secret. He didn't intend to say things that wounded Tessa to hear, but he was telling the truth.

The grandfather clock chimed and Felix realized how late it was. "I need to get back to Not Faxon's Farm. I left the boys to get themselves to bed and somehow I doubt that's happened."

Anna walked outside with him. Felix unhitched the reins and threw a leg over his horse.

"Felix," Anna said, her voice soft but firm. "Please tell Hans that Betsy is a strong girl, a wise girl. She knows that God is with her, even in this terrible tragedy."

Felix looked up at the bright stars. "Strange, isn't it? To think that Betsy is somewhere up north, possibly looking at these same stars. Just a normal April night for me, for you. But for Betsy, for her brothers, life has radically changed. I suppose for Hans too. " He clucked to his horse and gave her a kick to get her in a canter, eager to get home to his own little boys.

❧

Up the Schuylkill River
April 21, 1763

Only once did Betsy Zook look back.

A warrior had grabbed her wrist and pulled her across the

yard, past the burning barn. Before he could drag her into the thick forest, she yanked her wrist out of his hold and stopped to look back at her farm. She saw the bloody corpses of her mother and father, sprawled face up. Her eyes burned from the smoke, her mind swirled, as the vision seared on her mind.

When she refused to budge, the Indian yanked her arm, dragging her along a jagged, thin trail to a clearing under a canopy of trees where warriors had gathered together. There were warriors everywhere, and a dozen or more frightened captives, all children younger than she. She saw one warrior leading a cow, another one holding two frantic chickens upside down by their feet. Another pushed a wooden wheelbarrow, filled with farmers' tools.

Betsy searched for signs of her brothers, eleven-year-old Johnny and seven-year-old Willie. She caught sight of Johnny and made her way over to him. When she reached him, she pulled him into her arms.

"Mem and Da?" he asked, his voice clogged with unshed tears. "They are with you?"

Betsy choked on a wave of despair. All she could do was shake her head. She managed a whisper. "They have perished."

"Dead?" He wiggled out of her grasp. She saw him swallow, once, then twice. Tears filled his eyes. "Willie." His voice choked on the word. "What of our Willie?"

"I don't . . . know." Betsy wanted to provide comfort, to give him something to hope for, but in truth, she had no such assurance. How could Willie have survived? Most likely, he too had perished.

Johnny's voice was guttural with emotion. "Betsy, I'm scared."

A thorn pierced her heart. "Don't be afraid, Johnny," she said, though she was terrified at what fate lay in front of them. She reached for her brother's hand. He grasped it like a lifeline and squeezed so hard, her knuckles cracked softly.

As dawn broke, some kind of invisible signal had spurred the warriors to move into action. They pointed and shouted and pushed the children until they were strung out in a long line, then their hands were bound with twine. Then ropes were circled around their waists, to hobble them together. Some Indians were at the front and others at the back, and they started marching them through the wilderness. One warrior walked alongside the children with a whip, frequently lashing their feet to make them keep up. When one little boy begged for water, he made him drink urine or go thirsty. Children cried out for their mothers, but the warriors did not let them stop walking.

For two days, the Indian raiding party had made the captives march, providing neither food nor drink. Several times children tripped over tree limbs, rocks, or dropped to their knees from sheer exhaustion, and the entire line would stumble. Then the Indian would start whipping at their heels, until they recovered and started marching again. They were forced to march up, up, up into the Blue Mountains, an area that Betsy knew was not under British control. A plunging hopelessness descended over her.

❧

Beacon Hollow

Anna barely recognized the small boy who sat shivering behind her husband on the horse, so forlorn in his thin coat, somber eyes as large as horse chestnuts.

"Willie Zook!" she said. "What a welcome sight you are!" She reached up to help him down, and for one brief moment, as she felt the child's weight in her arms, her mind traveled to a memory when Tessa had gone on her first horseback ride with her father. But that was a lark, a joyful moment of childhood. This was nothing like that.

She set Willie on the ground beside her and looked up at Bairn, still on the horse. Even after all these years together, there was something riveting about the sight of her husband that caught her breath. The way he sat atop his horse, his back so straight and tall, the rigid set of his whiskered jaw. Such a rugged, capable face. And those gray eyes . . . a mirror to his soul. In them was such kindness.

Bairn tried to smile. His attempt failed miserably, and all she could be certain of was the grave solemnity of his eyes.

"I'm so glad you're home."

"As am I, darlin'." Bairn swung his leg over the horse and slid down, one hand holding the reins. "I promised Willie some of your famous johnnycakes."

Anna smiled. "The batter is already made and the maple syrup is warming." It was Bairn's request for breakfast, whenever he returned from travel. "Let's go inside, Willie. You can help me make the cakes."

"Where is our Tessa?"

"She was as restless as a colt, waiting here for you to arrive. I finally sent her over to Not Faxon's Farm to borrow some clothes the boys have outgrown. I thought Willie might need some spare clothing. She should be back soon."

"I'll see to the horse and be in shortly." He reached up and stroked her cheek with his thumb. In English, he added, "Anna, darlin', the laddie has not spoken a word since he told the story of the massacre. He told it once, then he just stopped talking."

Anna put her free hand on the boy's small shoulder and realized he was quivering. She didn't consider herself to be an overly imaginative woman, but even so, she shuddered at the thought of what this boy had been through. "First things first," she said in their dialect. "And the first thing is food."

As to the second thing, she had no idea. If only the heart and mind could be cared for as easily as the stomach.

Not Faxon's Farm

Tessa's heart never failed to race as she stepped up to the door of Not Faxon's Farm, where she knew Hans would be. But it was Dorothea who welcomed her inside, not Hans, not Felix, not Benjo or Dannie. Tessa was surprised to find her grandmother up; she had taken ill and spent the past month in bed. Her pallor had yellowed alarmingly since her illness, and her hand on Tessa's was cold as death. She encouraged her grandmother to sit by the fire.

"I'll make you some tea," she said as she wrapped a blanket around her lap. "Where's Felix?" *And Hans?* she wanted to ask but held back the question. She was desperate to see him.

"Felix and the boys are in the barn. They'll be back soon."

Tessa pushed coals around the fire in the hearth to get it blazing, then hooked the kettle on the trammel. She opened the crock on the hearth that kept tea leaves and found it to be nearly empty.

"Has your mother mentioned if she's received a letter from Catrina?"

"Catrina? Maria's daughter?" Tessa had to repeat herself a number of times until her grandmother heard her. She was deaf as a stone. "No. Nothing that I know of. But I was at Maria's and she said Catrina is coming to live with her." Tessa filled a piece of used cheesecloth with what was left of the tea leaves and let it steep in the kettle. By the time she had prepared the tea, her grandmother had nodded off in her chair.

This was a disappointing visit, all the way around. Even the tea was disappointing, stale in flavor. As she reached for her cloak, in swept Felix. He opened his mouth to greet her, but she shushed him and pointed to Dorothea.

Felix waved away her worry. "She can sleep through anything." He saw the loaf of bread she'd brought on the tabletop. "Just what I had a hankering for." He cut three pieces of bread and lathered them with rich, creamy, yellow butter from Anna's crock. He glanced up at her. "Hans should be back soon. He went to Lancaster Town to find out more information about the attacks."

"I didn't ask about Hans," Tessa said, irritably.

"Then why were you peering around every corner?"

"Just . . . mortified by your housekeeping." And that was no lie. The small house was not only cluttered and messy, but filthy. Dusty and dirty and dank smelling. *Too many males in one place*. Her grandmother let out a loud snore. *Not enough females*.

Felix laughed. "I will not take issue with you over that blunt assessment."

"Mem wondered if you might have clothes to spare for Willie Zook."

"Oh. Hmm. I'm sure I can scrounge up something." He

disappeared into the next room and came back with a few shirts and trousers. Dirty ones. "Here you go. The boys have outgrown these. I think."

The sound of an approaching horse drew his attention to the small window. "Here comes Hans now." Then he turned to her and tilted his head, curiously. "You always seem to get a nice rosy hue when Hans comes around."

Tessa turned away from him to douse the red blooming on her cheeks. Felix liked to tease and she hated getting embarrassed. "Mem expects me home. Dad should be arriving soon with Willie Zook." She reached a hand for the door latch.

"Tessa, you mustn't set your heart on Hans. He's not . . ."

She stopped and spun around. "He's not *what*?"

Felix looked at her, hesitating, then smiled. "You're so young. You've got much still to experience in life before you give your heart away." He'd told her such things before, but there was a warning tone in her uncle's voice.

Hans burst into the house, glancing briefly at Tessa but focusing his attention on Felix. He looked utterly stricken. Heartsick was the only word that suited his appearance. Dark circles rimmed his eyes, his face looked pinched and sickly, his shoulders were tensed in worry. "The sheriff has no plans to go after the raiders. He says since it didn't happen in Lancaster County, it's out of his jurisdiction."

Felix sighed. "Hans, it's out of our territory too."

Hans stood in the center of the small room, hands on his hips. He scraped a hand over his whiskered chin, dark with stubble. Tessa couldn't help but notice it was such a splendid chin—strong, square, clefted. "John Elder is creating a militia. He's made himself captain."

"Vigilantes," Felix said. "Not a militia. And we have no business getting involved with such things."

"No business with right and wrong? We're to stay out of exacting justice?"

"We're to stay away from vengeance. Bloodlust. Fear mongering."

A hard silence filled the room.

"I'll just be on my way, then," Tessa said quietly.

Hans jerked his head in her direction. He looked as if he'd just realized she was there. "I'll go with you," he said. "I want to talk to Bairn."

"Not today," Felix said sharply. "He'll be exhausted. Willie Zook will just be getting settled. They don't need you rushing in with your fury."

"My *grief*, Felix." Hans pounded his chest with his fist. "Imagine if this had happened to your Rachel."

That stung.

More softly, Felix added, "Tomorrow, Hans. You can see Bairn tomorrow."

Hans's chin jutted forward. "Are you speaking as a brother or a deacon?"

"Both. And you're not to go seeking after John Elder, either. He's nothing but a political firebrand. An agitator." The two men glared at each other.

She'd never seen her uncle Felix speak in that tone, not to his sons, not to Tessa, not to Hans. Nor had she ever seen such defiance in someone's face—Hans's eyes had a coldness in them that sent a shiver up her back.

Near the door, Tessa slipped outside and broke into a run through the woods to reach Beacon Hollow. About halfway along the trail, she slowed to a walk, feeling all churned up inside. The attacks might have occurred seventy miles away, but something essential had shifted in Stoney Ridge. Tessa did not casually dismiss feelings. A dweller, her father called her. She would have stood and puzzled for some time on the significance of the cross words exchanged between Felix and Hans, had it not been for the sound of a snapping twig behind her.

She jerked around to see Hans striding toward her. Her heart tripped over itself, and her skin flushed with excitement.

"Tessa, you forgot the clothes for Willie." He held out a bundle for her. He looked full of grief and sadness, and her heart went out to him.

"Hans, I'm so sorry."

"I cannot comprehend God's purpose in taking Betsy."

"But surely you know that God is watching over her."

He winced, closing his eyes. She studied him, struck again by his beauty. In an act of compassion, she laid her hand on his shoulder so lightly she was not even sure he felt it. Yet when she started to draw it away, he covered it with his own hand and held it there. She didn't know how long they remained in that position, but after some time his hand slid away.

"How selfish I am, Tessa. You and Betsy were such good friends. You loved her too."

Loved Betsy Zook? Tessa felt pinpricked with guilt. She had not loved Betsy, nor were they friends. She had envied her, resented her, wished her ill. And each time Tessa allowed herself to harbor a dark thought about Betsy, it revealed everything awful in her own soul. She was a terrible person. Truly terrible. But surely she didn't need to confess all that to Hans. Why add to his distress? "You must let me know how I can help you."

He nodded, his chin on his chest. And then quite suddenly he emerged from his sorrow, straightened his back, and looked at her. "Tell your father I must speak to Willie Zook as soon as possible."

"I'll tell him." To her own surprise, Tessa said, "Betsy's under the protection of God. You must believe that." Then she added, "All will be well." She wasn't sure what possessed her to add that since she had no reason to think so.

Tears filled his eyes and he blinked them back, reached out and pulled her to him. The embrace lasted no more than a brief moment, for he quickly drew away, turned, and headed back down the trail toward Not Faxon's Farm.

To Tessa, that brief moment felt as if she had fallen outside time and was no longer part of the ordinary world. A jolt of happiness traveled through her. Then, just as quickly as it had bloomed, it withered, and she was flooded with guilt.

She was a wretched sinner. Imagine benefiting from someone else's pain.

🌿

Blue Mountain

Finally, as the sun set on the second day, the Indians stopped the convoy for the night and untied the ropes that bound them. A warrior handed out provisions, bread and deer jerky. She held the torn chunk of bread in her hands and realized it was her mother's bread. The last loaf of bread that her mother had made, had kneaded, had pounded. The last loaf she would ever, ever make. As famished as Betsy was, her appetite vanished by that realization. Her mother, she knew, would tell her that she must eat, she must keep up her strength, for her sake and for Johnny's sake. And so she ate. As she chewed, she tried to make each bite last, painfully aware it was the last nourishment she would ever receive from her mother.

Johnny leaned against her. "Let's run away," he whispered. "When the big one falls asleep, let's run."

As Betsy rubbed her chafed, raw wrists, she looked around to see if she could recognize anything about their whereabouts. They had traveled along a ridge, climbing into the mountains, deep in the woods. They were in a wilderness unknown to them, without a path, without a guide. She had no idea of the direction or distance to their farm, or what was left of it. "We can't, Johnny. Remember what Mem told us. It would only cause more trouble. We must stay strong."

Betsy's father had prepared his children for a possible Indian attack. He had taught them to not resist violence but instead to trust God's protection. As the Indians circled their home, her mother grabbed her by her forearms and gave her a flood of warnings: "Don't forget the prayers that you've been taught. Say them often, and God will bless you. Don't forget your name, your English tongue. If you have an opportunity to get away, don't try to escape. If you do, they will find you and torture you. Stay strong and lean heavily on your faith."

Johnny curled up against her, eyes drooping. "I am glad that Willie is dead," he murmured. "He could not have survived this."

She looked at him, startled by the comment, watching Johnny fall asleep. Blessed sleep. How she longed to sleep! But her mind couldn't stop racing.

One of the Indians stared at Betsy, speaking a few incomprehensible words. His head was shaved, other than one section in the back from which a queue of greasy black hair hung down. He wore nothing but a breechcloth, leggings of deer hide, and a grimy blanket over one shoulder. His shiny black eyes reminded her of a devil as he studied her, his gleaming eyes resting on her hair.

Then he reached into a sack and pulled out a scalp with long, tangled blond hair, smeared with clumps of dried blood, and smiled at her in a queer way, pointing and jeering, and rattling off odd garbled words.

The warrior shook the scalp at her, tipping his head back, laughing as he shook it, enjoying her distress. Finally, he tired of the game, stretched out, and rolled to one side, his jaw slacked and he fell asleep, snoring loudly. The scalp lay by his side.

There was a small clip hanging on a lock of hair that hung from the scalp. Betsy began to shake. A chill settled over her, a cold that settled into her very marrow.

It was the hair clip from the passing peddler. The one she'd given her mother the day Hans had visited. The hair clip was just a secret between the two of them, for her father would not have approved. He was a stickler for rules, her father. But her mother appreciated a bit of fancy and wore it anyway, hidden under her prayer cap. The warrior must have known. He wanted Betsy to see it.

This was the warrior who had killed her mother.

This . . . this was her mother's scalp.

4

Beacon Hollow
April 23, 1763

Anna dropped black mustard seeds in a bowl and quickly ground them to powder with the pestle. She added the proper amounts of melted lard to make a plaster for the festering wound on Willie's arm. First she placed a piece of cheesecloth over the wound to protect it, for mustard could burn the skin. Then she spread the poultice over the thinly covered wound, wrapping his arm with a clean bandage. Willie was trying to be brave, though she could see he was nervous.

It was such a little arm. Anna had forgotten how small a child could be, and the Zooks were not big people. Betsy looked young, though she was seventeen. Johnny was small at age eleven, as was poor Willie at seven. He was a silent wraith of a boy.

As Anna tied the bandage on his little stick of an arm, she savored the time of mothering a young child. How she missed it.

Anna had never given up hope that she would conceive another child, not until this winter. Her flows had stopped, the end of being young and fruitful had come upon her. It broke her heart to realize she was now barren, that her yearning for another child—for many children—was not to be.

She had always dreamed of being surrounded by a houseful of children. Her elderly grandparents had raised her in Germany in a quiet, orderly home. She had envisioned her life with Bairn to be the opposite of her childhood—a home of happy chaos, lively laughter. She longed to hold an infant against her breast, to snuggle with a toddler near the warmth of the fire. She wanted little ones around her all the time, hanging on to her apron as she went about her chores. She wanted to hear their laughter in the house, listen to their silly questions. She wanted to hold on to chubby hands, wipe tears off round cheeks, smooth silky hair off foreheads.

She knew not to question God's mysterious ways, that if He were to deny her dream, He had good reason. But whenever she came across a woman whose belly was swollen with child, she felt again the emptiness of her womb, the longing of her heart.

Bairn had sensed her sorrow last winter. He asked her of the cause and she told him the truth, that her time for bearing children was over. "I'm sorry," she had told him. "You must be disappointed."

Bairn had taken her hands in his, tilted his head, and smiled at her, a familiar gesture that she cherished. He spoke in English with his Scottish brogue, full of rolling r's. "There is no other lassie on God's green earth whom I would want for m' wife, nor any other child but our Tessa." He had pulled her into his embrace, and she felt comforted by his words.

Willie shifted on the bench, snapping Anna back to the present. She finished the last tie of the bandage and rolled down his shirtsleeve. "All done for now, Willie. I'll change it again this afternoon." She smiled at him. It had been a few days since he had arrived at Beacon Hollow with Bairn, yet he still hadn't uttered a single word. He ate, he slept, he obediently did chores, but he did not speak. Nor did he smile.

❧

Beacon Hollow
April 24, 1763

Sunday morning meant church was held, this time at Tessa's stone house, the largest home in the Conestoga Valley. She sat on the bench next to her mother, near the window so she could watch the birds. She was convinced birds gathered in the trees the moment the little church began to sing its mournful songs. She would close her eyes and pretend to sing, when she was actually listening to the birdsong.

In the kitchen, the table was full of food, covered with linen cloths to keep the flies off it, waiting for the time of the fellowship meal. Tessa smelled the bean soup simmering on the raised hearth in the other room. Her mother had cooked the soup last evening in her largest kettle. Tessa had helped her boil eggs in a smaller kettle hung by an iron crane over the fireplace. The cheese, butter, and cider came from storage barrels in the root cellar of Beacon Hollow. Other families brought bread, plus their own wooden platters and pewter dishes and spoons. The spring day was so pleasant—warm, with a gentle breeze—that the meal would be eaten outdoors, beneath the trees in the front yard.

Across the room, Tessa took in the slump of Willie's thin shoulders, the restless tapping of his feet, awkward, like a young colt. Poor Willie. Tessa tried to befriend him, inviting him along with her when she went into the woods to hunt for the black stallion. He obliged her and came along, but he seemed lost in his own world, distracted and disinterested. She had to keep encouraging him to keep up with her, to look carefully for any telltale signs of the horse. That was no way to go stallion hunting! Her mother said to have patience, to not press him to talk, and to give him time to mend. Tessa feared his mind was disordered. She remembered him as a noisy boy, running and shouting, much like Felix's twin sons. The only spark of life in Willie was his affection for Tessa's old dog, Zeeb. The two of them had become inseparable. Even now, Zeeb sat at Willie's feet.

Next to poor Willie sat the twins—Benjo and Dannie— with Uncle Felix between them to discourage mischief making. Felix's wife Rachel had passed during childbirth, and his mother had moved to Not Faxon's Farm to help with the babies, though she was the one who seemed to need help. Tessa leaned back and glanced down the row to Dorothea, her sweet and frail grandmother. She had fallen sound asleep and church hadn't even started yet! Maria noticed and jabbed her with a bony elbow. Dorothea jerked awake, then looked at Maria, annoyed. Tessa had to bite on her lips to keep from laughing out loud. Maria and Dorothea treated each other more like irritable sisters than longtime friends.

The first hymn began when the Vorsinger, Simon Miller, the only male in the church who could sing in tune—and Tessa included her father in that assessment—opened his rather large mouth to release the first note. Before it emerged from Simon's lips, the front door opened and shut. Someone came clunking into the room, bumping into benches, whispering apologies, before plopping down on a crowded men's bench. The men had to shift down the row to make room for him.

Rumpled Martin? What was *he* doing here? He was a *Mennonite.*

When rumpled Martin saw that Tessa was watching him with a scowl, he gave her a big smile and waved his hand surreptitiously at her. Her scowl deepened.

After the first hymn was sung, there was a moment of quiet, of stillness, a time for reflection. Bairn, sitting on the front bench, gave Felix a nod.

In a loud voice, shockingly loud, Benjo said, "Why does Uncle Bairn disappear whenever church starts?"

Felix put a hand on his son's shoulder and whispered, "He goes off to a quiet room and prays for God's help to preach the sermon."

Dannie piped up in his own bellowing voice. "Then why doesn't God ever help him?"

Almost to the bedroom door, Tessa's father stopped, and the entire church froze, waiting for his reaction. His shoulders started to shake, then his whole body. He clapped a hand over his mouth. Tessa worried he was having an apoplectic fit—she'd seen someone in Lancaster Town have a fit once. It was a frightful sight.

But then a laugh burst out of her father, and he kept laughing, and most everyone joined in the laughter. Not Maria Müller, of course, but almost everyone else. *During* church!

Tessa looked across the room at Hans, to see if he might be amused too. She sat at an unfortunate angle and there were three stout women seated in front of her. She thought of them as the Stout Sisters, though they weren't actually sisters. She could not see Hans properly without stretching sideways and craning her neck. But when she did, she could see he wasn't laughing. He was staring at a spot on the floor in front of his shoes. Tessa stilled, and a pang of shame shot right to her gut. She was spending a happy Sunday morning in April thinking about birds and bean soup while Betsy was somewhere far away in the wilderness, held captive by savages.

And then she noticed that Willie Zook was watching Benjo and Dannie with a curious almost-sort-of-getting-close-practically-there smile on his face.

❧

Felix tried but couldn't hold back his amusement with his sons' remarks, inappropriate as they were. He knew he would get an earful after church from Maria Müller, but he thought his sons were a tonic to an ailing community. Leave it to those two boys to bring some levity after the week's distressing news. Why, those boys even elicited a near smile out of poor Willie Zook.

Felix adored those boys of his, loved their joyful spirit and enthusiasm for life. And how they made him laugh!

Just two weeks ago, Bairn had been preaching on Scripture based on Matthew 5:22. "Anyone who hates his brother will be guilty of murder," Bairn preached, then paused to let the impact of the words float through the church.

Apparently guilt ridden, both of Felix's sons had blurted out a loud "Uh oh."

On this spring morning, Felix kept his eyes away from Maria's disapproving grimace and locked down on the tops of his sons' carrot-red heads. Children were a blessing.

❦

Tessa should have been listening to her father's sermon, but instead she was captivated by how the sun streamed through the window and lit Hans's thick, wavy hair in such a way that he appeared like an angel. She suddenly sensed a change in the atmosphere, a brittleness. And then she realized her father had been talking about the massacre.

"The worst thing to do," her father said as he walked between the space that separated the men's side of the benches from the women's, "is to assume all people belong under a defining label. That all Indians are savages. All Scots-Irish are squatters. All French are bent on riling up the Indians to get back at the British. That is not God's view of man, nor of the massacre. Vengeance belongs to God alone."

Hans shot to his feet. "This was pure evil, Bairn. Nothing but evil! Betsy's family was brutally killed. Her parents were left in an inhuman manner."

Tessa almost gasped. Speaking out like that in church, it just wasn't done.

Tessa's father remained unfazed. He pivoted on his boot heels toward Hans. "It was indeed a truly evil act. It will not go unpunished. Perhaps not in this life, but in the one to come."

"But they're bloodthirsty heathens!" Hans said. "No different than Canaanites in the Promised Land. The ones the Lord God told Moses and Joshua to rid the land of."

"Hans, you must stop such talk," Tessa's father said in his deep, gentle voice. "Those warriors in the north, they're displaced from their hunting grounds and angry for it. It has made them conscienceless against the white settlers. But many Indians do not share their ways. Think of our Conestoga friends."

The Conestoga Indians, mostly converted Christians, were a peaceful tribe who lived nearby in Indiantown, on land that William Penn himself had deeded to them. Once Tessa had even seen the treaty, the actual treaty, signed by William Penn. It was a prized possession among the Conestogas. And they did not have much.

They were a poor people, drastically reduced in number in the last year. Their livelihood consisted of making brooms and baskets to sell locally, and they had to beg for food as they went from farm to farm. Will Sock was a leader of the Conestoga and had been a friend to the Bauers. Christy was an Indian boy who spent hours alongside Felix's sons; they were as close as brothers. Christy had taught Benjo and Dannie to track and trap wild animals with skill and daring as they explored the woods.

"You let them sleep at your hearth," Hans said, in a tone of ferocity and determination that shocked Tessa. He pointed at Bairn. "You bring them in your home. Would you still persist in that practice?"

That was true, but it was not unknown to others, and Tessa didn't know why Hans spoke in such an accusing way to her father. On cold nights, some of the Conestoga Indians who were on the road to sell handicrafts would stop at the Bauer home. They knew they could get a good meal and sleep by a warm fire. Betty Sock, mother to Will Sock, often helped Anna with household chores in exchange for food.

"We've always allowed that for the Conestogas," Bairn said, "and there's no reason to stop that practice now. You must not allow bitterness to take hold of you, to change your views about a man and lump all Indians together."

Hans's tone was sharp. "They're murderers. They plunder farms, burn houses, kill women and children."

Beside him Josef Gerber bobbed his head up and down, as did Simon and a few others. Rumpled Martin watched the exchange between Tessa's father and Hans with a thoughtful look on his face.

Hans lifted his arms. "And you think they should not be lumped together?"

"No more than we would want to be lumped together."

Hans shook his head in disgust. "But we *can* be lumped together. Because we do nothing to protect our own. *Nothing.* We are the ones who are lacking in conscience." He spoke rapidly, stressing each word, as if all were of equal importance.

And Hans walked out of church that day. Walked right out! Tessa could not remember anyone, ever, doing such a thing. She'd never even heard of such a thing ever happening. Through the window, Tessa saw him mount his horse and gallop away.

To walk *out* of church! It was like walking away from God.

🌿

Blue Mountain
April 27, 1763

Betsy was hungry all the time. She slept hungry and woke up hungry. Before her capture, she had never known a day without enough food to eat. Now food was dispensed to her by her enemies, bit by bit, scrap by scrap, only enough to keep her alive, moving along on this endless journey. Thoughts of food continually invaded her mind like whispers from the devil himself. She imagined tables laden with turkeys and hams and sausages and beef swimming in a thick brown gravy. Apple turnovers with flaky pastry, the sharp tang of newly cut cheese on her tongue, of crusty brown loaves of her mother's bread, slathered with thick butter.

As she walked, she catalogued meals in her mind, dwelling on each part of the recipes, distracting herself in the memories. With two brothers to work alongside her father outdoors—felling trees, clearing fields, caring for livestock— she had spent most of her time in the kitchen by her mother's side. They worked long hours preserving jams and jellies, baking bread and pies, churning butter, making cheese. They had lived in the house a scarce year, but with the generosity of good neighbors who shared their bounty, the cellar had filled up with loaded barrels of food stuffs.

The day of the Indian attack, she had spent the morning baking bread with her mother. The house smelled of bread, a sweet, yeasty scent. She remembered taking Hans's letter out of her journal and reading it whenever her mother sent her to the cellar to fetch something. Hans had sent word through the minister's circuit visit that he planned to come sometime in May to speak to her father about getting married. Early in the new year, he decided, they would be wed. As she went up and down the cellar steps, she remembered looking up at the sky, noticing the way the sun was shining through the newly leafed-out trees, making the green leaves appear almost glowing. She remembered feeling utterly safe, completely content.

And yet, not far off, a farmer was tomahawked in his

newly plowed cornfield. Later that night, all the neighbors would gather in the Zook house to fort up. Most likely, Betsy realized now, as she had stood on those cellar steps and read Hans's letter proposing marriage, her thoughts floating off to her wedding day, warriors were already in position, patiently watching the house, waiting for nightfall to attack.

Ironically, she had never been less safe than when she had last felt most safe.

When would she feel safe again? Or would she ever?

The convoy of captives walked west through the wilderness, stopping only to sleep when it grew dark, camping in the woods without shelter, and usually without fire for warmth. Extremely fatigued, weak with hunger, Betsy and Johnny lay upon the ground. Sheer exhaustion brought sleep, until at dawn they were roused to start off on the march again.

It was with great difficulty that Betsy helped the other children. She did not want to know their faces, to see the fear in their eyes. She did not want to care a whit about them. But she did. They looked to her as the eldest. They were all in the same terrible situation, and there was little she could do for them, but she could offer a reassuring smile, smooth a furrowed brow, give a soothing word even if her dialect was not understood. Betsy didn't falter. She wanted to. But never once did she falter.

On the eighth night after the attack, Betsy was startled awake by the sound of piercing cries in the darkness. She raised her head to see warriors dancing around a large fire, raising their elbows, writhing in obscene postures, chanting, shrieking, hopping, twisting, lifting knees up high. Their naked bodies were dark against the bright flames, and for a few disorienting seconds, Betsy thought surely she must have died. Surely, this was Hell.

She peered into the trees beyond the firelight. The Indians were wholly occupied with their wild reverie and paid no attention to the captives. She needed to relieve herself. She rose slowly, taking care not to wake Johnny. Suddenly, she found herself staring into her captor's dark eyes. He stood right up against her, grasping her forearms, so close she could smell the stink of his breath mingled with smoke from the fire. Black stripes were painted on his face; tattoos of wolves, bears, and other predators covered his bare chest. Feathers held in his hair queue fluttered with each movement he made. He said something in a rush of words that sounded to Betsy like the grunting of a wild sow. Then he lifted his hand and there was the shine of his knife.

Betsy was certain she was soon to die. "Don't," she begged in a tiny voice, even as she closed her eyes and steeled herself for the pain. "Thy will be done. Thy will be done." She felt the blade against her face, felt it slide along her cheek. But she felt no pain—nothing but terror. Then he withdrew his hand and released her, giving her an eerie, satisfied smile. As he left her to return to the dancers, she expelled a breath she hadn't realized she was holding. She lay back down on the ground and stifled her sobs, her only release. After some time she sank into a fitful sleep.

It was only in the morning that she realized what she thought were tears running down her face was her own blood. The warrior had sliced her deeply on one side of her face, a thin line drawn from below her eye all the way to her chin.

5

Days passed, yet there was still no sighting or word of the whereabouts of Betsy Zook. Nor of Handsome Hans. Everyone presumed Hans had gone to rescue Betsy.

Hans's absence distressed Tessa's father. For a young man to leave his work and his family in anger, vengeance driving his heart, was not the Plain way but the way of the world. And his disappearance left undone work for the others. Tessa's father had been counting on Hans's help to forge hardware, unique and essential to this new wagon. And then, of course, everyone was worried about Hans. Tessa, mostly.

She woke early one morning and heard her parents' voices below in the kitchen. She thought she heard her father say the name Hans, so she slipped out of bed and tiptoed to the fireplace, taking care not to wake Willie in his cot near the window. Long ago, by crouching close to the loft's fireplace, she had discovered she could eavesdrop on her parents as their voices floated up the chimney flue.

Her parents were discussing options about what to do—

should her father and Felix go after Hans? But that was a problem in itself, her father said, as he didn't even know where Hans had gone.

"He's running on emotion," Tessa heard her mother say. "He isn't thinking straight."

"He loves her," her father replied. "How could he just forget her and carry on with his life?"

Tessa sighed. They meant Betsy Zook, of course.

"Now, Anna." There was a long silence, until she heard her father say, "Anna, darlin'"—spoken softer this time, so soft that Tessa had to lean her head into the chimney to hear—"I dinnae forget y', darlin'. I just dinnae ken what t' do."

Since her father had brought Willie into their home, he had used English for many such private conversations, to Tessa's delight. She loved hearing his accent.

"That was cold comfort," her mother responded, "when I was up the Schuylkill, alone, while you were happily sailing away on the Atlantic Sea."

Tessa wasn't exactly sure what her parents were referring to—she could only catch bits and pieces of her parents' tumultuous courtship through eavesdropping because they were maddeningly private about their relationship. Once, she asked her mother outright, and her mother said, "It is our story, Tessa. What goes on between a man and a woman is theirs alone."

Such a response frustrated Tessa because everyone in the church seemed to know how she felt about Hans . . . except for Hans. He seemed oblivious to her ardor. Probably because he only had eyes for Betsy.

Tessa let out a sigh. Betsy Zook. Even gone, she was present. There was that zing again, a stab of conscience. She should be praying daily for Betsy Zook's welfare, not just for Hans's return. She heard her parents' mumble again and leaned closer to the fireplace.

"Why dinnae y' say what yer thinking? I can tell by the look on yer face that y've got something in mind."

"Hans was right about one thing. One thing. Being non-resistant should not mean being passive. We should be doing something to help locate Betsy. Hans stormed out of church because his anguish was not heard among us, or felt among us."

"But what 'tis there t' do?"

"I think you should go to Will Sock and see if he has any knowledge of Betsy and Johnny's whereabouts. Surely Will Sock has sources among the Indians in the north. We have none."

Tessa's father was silent for a long while. "Darlin', yer right. Felix and I will go speak t' Will Sock." She heard a chair scrape and knew her father had gone to embrace her mother. They were very affectionate with each other, so long as no one was nearby to observe them. "How did I get so blessed to have y' by m' side?"

She heard her mother laugh. "It was the rose. How could any woman resist a rose?"

What was the story about that rose? They wouldn't tell Tessa. Planted right by the front door, it bloomed profusely each spring, spreading its sweet fragrance over the front stoop. Her mother took exceptional care of it, covering it on freezing nights, adding tea leaves to the soil that covered its roots. She fussed over it like a baby.

"Tessa, y' can come down now," her father called up the flue. "I ken y've been eavesdroppin'."

She rose and tiptoed to the stairwell to peer down at her father.

"Would y' like to go with me to see Will Sock at Indiantown?"

She nodded. "Should I wake Willie? He might like to come."

"Nay," her father said quickly. "Let the laddie sleep."

Tessa thought going to Indiantown might be beneficial for Willie, that it might be helpful to see other kinds of Indians than those who had raided his home and killed his parents. To meet young Christy, perhaps to play with him. But by her father's quick refusal, he must have felt differently. Too soon.

Tessa's mother had gathered a flour sack full of food stuffs to take to Betty Sock, mother to Will Sock. A container filled with deer jerky, a bag of freshly milled wheat flour, another bag of dried beans, and two loaves of bread she had just baked yesterday.

As Tessa ate a quick breakfast, she said to her father, "After church on Sunday, I heard some of the men agreeing with Hans. I heard them say that all Indians are savage heathens who need to be civilized and converted and subdued and contained. Not necessarily in that order, they said."

His gray eyes peered at her over the top of his teacup. "Hans spoke those angry words out o' fear."

"What if he's right?"

"Right? About what?"

"That Indians can't be trusted."

He put down his teacup. "I think the same could be said of many white men."

"But you've always said that holy lives are a blessing to

those around them. Betsy's family hadn't done anything to hurt the Indians."

"Aye, not the Zooks, and hopefully not other Amish farmers, but there are many settlers who encroach on land that's been given t' the Indians. Greed drives them. Fear and greed can inspire tyranny in all men. Any man. Whatever color be his skin. While it's true that Indians have raided the settlers, far more often they're the victims of white men's greed. I ken of dreadful tales about how the Indians have been treated."

He leaned on his elbows to look right at her. "Tessa, when I was a sailor, I saw terrible things happen on a ship because of one man's hatred toward another, simply because of his skin color, or his religion, or his surname. I met all sorts o' people from all over the world, ones who treated me with great kindness, ones who did not. The worst thing is t' judge a man by the color of his skin, or by his allegiance. Each man must stand alone before God, and that is the same way we should consider him: standing on his own convictions."

She heard a horse gallop up the path and hurried to unlatch the door. She saw her uncle Felix throw himself off his horse and stride to the front door, all business.

"Felix! I was just coming t' get you," Tessa's father said, stepping in front of her. "We've got an errand to run."

Felix stomped his feet at the bootjack to get the mud off. "First, I've got news. Serious stuff."

"News about Hans?" Tessa blurted out.

"Hans?" Felix looked at her as if she had two heads. "No. He'll be back when he runs out of steam. This is far more serious." He plopped down in a chair at the kitchen table, hands flattened on its top. "Maria Müller arrived at the crack of dawn today." He slapped the table with his palms. "The crack of dawn!"

"She does that to us too," Tessa said with sympathy. "Rather a lot." She didn't look at her mother because she knew she would be frowning at her.

"Do you know what she wanted to tell me?"

"Oh, I bet I know! Catrina Müller is moving back."

"You knew?" Felix cried. "Wait a minute." He glared at Tessa's mother. "Is Catrina the tutor you've been threatening to hire?"

Slowly, Anna nodded. "Dorothea had the idea. Maria is lonely and Catrina needs a livelihood. Your boys need schooling. So does Willie Zook. It's a fine solution for everyone."

"Solution? Solution!" Felix was outraged. "Solutions are meant to fix problems. How can there be a solution when there's no problem in the first place? You've gone and created a *terrible* situation. The worst. Catrina Müller set her sights on me since the day I was born. I'm doomed."

❦

Anna had given Felix plenty of warning that she intended to hire a tutor to give his sons much-needed schooling. The stunned look on his face was comical. How many times had she brought this subject up to him? Dozens.

It was time those boys were taught to read and write and do their figures, to learn English, all things that Felix was entirely unconcerned about. They were nine years old and couldn't even scratch out their names. He gave free rein to his boys and they spent their time off in the woods or over at the Conestoga Indiantown playing with the young Indian boy Christy. They were boys growing up in the woods, with little womanly influence other than Dorothea, who was frail and elderly.

The lack of education imposed on Felix's sons reminded Anna of days on the *Charming Nancy*, crossing the Atlantic, as she tried to teach English to then eight-year-old Felix, when all he wanted to do was to explore the ship. To Benjo and Dannie, the deep woods were every bit as fascinating as a merchant ship on the high seas. They were entirely untroubled by the thought of reading or writing or doing figures. As was Felix. They were convinced all they needed to know could be learned by being out in the forest. With Christy, a boy nearly their age, as their sole tutor.

Christy had taught the boys the ways of the hunter—how to make snares and deadfalls, how to catch small animals. Even Anna couldn't deny that Felix's sons had acquired the eyes and ears of true woodsmen, alert at all times, instantly conscious of changes—a slight motion, an odd sound, or the faintest trail left by the passing of an animal or a man. They were thoroughly at home in the woods.

But put those two boys in a church service and they turned into restless, fidgety, impatient, mischievous little imps. They had become a trial to the entire church, unaware of how loud they could be, how easily bored, how distracting to others. Their lack of awareness for how they affected others was only matched by their father's amusement at their antics.

Anna was sorry Felix was raising his boys without benefit of a wife. It seemed as if he was raising his boys the way he'd wished he'd been raised—without anyone telling him to take a bath or read a book. Perhaps if his wife, Rachel, had lived, he would be more even keeled. As it was, he was appallingly indulgent as a parent.

Bairn thought Anna was a "wee bit too hard" on Felix, but she'd always felt more like a mother to him than a sister-in-law. Bairn asked her once if she might be taking on the raising of Felix's sons because she had no sons of her own. She was surprised by that question—she felt she expected as much from Tessa as she did from Felix's rascals. At the time, she didn't respond to Bairn because she didn't know how to answer him.

Then, a month ago, she caught Benjo and Dannie throwing tomahawks at Beacon Hollow's newly planted apple orchard—trees she had nurtured since saplings. She asked them why they were toppling her prized apple trees, and they said, "Because it was fun." That was the moment she realized what was at the root of her concern about Felix's sons. They were growing up wild.

She had marched the boys into the house and dropped the tomahawks on the kitchen table, right in front of Felix and Bairn. "This is no toy. Six apple trees—chopped down at the trunk."

"I'll replace them," Felix said, untroubled.

"I'm finding the boys a tutor. You've had long enough to find someone."

Felix was flummoxed. He felt his boys were beyond reproach and she was interfering. "They're frontier boys, Anna. They're learning what they're going to need in this life. One day, they'll be heading west to make their own way when they're grown. They're going to need to know how to hunt for food, not read books by the fireplace. Why, Benjo impaled a squirrel in a treetop yesterday. He's barely nine years old."

"An education is something that will benefit them all their

life, Felix. You've ignored it long enough. They should be reading by now."

In this, Bairn supported her; he agreed it was high time the boys learned to read. That very afternoon Anna wrote a letter to Catrina, whom Dorothea had suggested to her, and invited her to come back to Stoney Ridge. Soon, a letter arrived back in the post; Catrina readily accepted. Recently widowed and left with little means to support herself, Catrina had been seeking a way to secure the necessities of life. It was an ideal answer to a problem. Multiple problems, in fact.

Such as the problem with Maria Müller. Anna would never admit it to Tessa, but she was also exasperated by Maria's frequent, lengthy visits to Beacon Hollow. Once or twice, she'd even hinted at moving in with them. Anna shuddered at the thought. Maria needed someone of her own to fuss over.

And now there was Willie Zook to consider. He, too, needed schooling.

Anna smiled benignly at Felix. Catrina Müller was a perfect solution.

It exasperated Felix that no one took his worry about Catrina Müller seriously. He remembered her as a dedicated man hunter. And he was a contented widower. He loved his life. His mother, when she was up to the tasks (which he admitted, was not often), took care of cooking and cleaning, which left him all the time he needed to pursue the things he loved: horse breeding, hunting, fishing, having fun with his boys. It was a life that suited him quite nicely . . . and now Catrina was going to ruin it all.

He could see how it would all play out. Maria, Catrina's

bossy mother, would start pressuring from below, his mother and Anna would start pressuring from the sides, Catrina would show up at his house and endear herself to his mother, and then would start the pressure from above: Bairn, the minister.

He was suddenly facing a bleak and dismal future.

He thought of the pleased look on Maria's face early this morning when she told him that Catrina was moving back. "She can't manage the house on her own since her husband passed to his glory last winter."

"Wasn't he an old graybeard?" He thought he'd heard she'd married a geezer.

She fixed Felix in her hawklike gaze. "You remind me of Catrina's third husband."

"Third husband? How many has she had?"

She narrowed her beady eyes at him. "Two."

"Oh." Felix felt the collar tighten around his neck. Like a noose.

His mind replayed the morning's conversation as they rode over to Conestoga Indiantown. He barely heard his niece chatter on about the phantom stallion—a topic he normally found enthralling. Tessa was the only one who had seen the stallion up close, many times now. Whenever she had a sighting, Felix would quiz her about every detail, gathering information for his horse breeding. The first time she'd seen it, he listened attentively but was fairly certain she was spinning a yarn. Tessa had a vivid imagination, much like his own. But that spring, an unusually large foal was born to him that looked exactly like Tessa's description of the mysterious stallion, right down to the shortened tail. Then another foal arrived. Then four more.

The following spring, eight more foals were delivered. They, too, showed characteristics of the phantom stallion. And as the first yearlings grew, he realized that their size was going to be off the charts. The legendary phantom stallion had found his way into his broodmares' pasture and he couldn't be more delighted. A gift from above!

Three years old now, the first colts were nearly full grown. A breed perfectly suited for the farming life—gentle giants, with hooves the size of dish plates. His brother Bairn eyed the six colts and claimed them for his custom-designed wagon— the one that looked a little like a ship.

Bairn had been working on that wagon for the better part of a year now, tweaking, fine tuning, adjusting. Felix wondered what Bairn would end up charging Faxon Gingerich for the wagon. Bairn's policy was that the price of goods should be its cost plus an honest profit, and that's how he priced his work, no more, no less. He was an honest tradesman in a dishonest colony. Felix was an honest tradesman too, but he had a different idea about bartering. He liked having a contest of wits between a buyer and seller. If it were up to Felix, he would have taken out a patent on this wagon of Bairn's, so that the Bauers could receive a portion each time a copy was manufactured.

But that was assuming the first protoype wagon would ever get completed. Hans's disappearance put a serious wrench in Bairn's plans. Hans was the only dedicated smithy for Stoney Ridge, arguably the most important artisan in the area, because few men had the ability to do the ironwork for themselves. Bairn, trained as a cooper, had started the forge fire when they first bought the land, twenty-five years earlier. Most of Bairn's practice had consisted of shodding horses. Some oxen, too.

At an early age, Hans had shown an interest in the work. When he was of age to be apprenticed, Bairn taught Hans all he knew. Hans had a talent for the work, quickly surpassing Bairn's abilities. He did much more than act as farrier; he became the preferred toolmaker for the local farmers, the pot and kettle maker for the farmers' wives, and when necessary, even pulled out neighbors' aching teeth.

The wagon was at a standstill until Hans returned to Stoney Ridge from wherever it was he went. Felix and Bairn had been working on making wheels, large hubs with spokes that radiated to the wooden rim. Bairn had the idea of making the wheels in the back of the wagon much larger than the front. He thought it would help the wagon manage muddy roads. But he needed Hans's help to shod the rim with strakes—curved strips of iron. He was the only one with the skill to trim a wheel with a ribbon of iron. But Hans was nowhere to be found.

6

Conestoga Indiantown
April 29, 1763

Tessa had been coming to Conestoga Indiantown as long as she could remember. She felt quite at home among these Indians. Will Sock, along with tribal elder Captain John, emerged out of the longhouse to greet their wagon. Will Sock had twinkly eyes, Tessa thought. They actually twinkled, like stars. He was a short man, small even for an Indian, and he wore his hair clipped and fringed like most white men. Captain John, who followed behind Will Sock, was elderly, gray and wizened with brown crepe-paper skin. He was the leader of the Conestogas, highly revered and equally beloved.

The longhouses were fascinating to Tessa. Each family lived separately in their own longhouse; they were made with pole framing, shaped like a hoop, covered in tree bark. Inside, raised platforms along each side were used for sleeping and storage, and a round firepit was in the center. Unlike Tessa's own home, there were no smooth wooden boards under one's feet; the floor of the longhouses was made of packed earth.

The Conestogas were farmers, dependent on the Susquehanna River for its rich soil and ever present supply of water. As a child, Tessa had loved visiting here. No longer. A once-lovely village on the river—if not thriving, at least stable—it had become a depressing place for her. The encroachment of immigrant settlers had taken its toll on the small tribe, and the village dwindled. Whenever some Conestoga arrived at Beacon Hollow, Tessa's mother would buy their brooms and baskets and send them home with as much food as they could carry.

Last fall, an outbreak of smallpox devastated the tribe even further. Tessa's father insisted that no Conestoga be allowed in their home, nor could anyone go to Indiantown. He went unaccompanied to the village during that time to drop off food supplies and medicine, for he had survived a bout of smallpox as a boy on the *Charming Nancy*, but he burned his clothes when he returned home. It was called the Time of Great Sickness. The village consisted of only thirty people now, mostly women and children.

Betty Sock, Will Sock's mother, was the matriarch of the village. She had lived her entire life in the same longhouse. Sixty people had once lived in her longhouse, she had told Tessa, each one related to her. Her family. Now there were only five.

"Greetings to you, Chief Bairn," Will Sock said, smiling broadly. "Will you eat with us?"

"Thank you," Bairn said, "but we have just eaten. In fact, I was hopin' I might be able to ask you to take some food off our hands before it spoils. You would be doin' us a great favor."

Will Sock dipped his chin. "It is sinful to waste food. Yes, we will help you with this favor."

That was their way. Will Sock would offer food though he had none to spare. Tessa's father always declined, saying he had just eaten, even if he had not, and offered spare food to Will Sock in a roundabout way. It helped Will Sock to save face, her father said, and that was important to a man's pride.

It was the only time Tessa knew her father to allow a man his pride.

Will Sock's twinkly eyes smiled at Tessa. "Where is Zeeb?"

"He's at home with our new houseguest. A little boy named Willie." Old Zeeb wouldn't leave Willie's side. Or maybe Willie wouldn't leave Zeeb's side. Tessa wasn't sure who was more devoted to whom. All she knew was that she was now second fiddle to Willie in Zeeb's eyes. That was fine with her. Willie needed him.

"You have grown even taller since you were last here, little one. Soon you will be taller than your father."

Tessa groaned. Her father was six foot six inches in his stocking feet. She glanced at Felix, her father's brother, who was only five foot nine inches. She had surpassed him last winter. He took after Dorothea's side of the family, not Jacob's.

"I wish I could trade you my height," Felix often told her. "It's not easy for a man to be short."

Tessa would roll her eyes at him. "It's worse for a girl to be tall than a man to be short."

That was usually the point when Tessa's mother intervened and told them both to stop complaining, that a person's height was neither a shortcoming nor an achievement. It was God's doing and they were insulting the Almighty with their foolish grievances.

Tessa thought that was easy for her to say when she stood at five foot two inches, an average height, and would have no idea how it felt to be on the fringe of average. Not even the fringe—far from average!

Betty Sock emerged from the flap that covered the entrance to the longhouse. She looked at Tessa's father with a steady gaze. "You have come with news."

He smiled. "Not so much news, as a request. I came t' ask for Will Sock's help." He turned to face Will Sock and Captain John. "There has been an attack on an Amish family. A girl, about Tessa's age, was taken captive along with her brother, about Christy's age. I'm hopin' someone from Indiantown might be able to find out where they might be, and what it would take to get them released."

At the exact same second, Will Sock and Captain John both closed their eyes and Tessa wondered what was running through their minds. The Conestogas were not regarded highly by the powerful Iroquois Confederacy. The Conestogas were of the larger Susquehanna tribe, once a fierce tribal people who had defeated the mighty Iroquois. But as the Iroquois developed a confederacy among tribes, the Susquehanna remained independent. It left them weak and vulnerable; they were not strong enough to withstand the sweep of colonists, nor of other warring Indian tribes. Betty Sock had recited to Tessa the story of her people countless times over the years, that there were once as many Susquehanna warriors as trees in the forest. No longer.

Tessa adored Betty Sock. She was fond of Will Sock and his wife, Molly, and their two children, but Betty Sock enamored her. She was never in a hurry, unlike most everyone in Tessa's world, who moved from one chore to the other as if they were always late and trying to catch up. Betty Sock saw time differently; she had an abundance of it and was always willing to share it with Tessa. She gave her the history of her people, taught her how to make baskets, how to catch a fish with her bare hands, how to start a fire using a stick and a rock. She tried to teach Tessa how to cook boiled cornbread, a staple among her people, but after four tries, Betty Sock gave up. "White women cannot cook Indian food," she had declared.

Tessa thought that was tommyrot. Cooking was cooking. Then her mother explained that most of the food that made up their diet was introduced from the natives: maple syrup, maple sugar, peppers, sassafras, corn, and everything that came from corn—grits, hominy, cornbread. It shocked Tessa to realize that her parents had never even seen corn before coming to the New World. She had grown up with it; Beacon Hollow was heavily dependent on it—for their livestock and for their own daily fare.

Will Sock and Captain John walked over to their totem pole. They knelt and bowed down low, foreheads touching the ground, and remained in that pose a very long time. Tessa had heard people in her church complain about those poles, wanting them removed because they were convinced totem poles were heathen, as suspect as the Asherah poles in the Old Testament, but her father held different ideas. It was the Conestoga's place of prayer, her father explained, like an outdoor church. A place they sought answers.

There were many similar traditions among the Conestoga Indians that caused grumbling among Tessa's church but with which her father had no quarrel. And that, in turn, caused a great deal of grumbling about her father. Mostly, that he strayed appallingly far from the straight and narrow path.

After a long time, a very long time, Will Sock and Captain John rose from their posture of prayer. They returned to Bairn, Felix, and Tessa, who had waited patiently in front of the longhouse.

Captain John spoke first. "You ask a difficult thing, Chief Bairn. It will not be simple to find this information." He looked to Will Sock to continue.

"I will do what I can do," Will Sock said, but Tessa noticed that his eyes were no longer twinkling.

Tessa's father dipped his head in thanks.

On the way back to Beacon Hollow, Tessa asked her father if Will Sock was worried he could be in danger from other Indians if he left his village to go north to find information about Betsy.

"I think," her father said, "that he is not as concerned about other Indians as about other white men."

The Scots-Irish, he meant. They were immigrant settlers who moved west into the frontier, past the Susquehanna River. They had little tolerance for those who did not share their Presbyterian views, and even less tolerance for Indians. Any and all Indians. Her father's Scottish accent had caused wariness among the Conestogas for a long time, until the Time of Great Sickness when he came to the village to help treat the sick and bury the dead. He won their hearts during that time.

"Papa," Tessa said, "do you think that Betsy and Johnny might have been taken captive by kind people, like Betty and Will Sock?"

He gave her a sad smile and answered her in English, though she had asked it in their dialect. "Let's pray for exactly that, Tessa darlin'."

Blue Mountain
May 2, 1763

Betsy had lost track of how many days it had been since the attack, or which day it was. Her legs ached, her stomach cramped from emptiness, the cut on her cheek burned hot and sore. There were times when she wondered if the warriors had no destination in mind at all, that their plan was to drive the captive children until they all fell down dead.

And then one afternoon the convoy's pace picked up. Some of the warriors ran ahead, up the hill, while others hurried the captive children along. When they reached the top of the hill, Betsy looked down and saw the junction of two rivers.

The warrior pointed. "Monongahela." He moved his hand and pointed to the other river. "Allegheny." Then he clasped his hands together. "O-hi-o." He smiled at her in that peculiar way that made the hair on the back of her neck rise. "Bloody. O-hi-o. Bloody."

She had heard of the great Ohio River, far west of the Schuylkill River. It was the first time since the attack that she had some kind of bearing of where she was, but she had little time to ponder, for in the next instant he shoved her roughly to keep moving.

They came to an open place where there were Indians milling around, talking to each other in their clickity-clack language. The ropes were taken off the captive children, their hands and their waists. Her captor grabbed Betsy's forearm and pushed his way through the crowd. She looked behind her for Johnny's whereabouts and saw him a few rods away, his gaze fixed on her as she was led away. The warrior stopped in front of a shelter covered with animal skins. He lifted a flap and gestured for her to go through the opening. Betsy did not move. She felt a rush of panic and stepped back, away from her captor, away from the shelter, and turned to look back at Johnny. She heard him yell out, "Don't go in!" but then a warrior whipped out a knife and held it to her brother's throat. The boy's eyes widened in fear.

Betsy dipped her head, indicating that she would cooperate. She would not resist.

Her captor plucked off her prayer covering, sneering, and flicked it into the air. It landed on the ground and he stepped on it with his filthy moccasin, grinding it into the dirt. Laughing, he gave her a hard push and she stumbled through the opening. Behind her, the flap thumped back across the opening and the interior of the shelter went dark. Strong, musky odors overwhelmed her—smoke, grease, rotting fish. At first, she could see nothing, but as her eyes adjusted, she saw a small fire, sunk in a stone-lined pit. Curls of smoke rose straight up and disappeared through a small opening in the shelter's roof.

And she realized she wasn't alone.

7

Not Faxon's Farm
May 2, 1763

Felix had been a deacon for ten years now, ordained right after he'd been married to his Rachel. And he meant *right* after. It was the same church service. Married one moment, deaconized the next. His life was radically altered on that one day.

Ten months later, he'd had another life-altering day. He'd become a father to Benjo and Dannie, and on that same day, he'd become a widower. It was an excruciatingly painful time of life, but it was not without joy too. His Rachel had left him with a precious gift: their twin sons.

Being a deacon was less of a gift. Much, much less. He didn't know how Bairn stood the burden of being the church's only ordained minister. Everything, good or bad, rested on his shoulders.

But anything in between good or bad sat at Felix's door. Bairn felt free to pass plenty of tasks on to his deacon: collecting alms for the poor, paying calls on certain church members who did not live the straight and narrow life.

It wasn't all drudgery and doom. It was Felix's job to publish the news of a couple who sought to marry. That was his favorite part of deaconry. He was a romantic at heart—as long as it wasn't his heart that was getting snared in a trap.

On this beautiful spring morning, Bairn had asked Felix to stop by Sam Weaver's farm and prompt Sam to pay the cat whipper what was owed to him for making shoes for his seven children. The shoemaker had repaired or made new shoes for each family member, and Sam had promised to pay him for over eight months. An empty promise. It was time for Bairn to step in, so naturally, he sent Felix to handle it.

Felix had dropped by Sam Weaver's house, and as he expected, Sam had made himself scarce. Sam had a knack for disappearing whenever anyone mentioned the settling of debts. One of Sam Weaver's sons met Felix at the door, a guarded look on his face. "My father is out . . . hunting."

Felix was not so easily fobbed off. "So, then, what of your mother?"

"Uh, she went shopping in Lancaster Town."

Felix frowned. He rubbed his hands together. "Mind if I warm my hands by the fire for a few moments?"

Reluctantly, the boy opened the door and let Felix in. Out of nowhere, children started to slip into the kitchen, watching Felix with the same guarded look as the older boy. It was like they came out of the woodwork.

Felix turned in a circle to look at each child. All seven, ranging in age from five to thirteen. "Children, I'm worried about your mother."

The children exchanged nervous looks.

"It's the saddest story I've ever heard," Felix said, in as

loud a voice as he could manage. "The good woman went shopping and left her legs behind."

Seven pairs of eyes shifted to the bed, tucked against the wall. There were two large feet sticking out under it.

His errand at the Weavers' had finished up quite well, deacon-wise, and Felix felt pretty pleased with himself. His horse knew its way back to Not Faxon's Farm, so he settled deep in the saddle and reviewed the day. Sam Weaver's wife rolled out from under the bed, dusted herself off, went to a crock kept on the hearth's mantel, and reached a hand into the crock to pull out money. Without a word, she counted out every shilling and pence owed to the poor cat whipper and handed it to Felix. The money was now in Felix's coat pocket, soon to be delivered. Account settled.

He didn't like to brag, but he thought he was a very effective deacon. Take the Tom the Tailor situation.

A few months ago, Bairn had been concerned that Tom Miller's church attendance had become rather spotty. No Plain family ever missed a preaching if they could help it. So, naturally, Bairn sent Felix to deal with Tom.

Felix had knocked and knocked on Tom Miller's door, to no avail. Tom's horse was picketed in the front yard and Felix heard someone scurry upstairs. He knew the tailor was inside. So finally Felix left a note on the door: *Revelation 3:20*. If Tom bothered to look it up in his Bible, he would find the words: "I stand at the door and knock."

The following Sunday, he was pleased to see Tom Miller arrive at church right on time and plunk himself down right next to Felix. In the middle of Bairn's sermon, Tom Miller leaned to one side and passed the note that Felix had left on his door, the one with Revelation 3:20 on it. Below that verse was scrawled Genesis 3:10: ". . . and I was afraid because I was naked."

Felix tried his best to hold himself together but his eyes started to water, his chest heaved, he could barely contain his laughter. Tom Miller struggled to tamp down his own mirth; his face was bright red, and tears streamed down his round cheeks. It was a fine moment.

And best of all, Tom the Tailor hadn't missed church since. Not once.

Felix really was a very effective deacon. Possibly, the finest deacon in the New World, though he knew it was prideful to think such a vain thought. Plus, he was the only deacon in the New World.

After stopping by the cat whipper to settle the Sam Weavers' sizable account and receiving profuse thank-yous from the cat whipper's wife, he decided to drop by Beacon Hollow to share the good news of his completed task with his brother. He wasn't always sure Bairn realized what a fine deacon he had, and it wouldn't hurt for Anna to hear that Felix had actually finished something. She did not always appreciate Felix's style of deaconry leadership. He still felt a burning sensation in his gut when he thought about the tutor who had been hired for his sons without his knowledge or permission. Catrina Müller. Of all people on this earth!

His horse turned up the lane to Beacon Hollow without any prodding, and Felix closed his eyes to enjoy the warm sun on his face. He took another deep breath, then opened his eyes as the horse abruptly stopped, then danced on his feet.

Galloping behind him on the lane, without even a nod as his horse sailed past Felix, was his foster brother, Hans, the missing smithy.

Beacon Hollow

Tessa and Willie had been giving the henhouse a much-needed spring cleaning when they heard the sound of pounding hooves approach the house. She rushed to the door. And there was Hans! He looked a mess: scruffy whiskers, dirty clothes, mud-caked boots.

Her father hurried over from the carpentry shop, her mother flew out of the house, and they were soon both by his side, questions tumbling over each other. "Hans, where have you been?" "Why didn't you send word?" "Did it not occur to you how you worried Dorothea?"

Hans slipped off his horse and turned to them. "I went to the Zook farm up the Schuylkill River. All that remained were the charred timbers of the barn. The house is completely gone."

Her father folded his arms against his chest. "I could have told you as much."

"I had to see for myself."

Tessa's mother turned and flashed her a warning look. Willie! Tessa took his hand and tugged him back into the henhouse. "Let's go finish up the henhouse, Willie." His eyes were on Hans; he wasn't budging. "Let's go." As soon as they went back inside the small structure, Tessa sent Willie to the far end with a broom and she placed herself by the little opening. She wasn't about to miss anything Hans had to say.

Her father's voice was easy to hear. "Was there any word of where the warriors took the captives?"

"I spoke to some neighbors, but they had no information."

"But they're alive," Tessa's mother said, quietly. "If not, the neighbors would've known. Someone would've have known. It's been over ten days now since the attack. Surely, someone would've come across . . ."

Come across what? Then a shudder spread over Tessa. Come across dead bodies was what her mother was about to say.

Hans nodded. "Betsy's alive. I'm sure of it. I'm going to keep looking."

Her father put a hand on Hans's shoulder. "No you're not. I'm sorry, Hans. You're a member of this church and we need you here. Many parts of the wagon are waiting for your help. It's a project that belongs to the entire church. We need you here. You're going to have to leave Betsy's fate in God's hands."

Hans was shocked. "You're saying that I can't go?"

He nodded. "You can't go."

Hans jerked his hand off his shoulder and stepped back a few feet. He mounted his horse, turned it around, and galloped off in the direction of Not Faxon's Farm, passing right by her startled uncle Felix.

❧

Later that afternoon, Anna opened the knock at the door to find Hans, clean shaven, freshly clothed, and less angry. He said he had come to speak to Bairn, that he wanted his blessing to head out and seek for Betsy.

Anna's first thought was that she was pleased Hans wanted his minister's approval. But as soon as Bairn and Hans sat at the table, facing each other grimly, Anna could see this was going to be a contentious meeting. Swiftly, she sent Tessa and Willie out to the barn to feed the animals. Tessa was openly disappointed to be sent out the door, but there was no need for Willie to hear anything more that Hans had to say. How much could a little boy bear?

"Hans, you're needed here," Bairn said. "You're the only smithy in all of Stoney Ridge. Horses need shodding, tools need fixing. Even Tom the Tailor can't do his work because his scissors need mending. And I've already told you that the wagon is on hold, waiting for your hardware."

"Then let us make a compromise," Hans said, eyes pleading. "I'll finish up the wagon, take care of the horses, get caught up on the tools. But then I want to head out again. One more search for her."

"I've told you no."

Hans opened his mouth to object and Bairn cut him off. "That's the end of it, Hans. I'm sorry, but you're needed here. You've done all you can for Betsy Zook. She belongs to God."

Hans slammed his palms on the table. "Why can't I go look for her?"

"For more reasons than I can count. You don't know where she is. You're alone. What's driving your search is vengeance—" Bairn lifted a hand to silence Hans's indignation—"don't think I don't know what's fueling your heart right now. Vengeance is a dangerous master to feed. Its appetite has no end."

Hans was visibly outraged. "I am seeking clues to Betsy's whereabouts."

"I don't know what you were thinking—running off to the Zook farm as if it would provide those answers."

Hans lifted in his chair and thumped his chest. "At least I did something!" He pointed at Bairn. "You just sit here, fussing over your wagon. You don't even care about what goes on up north. You moved the church down here and act like an ostrich with your head in the sand."

Bairn's jaw stiffened. Anna was surprised he let Hans talk to him like that. He took his time answering. "I have done something. I have gone to Will Sock and asked him to see what he can find out."

Hans settled back into chair. "So what did he say?"

"He hasn't brought word yet."

Hans shook his head in disgust. "You'd trust an Indian to bring you the truth."

"I do. I trust Will Sock." Bairn sighed. "Hans, we have no business going up north. The frontier is getting more dangerous. I won't be traveling on circuit for a while."

Quietly Anna added, "There aren't many Amish left up there. Not any more."

"Not any more," Bairn repeated.

Hans covered his face with his hands and leaned his elbows on the table. He was silent for such a long time that Anna thought he might be trying not to cry. "She's never coming back, is she?"

Bairn exchanged a look with Anna. "We don't know what the future holds. For whatever reason Betsy has had to endure this terrible thing, we trust that God is sovereign over all things. All things, Hans. Even over these bleak circumstances. His presence will never leave Betsy. His purposes for her life will endure. It's time to give Betsy's fate over to God."

Hans did not protest. He picked up his hat and walked to the door. Anna stopped him as he put a hand on the door's latch. "He is with you too. God has not gone missing, even in this."

He stared at her with an odd expression in his eyes, a look

she couldn't read, then he shoved his hat on his head and slammed the door behind him.

🌿

Junction of the Monongahela, Allegheny, and Ohio Rivers

Betsy's legs wobbled beneath her. There seemed to be people in the shelter—squaws—who had been waiting for her. The squaws advanced upon her, circling her, crowding around, jabbering in their strange tongues, plucking at her clothes to pull them off. She resisted, thrashing and grappling, trying to break free. An older squaw grabbed a handful of Betsy's tangled, matted hair, then let loose a stream of angry Indian words. Her meaning was clear—Betsy must remove her soiled clothes and wash in a pot of water warmed by the fire. Shaking, Betsy obliged, peeling the layers away one after another. A chunk of bristly moss was thrust into her hand by the old squaw. The old squaw put her hand on Betsy's shoulder and pressed her down until she crouched near the fire. Then she dipped the moss into the water and started to scrub the grime off her body.

She didn't notice her clothes and shoes had been taken away until she finished washing. She looked for them, panicking, but the squaws handed her an Indian dress and moccasins, both new, made of white deerskin. The dress slipped on easily and draped over her, surprisingly soft and comfortable against her skin. The moccasins felt like slippers.

A girl dipped a bowl into a clay pot simmering over the fire and handed the bowl to Betsy. She would never have dreamed she would eat something that smelled rancid, or put something in her mouth without any idea what it was, but consuming hunger drove her. It was some kind of boiled fish in a putrid broth, and she scooped the flesh into her mouth with her fingers, then drank the greasy liquid. Exhausted, she sank to the ground near the fire. They must have walked hundreds of miles to get to this place.

But where was this place? And why was she here? She still didn't know what was going to happen to Johnny or to her, or to the other children.

Betsy sensed someone come up behind her. She tensed, drew up her shoulders, stiffening them as if to protect her neck from a blow. Desperate thoughts flitted through her mind, desperate but shockingly clear minded: Why would they feed her, bathe her, only to kill her?

But with the gentlest of touches, the same Indian girl who handed her a bowl of food now combed the tangles out of her hair, then braided it into a plait, Indian style. She came around to the front of Betsy and peered at her with a serious look on her face. She took the lid off a wooden container and dipped her finger into a powder of red ochre. Gently, with her finger, she spread the powder over Betsy's face, taking care over the oozing cut on her cheek made by the warrior's knife, and rubbed the powder into her hair.

Betsy's mind was filled with questions, but what could she say? Nothing. How could she make herself understood, or try to understand anything these squaws could tell her? And so her questions fluttered away, like moths in the night, and she felt herself relax ever so slightly with the girl's calm touch.

She wasn't aware of how much time had passed when the flap opened and her captor appeared, shouting angry words. The young Indian girl pointed to the door, indicating Betsy should leave. When she walked outside, her eyes blinked from the bright afternoon sunlight. Her heart caught in her throat—there was no sign of the other white children. None of them. She looked in vain for Johnny.

Where was he?

Betsy began to shake. "Where is my brother? What have you done with him?"

Her captor lifted his fingers and made a gesture like a bird flying away. "All gone."

"Please, tell me what's happened to him!" In despair, she fell to her knees and begged, but the warrior only tilted his head back and laughed.

A hand gripped Betsy's shoulder, gently but firmly. She looked up into the face of an Indian she'd never seen before—his eyes were not the black of the devil warrior's eyes, but blue.

"Whom do you seek?" he said.

She stared at him, stupefied, as it slowly dawned on her that he was speaking her dialect. "My brother. Please. Tell me where he is." Her voice was little more than a whisper. "Is he dead? Have they killed him?"

"The captives are gone. They have been offered in tribute to Indian families. Most likely, your brother will not be killed. He will be treated as a son. The same fate awaits you." There was a kindness in his expression that she had not imagined possible in an Indian. She had perceived Indians to be a depraved people, polluted by their paganry. But here was this man, looking down at her with eyes filled with compassion. There was something about the set of his chin, his straight dark hair, his thick brows, his high forehead, features that could make him appear thoroughly intimidating were it not for the kindness she saw in those blue eyes.

"Please, help me."

"Do not fear." He gave her a gentle smile. "The same sun that hardens the clay melts the ice."

But she was afraid. She was terrified. A coil of anxiety began to tighten in her stomach and she felt close to heaving the peculiar contents of the broth. He lifted her under her arms, pulling her to her feet.

With great reluctance, she stood.

8

Junction of the Monongahela, Allegheny, and Ohio Rivers
May 2, 1763

Trembling with fear, Betsy let the blue-eyed Indian take her elbow and gently lead her to stand before two Indian squaws. As she approached them, one squaw—the older of the two, clearly in charge—peered at her, eyes narrowed.

The older one was tall and thin, with a long face and a straight nose, wide-spaced eyes, a strong chin. An intricate silver headpiece gathered her hair. She wore a queenly air, though she kept her face without expression. The younger woman was short and stout, round as a pumpkin, with merry eyes, as if she found life to be amusing. She carried an infant on her back, strapped on a cradleboard, and the baby gazed out like a little doll.

The older squaw came forward and took Betsy's chin in her hands, studying her infected cheek. She spoke to the other squaw and then to the blue-eyed Indian, who stood deferentially to the side. He said something in their tongue and then they all looked at her. Betsy realized something important had been decided.

They led Betsy down the hillside to a canoe on the river's beach. The blue-eyed Indian pushed it into the river. The two squaws waded into the water and climbed into the canoe, then turned to Betsy and made motions with their hands that she should get in. The blue-eyed Indian helped her into the stern of the canoe, but then he stepped back.

"Where are they taking me?" she asked him.

"Home." His tone was calm but firm. "You are going home."

Home? She had no home.

***

Not Faxon's Farm
May 3, 1763

After much tinkering, Bairn had found ways to outfit the Conestoga wagon with several unique features to help handle heavy hauling. Felix thought his brother might be an engineering genius.

For one thing, Bairn had designed the wagon with brakes. No wagon Felix had ever seen had brakes built into it, other than latching a chain through the spokes of wheels on a descent so that the locked wheels skidded down a slope. A primitive braking system that worked for a farmer's light loads to market and back. It would never work hauling the heavy freight in a Conestoga wagon.

Bairn spent a long time figuring out a better brake system, trying out several options until he settled on a lever that pressed blocks of woods against the wheel to slow the wagon. To keep the brake on, the teamster fastened a chain on the brake lever to a pin under the wagon.

Another distinctive feature of Bairn's wagon design was the wheels. They had to be large and strong to hold the wagon together over rough terrain, including rivers and streams, as there were pitifully few bridges on the route from Lancaster to Philadelphia. The rear wheels stood about six feet tall, the smaller front wheels at four feet.

Bairn angled the wheels so the part below the axle was pitched inward, while the part above the axle turned outward. At first Felix thought Bairn might have made a mistake, perhaps his vision was failing him. But then Bairn showed him that when the wagon was filled with freight, the load pushed on the wheels, forcing them upright or vertical. *Brilliant*. He was brilliant, that brother of his.

Those wheels, though, they were difficult to construct. Time-consuming and complicated. Bairn had already built the rims out of oak plank and pounded the spokes into the tight mortises. This afternoon, he brought the wheels over to Not Faxon's Farm so that he and Felix could help Hans make tires, strips of iron, to wrap around the wheel and solder the joint. To put the tire on the wheel, Hans heated the iron strip until it glowed red. Then he bent the hot metal around the wheel and joined the two ends.

The moment Hans began hammering the tire on the wheel, smoke and flames danced up from the wooden wheel. With the tire in place, he doused the wheel with water, causing the metal to hiss and spit steam. While the wheel cooked, it squeaked and groaned as the iron tire shrank, squeezing and tightening the wheel joints. A long and laborious process.

The three men had just completed the tire for one wheel

when they looked up and found Will Sock standing at the door.

"No news," Will Sock said.

"No news about Betsy Zook?" Bairn asked. "No news about Johnny Zook?"

"No news." Will Sock turned and left as silently as he came.

The three of them remained silent for a long while, watching Will Sock until he disappeared into the woods.

"I don't believe him." Hans crossed his arms, staring at the woods as if he could still see Will Sock. He spun to face Bairn. "You shouldn't have gone to an Indian to find out about other Indians. Of course you're not going to get a straight answer."

Bairn glanced sharply at Hans. "If there were news to report, Will Sock would bring it."

"You don't know about Indians, Bairn. You think you do but you don't. You don't know what they're capable of."

Bairn straightened to his full height. "Sounds to me like words straight from the pulpit of John Elder."

"This has nothing to do with John Elder," Hans said, steaming mad. He stiffened his spine, trying to match Bairn eye to eye, but he had to lift his chin and Felix thought he looked mighty silly. "This has to do with you. You've given up. You've given her up for dead."

Bairn was never one to sugarcoat things. He slipped into English, which Felix knew was an indication that he was speaking from his heart. "Nae. Nae for dead, Hans. I have nae given Betsy Zook up for dead. But I doot y'll ever see her again." He took off his leather gloves. "I'm sorry. Truly I am. I ken how keen y've been for her."

"Whether she's dead or alive, at least John Elder would have done something. Not just carried on with building a wagon." Hans untied his leather apron, tossed it on the ground, and started toward the door.

"Hans!" Bairn said in a harsh tone. "We need to finish this. Heed my word, lad."

For a brief moment, Felix was eight years old again, tucked on the *Charming Nancy* as it lurched and chugged across the Atlantic Ocean, watching Bairn, as ship's carpenter, chastise a lazy sailor. All that was missing was salty sea air and the sound of flapping sails.

Hans stopped at the door and shook his head. He seemed very far away, sunk deep in his own anguish, angry and injured. "I need time to sort this all through." He mounted his horse and rode off toward the road.

Bairn sighed, staring sightlessly at a spot on the floor, then put his leather gloves back on. Back to work.

"Did you have to take all hope away from him?"

Bairn looked up at Felix, surprised. "Hope can n'er be taken away. But hope should nae be misplaced. We hope in an eternal life, we hope for Betsy to be sheltered by the Lord God's lovin' presence."

"But we don't know that she's gone for good. Why not let him believe she might return?"

"Most likely, Felix, she is gone for good. But even if she were to return one day, she will nae be the girl he once ken. Look at how Jacob Hochstetler's sons had adjusted to their new life and dinnae want to return even when given freedom." He picked up the traveler, a tool made with a small wheel to measure, and started rolling it along another iron strip. "When one did get released—Christian, I think 'tis his name—he went to his old home and knocked on the door. Jacob dinnae even ken him." He stopped marking the iron strip and looked up at Felix. "His own father dinnae ken him. Jacob made him wait outside, like a pesky peddler, 'til he was finished with his supper."

"But those boys were gone a long time. Betsy's only been gone a few weeks."

"Aye, but Hans needs to do his grieving and get on with it. Y' ken him as well as I do—he will focus on his loss. It will consume him. I am sorry for this trial, truly sorry, but mayhap 'tis meant t' test him. T' give him experience with spiritual matters. Mayhap this will be a great fork in the road for Hans. A trial and tribulation. In m' own life, those were the times when I learned t' depend on God in ways I had nae considered.

"A sea captain once told me something very wise, something I've never forgotten: 'What life does t' you depends on what life finds in you.' This terrible trial, 'tis an opportunity for Hans to find out what is in him. His faith will be tested. And found proven, I trust, like those wheels." He pointed to the three unfinished wheels resting on the wall. "We must find out if they are able to take the weight of the freight in the wagon."

Hands hooked on his hips, Bairn's gaze swept the blacksmith shop and he let out an exasperated sigh. It was a mess, with jobs started, none finished. "And now I must go tell Faxon Gingerich that the wagon's completion will be delayed a wee bit longer."

"So that's it? Just . . . get on with the wagon? Hans had a point, Bairn. It does seem a little coldhearted."

"Nae, not coldhearted at all. I spoke to Hans as I did so

he will get on with his livin'." Bairn picked up the tongue of the wagon, a long pole of iron that would fit between the horses, a project he had asked Hans to finish months ago. "So we all can get on with livin' the lives God has given us."

"Do you truly believe we've done everything we could do?"

"Aye, Felix. I do."

"If the girl taken had been our Tessa, would you still give up so easily?"

Bairn sent him a frustrated glance. "Givin' the matter of Betsy Zook over to God's good hands is nae the same as givin' up. And I would thank you t' stop questionin' my judgment on this. 'Tis hard enough, Felix. I'm doin' m' best. And now I'm gettin' back to work."

He picked up an iron latch and put it in the fire. "I've prayed mightily over this and the answer I keep getting is that Betsy is in God's hands. I feel peace about it. So does Anna, if that makes you feel any better."

"I suppose it does," Felix said, sorry to add to his brother's burden. At times, he forgot the pressures that were on Bairn. There was no simple solution. If they were to join Hans and spend all their time pursuing Betsy Zook's whereabouts, then what would happen to their farms, to their harvest, to this never-ending wagon project?

Yet to not find an answer about Betsy—wasn't that wrong too?

Then Felix realized that his brother had found the middle ground. He had tried, with Will Sock's help, to see if there was any possible clue to pursue about Betsy's whereabouts. There wasn't. So that might be the answer. "I'm sorry. I know it's a troubling thing. Thinking about this whole thing makes me feel worn out."

Bairn took the piece of iron latch out of the fire and set it on the anvil. "What will make y' feel even more worn out is that yer going t' have t' set aside training those colts to get Hans's unfinished tasks caught up." He handed a hammer to Felix. "Thank you, brother."

Felix looked around the smithy shop at all the work piled up. He had some basic smithy skills but nothing like Hans.

And then up drove Maria Müller in a pony cart, with her meanest, ugliest pony tied to the back of the cart, the one that was known for biting and kicking. It was walking a little odd, favoring a foot. Felix squinted his eyes and saw that it was missing a shoe on its back leg. Its kicking leg.

❧

Not Faxon's Farm

Tessa was in the woods behind Not Faxon's Farm, scavenging for wild ginger, when Will Sock appeared, out of the blue.

He looked in her basket. "Very good medicine."

"It's for my grandmother. She suffers from dyspepsia." When his sparse eyebrows lifted in curiosity, she rubbed her tummy. "Stomachaches."

He nodded solemnly, then his gaze shifted past her. "Are you not frightened to be alone in the woods, little one?"

She smiled. "No. I know every tree in these woods."

"It is not the woods you should fear, but the man who pretends to be a strong tree when his core is rotting within."

She looked around her, squinting her eyes to penetrate the forest gloom. "I don't see anyone but you and me."

He gave her a sad smile. "You are not Indian. You look with your eyes. If you were Indian, then you would see with your heart." He left her then to continue along the narrow path that led toward the main road. She spent the next few minutes turning his words over in her mind, flummoxed by them. Will Sock often spoke in riddles.

She went back to the task of gathering wild ginger when not more than ten minutes later, Hans galloped down the path and went right past, not even seeing her.

❧

Not Faxon's Farm
May 4, 1763

Felix awakened to a rose-hued sunrise creeping over the sill. Startled by a sound, he sat up in bed. A new horse was nearby—he could tell by the anxious back-and-forth nickering of his pasture horses. The mysterious stallion! Maybe he'd come to do his business. Maybe Felix could finally get a look at him.

Barefoot, he padded to the window and peered out. Coming up the long winding lane was a horse and carriage. He scratched his head. None of the neighbors had carriages, only wagons. Carriages belonged to city folks, where roads were cobbled. Out in the country, roads were steep, rocky, and full of washouts. He rubbed his eyes and squinted. Could it be him? Felix opened the window and leaned out. "Why, Benjamin Franklin, do my eyes deceive me? Is it really you?"

The man snapped his head up to locate the voice. "Indeed, young Felix! 'Tis me!"

Felix pulled his nightshirt over his head and yanked on his britches and shirt, then bolted down the stairs, still barefoot. The front door slammed behind him and he bolted down the steps. He hadn't seen his old friend in years, not since the last time he was in Philadelphia, and he had certainly aged a bit. Still tall and straight backed, his belly had rounded and his hairline had receded. He waved his tricornered hat, greeting Felix warmly with a smile that lit his steady gray eyes.

Felix reached for his hand to shake it. "What brings you to Not Faxon's Farm?"

A confused look flitted over Ben Franklin's eyes. "'Tis not Beacon Hollow?"

"No. It's about a mile down the road. Shorter through the woods."

"Ah." He peered out the carriage and down the lane. "My sense of direction has never been stellar."

"What takes you to Beacon Hollow?"

"While in Lancaster Town, news of this Conestoga wagon reached my ears. I had to come see it for myself."

How about *that*. Bairn's wagon was gaining notice. "It's housed over at Beacon Hollow, over at my brother Bairn's property. I'll take you there myself, but first let's have breakfast."

"I won't refuse your hospitality, my friend. I started out from Lancaster Town long before dawn and I am rather famished."

Felix's glance swept the house, at the chimney that showed no sign of smoke; he thought of what breakfast would look like in his house on this gray morning—Hans hadn't returned home last night so he would be of no help, his mother slept late so she would be no help. His mind made a quick inventory of the larder. Near empty. The boys could run to the henhouse and fetch some eggs, hopefully fresh. Felix would crack them in lard over his lone iron skillet (still caked with soot from the previous evening's meal), watch them sputter and pop until the yolk turned rubbery and the edges were burnt and he was sure they were done. He looked back at Benjamin Franklin, whom he knew had a fine palate and a love of good food. A greasy fried egg might not be the proper victuals for this esteemed visitor.

Ben smiled at Felix. "A cup of chamomile tea to warm these old bones sounds delightful."

Chamomile tea? Felix never heard of such a thing. Tea was tea. Then he remembered that he had run out of tea leaves and hadn't bothered to replace them.

Felix's pant legs were wicking up the morning's dew. "I have a better idea. Let me get my boots on and we'll breakfast at Beacon Hollow. It will save you time."

"The mistress of Beacon Hollow won't mind?" But Benjamin was already scooting over in the carriage to make room for Felix.

"Anna? No. She's accustomed to me." He hurried back into the house, grabbed an old rag to wipe off his feet, yanked on a pair of socks—with holes, he noticed—jammed his feet into boots, and was about to leave when he remembered his boys. They would need to eat. He found two red apples and set them in the center of the table.

It was a short ride to Beacon Hollow, far too short, Felix thought, as he enjoyed the time alone with Ben Franklin. He had retired from printing years ago, and although he was involved in politics, it gave him more time to tinker, his true love. Besides good food.

Franklin was a born inventor. Felix's favorite story was about Ben as a boy—a hint of what genius lay in that mind of his. At age eleven, he had wanted to make swimming an easier endeavor, so he built wooden paddles to fit on his hands. They looked like a painter's palette and acted like fish fins. And they had worked! Last summer, Felix made pairs for his own sons based on his recollection of Ben's paddles. Unfortunately, they did not work. He used balsa fir wood—soft wood, easy to whittle but good for little else; the paddles swelled up and disintegrated and his boys had to be rescued from the middle of the pond.

Those things happened. Trial and error was part of the inventor's labor. Felix fancied himself an inventor, much like Ben Franklin. His barn was littered with good ideas in the making.

Just as expected, Anna and Bairn were pleased to have unexpected visitors for breakfast, and it was a far better serving than anything Felix could've mustered up at Not Faxon's Farm. Tessa and poor Willie listened wide-eyed as Ben regaled them with story after story. Felix couldn't stop grinning; he could listen to this man all day long.

He had done that very thing when he was just a boy himself, not much older than poor Willie. The *Charming Nancy* had docked in Port Philadelphia, but the German immigrants were held up from entering the colony. They had spent their days haggling over naturalization at the Court House with processing agents. Felix, a curious boy at age eight, had no patience for waiting. He'd spent months on that leaky vessel and was ready to explore the young city. He happened upon the printer at his shop on Market Street and returned to it as often as he could slip away. Felix had been an ardent admirer of Ben Franklin ever since, supporting him even when other Germans disavowed him.

Too soon, breakfast was over and the day was under way.

Anna took Willie to Not Faxon's Farm with breakfast for Dorothea and the boys, Tessa set off for barn chores, and it was time to show off the wagon. Bairn gave Ben Franklin an overview, walking him from stern to bow.

He studied every inch of it, just as Felix knew he would. He questioned Bairn on each aspect, those parts that were completed, and the parts that remained unfinished—the brakes, the weatherproofing of the canvas, the hitch at the back to make loading easier—and finally gave it his stamp of approval. "I am duly impressed," he said. "It surpasses the rumors that surround it."

Bairn was pleased by his assessment, Felix could see that. Though they would not say it aloud, they were both thinking the same thing: It would be a fine thing to have such high praise for the wagon spread through Philadelphia, coming from Benjamin Franklin's eyewitness account.

They walked Ben out to his carriage. "Before I take my leave," he said, fidgeting with the brim of his hat, "I hope I can count on you to defend me against my foes."

This was a tetchy subject. Ben had written a pamphlet called *Observations Concerning the Increase of Mankind* about the influx of immigrants into the colonies. In the manuscript, there were a few paragraphs in which he wrote of his alarm about the Pennsylvania Germans, whom he felt did not adopt the English language or customs or politics. It was true that his pamphlet had fostered a negative view of Germans around the colony, but it also caused a marked decline in German support for him, as well. Felix believed he regretted his words.

"I do not always share the opinions of my colleagues."

"Aboot what in particular?" Bairn asked.

"About the natives, for example. If one Indian injures another, I do not agree that all Indians must have revenge visited upon them." He set his hat upon his head. "I suspect you hold the same view."

"I do," Bairn said. He reached his hand out and Franklin took it in a prolonged handclasp.

"I trust you will bear my thought to others, Bairn." He meant the Amish church, Felix knew. He meant the local German Mennonites, over whom Bairn had great influence. He climbed into the carriage. "And I will certainly remind others to watch with bated breath for the arrival of the mighty Conestoga wagon." He raised a hand and waved a farewell.

It dawned on Felix that Benjamin Franklin had come not just to see the Conestoga wagon on this morning but to share his politics.

As Franklin's carriage rolled down the lane, Bairn returned to the carpentry shop. Felix stayed where he was, hands on his hips, watching the carriage until it was out of sight.

Tessa eased up behind him. "So the chatty man with the droopy eyes left?"

"Yes."

"He came to see the wagon?"

"Yes." He dropped his hands and turned to face Tessa. "That, and maybe to do a little politicking."

She shifted a basket filled with chicken eggs to her hip. "About what?"

"What else? Indians."

9

Along the Monongahela River
May 4, 1763

One day passed, then another. The two squaws spoke in low voices to each other as they paddled the canoe along the river, and while Betsy couldn't understand them, at least their sounds were soothing, so different from the angry, shrieking sounds of the warriors. Only once or twice did the wide-eyed infant in the cradleboard cry out. The young squaw gently unwrapped the baby, and to Betsy's surprise at first—because she had assumed the baby belonged to her—she handed the baby to the older squaw, who folded him in her arms, tugged down one side of her dress, and held him to her breast. They made camp each evening along the river's shoreline. The younger squaw caught a fish in her bare hands and they roasted it over an open fire, sharing all with Betsy. Like manna from heaven, it was the first fresh food she had tasted in weeks. Not plentiful but oh-so-satisfying.

At long last the canoe came round a bend in the river and the young squaw tugged on Betsy's sleeve, pointing up ahead. There along the river's shore was what looked to be an Indian village, dozens of clustered domed huts. "Wigwams," the squaw told her. "Wigwams." Threads of gray smoke rose from the dwellings into the air. Apparently, this was "home."

Squaws in the village hurried down to the river's edge to greet them, nearly a dozen or more. They surrounded the canoe and started to cry, keening in agony, as if they had arrived with a death message. The sound was dreadful, worse than the howling of wolves. Almost as ear splitting as the warrior's death halloo.

They pulled Betsy out of the canoe and onto the narrow shore, circling her, crying and screaming, plucking at her hair and dress. Terrified, Betsy held her arms against her body, not understanding what caused them such distress. Then the sounds stopped, like a flame was blown out. And new sounds began, joyful ones. The older squaw pointed to her and said, "Hurit." Then women rejoiced over her, calling her Hurit, as if she had been lost to them and now was found.

It dawned on her that she had been brought to this village to fill a hole in the bereaved family. She was the new sister to the squaws. She was the atonement.

But what about *her* grief? Who was going to replace the anguish in her heart? Who was going to replace her family? Her life had been stolen from her, her parents and brother Willie had been murdered, her only remaining sibling had been taken captive. Everything—*everyone*—near and dear to her was gone.

How she hated them!

Beacon Hollow
May 5, 1763

Anna was outside when she saw John Elder ride up to the farmhouse, looking for Bairn. From the nearby town of Paxton, he was a leader among Scots-Irish settlers.

John Elder dismounted and started toward Anna, then stopped with disgust when Zeeb ran up to greet him. "I hate those sharp-nosed, droop-tailed Indian dogs." He swatted Zeeb away as if the poor old dog was a repulsive insect caught climbing up his trousers. He frowned at Anna. "Those blasted dogs are makin' strife between neighbors over in Paxton. They kill sheep and calves."

"Sweet old Zeeb has never killed anything," Anna said, clapping her hands so the dog would leave sour John Elder and come to her for a pat. She tried to find good in all people, to appreciate the image of God that was imprinted within, but John Elder sorely tried her efforts. The gray-and-white tangle of his hair gave him the appearance of a sage, but he was far from that. Anna thought of him as a rabble-rouser. He circulated alarming rumors on every visit and seemed eager to create unrest. He carried just enough truth to be dangerous. She always felt a swirl of distress after he left their home.

She pointed across the yard. "My husband is in the carpentry shop."

"Might I trouble y' for a cup of yer finest tea?" John Elder said, now recovered from Zeeb's greeting enough to grin.

Anna nodded. "I'll bring it down to the shop." She didn't want him in the house.

"I've come t' see this wagon that is causing so much chatter." John Elder pulled off his hat with a flourish and bowed low, a gesture that Anna felt smacked of mock humility. He handed her his horse's reins and strode across the yard to the carpentry shop. She doubted he came for the sole purpose of seeing the wagon. Whenever there was an Indian raid, John Elder seemed personally to make it his business to spread the news far and wide, to increase the terror, embellishing the story with as much finesse as his imagination could furnish.

As Anna tied his horse's reins to the hitching post, she stroked the horse's long neck. "I'm sorry for your master," she said. "You deserve better." She filled a bucket of water from the well and set it under the horse's nose.

Tessa appeared on the front stoop. "Mem, he's brought those horrible caterwaulers."

"I noticed." Tied to John Elder's saddle was a felt bag containing bagpipes. He ended each visit to Beacon Hollow with a personal concert, which he felt was a fitting benediction. The haunting sound of the bagpipes set Anna's teeth on edge; Tessa deplored them. She said it caused the birds to leave the trees, the sows to vanish deeper into the forest, and her beloved mysterious stallion to head for the hills.

After brewing tea, Anna carried the mugs to the carpentry shop. She set them on a workbench and turned to leave, but Bairn stopped her. "Stay, Anna. John Elder has some things t' say that I'd like y' t' hear."

John Elder lifted up a copy of the *Pennsylvania Gazette* and read from it: "'A thousand families in Cumberland County have been driven from their houses and Habitations, and all the Comforts and Conveniences of life. Large numbers are living in barns, stables, cellars, and under old leaky sheds, the dwelling-houses being all crowded.'" He looked straight at her, as if daring her to defy the *Gazette*. "The barbarians are startin' up war again."

Anna did not allow herself to show alarm, though she felt it. "Cumberland County is quite a distance from here."

John Elder held up the *Gazette* high in the air. "'If Cumberland County is lost, then Lancaster or even Philadelphia will become'"—he read from the article—"'the frontier of this Province.'" He pushed the paper to Bairn. "Have y' not heard of the barbarian siege upon Fort Pitt?"

Bairn and Anna exchanged a look. Word had trickled down that the Senecas and Cayugas had declared war against the English, intended to take Fort Pitt, then march down the country. Fort Pitt, established by the French in 1753 as Fort Duquesne on the spot where two rivers joined together, had been destroyed by the British in 1758, then rebuilt and renamed. Whoever controlled that strategic fort controlled the entire Ohio country, for both settlement and trade.

John Elder tossed the *Gazette* on Bairn's workbench. "I heard the tragedy about the Plain farm up the Schuylkill. The wee ones taken captive, the parents kilt right before their eyes. The farm burned, the livestock butchered or stolen. I heard the woman was reduced to a smokin' pyre, that the man had been mutilated, awls thrust in his eyes and a pitchfork and spear stuck in his body."

Bairn kept his gaze fixed steadily on John Elder. "Aye, y' heard the truth."

Stunned and sickened, Anna clapped her hands against her mouth. Bairn had not given her those details.

"Had the government removed the Indians as they had been urged to do, this painful catastrophe might have been avoided. Those poor people—they're *yer* people, Bairn Bauer!

These children, they belong t' yer Plain clan. It's high time we put a stop t' this kind o' thing."

Bairn looked away and Anna knew what he was thinking. John Elder could be very persuasive.

"So what are y' proposin', John?"

"I have given myself t' the task o' raising two companies. 'Tis time to provoke the Assembly to protect the frontier. They're blind t' the troubles and tribulations o' the frontier settlers."

"Y' ken we are nae people who will take up arms."

"There is a great danger in such apathy. People are dying out there, after all. *Yer* people."

"Apathy is nae the same thing as tolerance. We have a commitment t' toleration. Pennsylvania is a story of how different sorts of people get along. Yer people are part of that story too, John."

"Aye, but there is such a thing as being too tolerant." John pointed at Bairn. "Such apathy leads innocent victims as prey t' invaders."

Anna knew this conversation was a stalemate. John Elder and his friends despised any and all pacifists, particularly Quakers. They believed the Quakers, who had the strongest voice in the Pennsylvania government, were not protecting the citizens, especially those at the frontier.

"'Tis why y' Germans are considered t' have a lack o' interest in political things. 'Tis why y' have the reputation for apathy and ignorance. 'Germans are considered a betrayer of this country, to be hated and despised.' Those are the words o' Benjamin Franklin himself."

"'Tis nae the words o' Benjamin Franklin. Y've twisted his meaning, John."

John scoffed. "I dinnae think so. He called all of y' Palatine Boors. Swarthy and dark. He said Germans were planning t' turn this country into another Germany."

Anna dropped her chin to her chest. *Not this again.*

This New World, intended to be a holy experiment of tolerance, was anything but. All these devout people—Scots-Irish, Quakers, Mennonites, Moravians, Lutherans—they all distrusted each other. But let the talk turn to Indians, and they were instantly thick as thieves, united in their hatred.

John Elder sighed. "Many Quakers are setting aside their pacifist tendencies, Bairn. They ken this t' be a matter of life and death."

"I dinnae want strife with y', but no man in our church will be joinin' yer companies."

John Elder jabbed his finger in Bairn's direction. "I know that whatever Bishop Bauer says, people do. Yer a respected man, Bairn. The Mennonites will follow yer lead."

"I'm not a bishop, John. I've told y' that over and over. And I dinnae think that the Mennonites would pay me any mind."

"Not true." John Elder took a few steps around the front of the wagon, then spun around to face Bairn. "Everyone is talking about this wagon. They believe it will revolutionize transportation of goods. Everyone from Lancaster to Philadelphia knows of y' and yer building prowess."

On this one topic, Anna knew that John Elder was not exaggerating. There was much ballyhoo about the Conestoga wagon throughout the county, and it was spreading quickly. On a weekly basis, curious neighbors and interested townspeople arrived at Beacon Hollow to have a look.

Bairn frowned. "The Conestoga wagon was created with many hands."

John Elder waved him off. "Dinnae bother servin' up false modesty. Y' built that wagon from the experience y' gleaned after living half yer life on the sea. No German farmer could have thought of that keel-shaped center. Everyone ken who designed this wagon." He looked at Anna. "Have y' no influence on yer man?"

"Our people think for themselves," Anna said. "The intention of our church is to honor God, not man."

John Elder kept his eyes on Anna. "A church needs a strong leader, and that's who Bairn Bauer is, its leader. A true leader guides his people t' make the right decisions."

"And what decisions would those be?" Bairn said.

John Elder shifted his gaze to Bairn. "We need t' press the government t' contain the Indians. Washington's War has nae done enough."

"Pennsylvania is committed t' tolerance, John. William Penn treated the natives rightly and fairly. He bought title t' their land."

"Aye, because he was an *Englishman*. Penn purchased land from the Indians fairly and openly, but he dinnae so simply out of benevolence. He needed to free the land of prior titles so that he could sell it t' settlers and recoup the expenses he incurred in settin' up his colony. Penn might've wanted harmony with Indians, but he also needed t' own their land outright."

"John Elder, this land you feel so entitled to—most of yer own parishioners are squattin' on that land. They have nae title to it."

His jaw hardened. "'Tis unused land."

"'Tis land set apart for the natives to hunt in. John, I heard you led a game drive a few weeks back."

"'Twas a hunting expedition."

"Yer people farm—they do not need to hunt. When you drive the wildlife into one area and then hunt them down, the natives believe you're taking their livelihood. You offend them. They view land differently than you do—they use it to sustain life."

"And how do I view it?"

"To make a profit."

"Whose side are y' on, Bairn?"

"On the side of what's right. On the side of truth."

"It is imperative t' seek their removal."

"John, do y' make any distinction between friendly Indians and enemies?"

John Elder was quiet for a moment. "This is a Holy War. A struggle that God has ordained."

Quiet crackled through the shop. Bairn Bauer stood at his full height, impressive, radiating purpose. "I dinnae argue that the Indians have killed settlers, but far more often they are the victims. I am concerned you are preachin' a rhetoric of fear."

John Elder snorted. "Hardly that. Not fear. Only caution. Preparation."

"You can incite entire populations to violence with that kind of talk."

"I think he's right."

Everyone turned to see Hans, standing at the open door. "John Elder is right." He looked directly at the Paxton preacher. "This is a holy struggle that God has ordained."

John Elder was delighted. "Perhaps we could talk outside, Hans Bauer. I cannae see any point in continuin' the discussion with yer brother. His mind is closed." He put an arm around Hans's shoulder and led him outside.

Bairn and Anna looked at each other. She crossed her arms against her middle. "You neglected to tell me those details about the Zooks."

Bairn glanced away. "I wanted t' spare y'."

"Why was it so . . . especially brutal?"

His voice was crisp. "To inflict maximum terror on settlers who might intrude on Indian land."

Anna covered her face with her hands. "Oh Bairn, no wonder our Willie won't speak. He can't."

"Aye," he said, wrapping his arms around her and pulling her close against him. "Aye, our poor wee laddie."

❧

Tessa and Willie were deep in the woods behind Beacon Hollow. She'd found the horse eating the spring carrots she'd pulled from her mother's garden and left in a place she knew he had slept in—she'd seen him there twice. This afternoon, she had Willie stay far away, hidden behind a tree, as she slowly approached the stallion. In her hands were more carrots. The horse saw her, watched her, yet he kept munching on the carrots and didn't seem at all skittish.

She was in awe. This horse was majestic—unusually large yet well proportioned, with a glossy black coat; bright, intelligent eyes.

Slowly, slowly, she moved closer to him, holding the carrots out to him. The horse sniffed the air around her, then sniffed her. She froze, letting his velvety nose take in her scent. Inside, she wanted to jump in the air for joy. The horse took a carrot from her outstretched hand and chewed. A victory!

All of a sudden, the horse pricked his ears, huffed, and vanished. Then she realized what had startled him—off in the distance, she heard men's voices approach. She hurried to join Willie behind the thick trunk of an old poplar tree, feeling foolish when she realized one of the voices belonged to Hans. She nearly revealed herself, but as soon as she saw that John Elder was with him, she stayed hidden and put her hands on Willie's shoulders. She couldn't abide John Elder.

John Elder stopped his horse, not more than a few rods from where Tessa and Willie remained hidden behind the poplar tree. For once, she was grateful for Willie's silent tongue. If John Elder saw her, he would no doubt offer to serenade her with his horrible bagpipes.

"You've been beneficial in the past, Hans," she heard John Elder say. "We could sorely use your help again."

Hans made a jerking movement in such a way that Tessa thought he must have spotted her, but then she realized he had merely bowed his head. "I did not know the extent of the errand I was sent on."

"Hans, do y' happen t' ken an Indian named Will Sock?"

"Yes, of course. Everyone knows him. He's got a lot of influence."

"He's under particular suspicion."

"Will Sock? Most of his time is spent going from farm to farm, selling his brooms and baskets. How credible are these accusations?"

"He was recently observed while visitin' Seneca Indians . . . and y' ken how they lean toward the French."

"Bairn had asked Will Sock to seek out information about Betsy Zook. She was captured in the recent attack." He rubbed his forehead, chin to his chest. "We were to be married."

"Ah, Hans. I dinnae ken. My heart goes out t' y. But y' see now, dinnae y', why our efforts are so vitally important?"

Hans lifted his head. "I do. I see exactly why."

"Will Sock has also been found t' plan and participate in attacks on local settlers. Watch him carefully, m'boy. He's a marked man. Send word t' me o' anything suspicious." As he mounted his horse, he added one last thing. "Soon, y' will hear word from me with more plans."

Tessa held her breath until Hans finally turned and walked back down the narrow path that led to Beacon Hollow. She waited until he was out of sight before she came out from behind the tree. She gave Willie a reassuring smile. Hans and John Elder had been speaking in English, which Willie did not understand. Even still, he seemed troubled.

As was Tessa.

What did John Elder mean when he said that Hans had been beneficial to him in the past? And what errand had he sent Hans on? Probably nothing, she decided. She wondered if John Elder had gone mad. Crazier than a loon, she considered him to be.

But she was suddenly afraid and could not fathom why.

❧

Not Faxon's Farm
May 6, 1763

Crows and blackbirds had become such a nuisance to the farmers that the Lancaster Town sheriff put a bounty on them: three pence apiece for a single crow or for a dozen blackbirds. When Felix's sons, Benjo and Dannie, learned of the bounty, they implored him to let them borrow his shooting rifles. Felix was sorely tempted, especially after he carried a bucket of water to his garden this morning and discovered that the crows had made a mess of his just-planted corn seeds. Something had to be done. Felix's mother, Dorothea, pitched a fit at the thought of Benjo and Dannie using rifles, convinced the boys would kill them all.

There was some truth in that worry—the boys used ammunition like it was popcorn and had recently blown out two windows in the house. So Felix and his mother arrived on a compromise: a slingshot and rocks, of which there were plenty. The boys went straight to work.

Felix sat on the farmhouse steps to watch the boys practice slinging rocks. They had yet to hit a bird but were starting to get the hang of the slinging part. Rocks went sailing all over the yard, and Dorothea stayed inside, far from the front of the house, to stay safe.

Unfortunately, Felix and the boys were so engrossed with slinging rocks that they didn't notice Maria Müller's pony cart turn up the lane. One errant rock flew too close to the pony and caused him to bolt. Felix jumped off the steps and ran to grab the pony's reins to catch him. He hung on to the pony's reins with all his might, despite thinking his arms might get yanked out of their sockets. The pony settled down and Felix let out a deep breath of relief.

"Crisis averted," he said cheerfully.

"Crisis averted, my eye," Maria spit back. "You and your boys *create* crises."

The boys, Felix noticed, had vanished. Disappeared into thin air. They had a knack for that.

He turned back to Maria and suddenly realized she wasn't alone in the cart. Beside her on the seat was her daughter,

Catrina, an inquisitive look on her face. Imperious as always, was his first thought.

Maria climbed down from the cart and gave Felix an appraising look, up and down, her eyes resting on the patches on his knees. He'd sewn them himself and was rather proud of his efforts. "Is Dorothea home?"

"Yes. She's in the house. She's having a good day. It'll be a treat for her to see you." As Maria bustled past him and into the house, an awkward silence remained as Felix offered a hand to help Catrina down from the cart. He wiped sweat off his forehead with his wrist. "Welcome, Catrina. Your mother said you're returning to Stoney Ridge."

"Yes." She looked him right in the eye and he noticed that her wandering eye didn't wander anymore. Not so much, anyway.

"Apparently you've been employed to teach my sons to read and write and do sums."

"Yes. Exactly that. And English. Plus more, I hope, assuming their minds are nimble." Her brows knit in a frown. "Are they?"

"Of course! Of course they're nimble minded. Who said they weren't?" Who would give the impression that his boys were feebleminded? Maria, most likely. How dare she!

"No one said they weren't. I was just concerned, after I heard that they're already ten years old—"

"Just turned nine. Barely nine."

"—and they aren't able to read. I hoped they would be . . . teachable. That it isn't too late." Her lips curved up a little on one side, as if she found him amusing. Like he was a silly child—that kind of amusing.

What a ridiculous notion. Too late? How could it be too late for two nine-year-old boys to learn to read?

For a long moment, Felix considered Catrina, trying hard to discern her motives. Was she sizing him up? Estimating the value of his farm? Already planning her next wedding? Felix couldn't tell. It would be naïve of him to think Catrina had anything but her own self-interests at heart.

She lifted her eyebrows as if she were reading his thoughts. "Pay no mind to my mother's attempts at matchmaking, Felix. I'm not at all interested in you." And she strode past him into the house to visit with Dorothea and Maria.

Good, Felix thought. *Excellent*. Then, *And why not?*

10

Betsy woke in the night to realize that she was warm. For the first time since the attack, she had not woken shivering, numb with cold and fear. It was dark, some time had passed since she fell asleep, but she couldn't tell if it was minutes or hours.

She heard the heavy, steady breathing of the two Indian women who had adopted her. The older one was called Nijlon, meaning "mistress." The younger one was Numees, or "sister." On the first day they had arrived at the village, Numees had made a compress of wild tansy for Betsy's face wound, which had started to throb with pain. Numees applied the compress with tenderness, reapplying it several times that day. Betsy put a hand to her face. It felt less swollen, less tender to the touch.

Outside the wigwam, Betsy heard the hum of voices. With one large central fire continually burning, family groups would feed their fires off the main one, and Nijlon's wigwam was closest to the fire.

Betsy assumed the proximity of Nijlon's wigwam had

something to do with status; the squaw was treated with unusual respect. When they arrived at the village yesterday, most everyone in the village—men, women, and children alike—stopped what they were doing and stood at attention, waiting and watching quietly as Nijlon walked up from the river and disappeared into her wigwam. Then they resumed their activities.

Betsy had seen such a sign of reverence only once before. It was in Port Philadelphia when her family had newly arrived, and they happened upon General George Washington on horseback. Shop owners and customers came out of the shops to quietly watch the general as he went along the cobblestone road.

Burrowed deeper under the skins given to her by Nijlon and Numees, Betsy tried to shut out the sounds, to shut off her mind. She couldn't stop worrying about Johnny, wondering if he were being treated well, and she grieved over Willie, sure he had been killed alongside her parents. Grief was a sin. Her father had warned continually against it when they left Europe because her mother had felt such sorrow over leaving behind her parents and sisters, knowing she would never see them again. She could hear her father's voice as clearly as if she were on the ship that brought them to Port Philadelphia, with her mother's head bowed low to take his scolding. "Do not attach yourself to the things of this earth," he told her nearly every day, "but to heaven alone."

It was a sin to grieve, and yet Betsy couldn't help it, just as her mother couldn't help her great sadness as she left Europe. Her thoughts traveled to Hans. Would he forget her and find someone else to love? Perhaps he already had.

She quietly wept, swallowing her sobs so she wouldn't

awaken Nijlon, Numees, or the infant. Finally she drifted off to sleep, moving away from her sadness, sliding into a blessed darkness.

※

Not Faxon's Farm
May 11, 1763

On Wednesday morning, Anna made a point of stopping by Hans's forge after dropping poor Willie off at Not Faxon's Farm. She watched Hans at work for a long while, noticing his intense concentration on his task. She could see how young women, girls like her own Tessa, easily gave their hearts to Hans. The entire church had waited to see which girl might catch the elusive Hans Bauer. A year ago, when Anna first learned that Hans was courting Betsy Zook, she breathed a sigh of relief. She had known Tessa would be crushed, but she was so young. Much too young for Hans to notice her, thank goodness.

Anna caught herself. Why did she feel such a catch in her spirit about Hans? She couldn't say. He had been a beautiful boy and was now a strikingly handsome man, charming and winsome. But Dorothea had pampered him and he was accustomed to getting his way.

Long ago, when Hans was only a boy, he had captured a beautiful monarch butterfly and asked Anna for a crock to keep it. She warned him the butterfly could not survive without air and light. But Hans insisted, convinced that if he wanted something enough, it would happen. Within a day, the butterfly died. Furious, he threw the crock against the kitchen wall, shattering it, and ran off when Anna asked him to sweep it up. He was only a boy, but Anna had never forgotten that incident. It seemed to portend something, though she had no idea what.

On this rainy morning, Hans was focused on finishing the iron tongue to fit on Bairn's wagon, which would please her husband to hear about. Bairn was spending long days on that wagon, eager to complete it but equally compelled to make it perfect in every way.

Hans finished hammering the handle of the tongue and thrust it in a kettle of water with his tongs. Clouds of steam billowed up from the kettle. He looked up and noticed Anna, standing a few feet away. "Anna! I didn't realize you were standing there. You should have said something."

She smiled. "I didn't want to interrupt you."

He set the tongs down and put his hands on his hips. "You can tell Bairn that I will bring the wagon tongue over tonight."

"He'll be glad to hear it." More than glad.

"I thought you'd left long ago."

"I dropped Willie off for school and then I tarried. I wanted to see how Dorothea is faring."

"She's better, don't you think?"

Actually, no. The opposite, in fact. Anna had noticed that the whites of Dorothea's eyes had a slight yellow hue, and she didn't want to get out of bed. She started to say as much to Hans, then hesitated as she caught the hopeful look in his eyes. He had enough woes and worries to deal with lately. "She seemed quite cheerful."

He gave her a slight grin. "I think she's doing much better too."

She took one step closer to his workbench but backed

away again, startled by the intense heat of the fire. How did he stand it? And this was only May. "Hans, I thought of one way you could help Betsy Zook."

His grin faded and he leaned toward her. "Tell me. What news have you?" In his voice was a quiet desperation.

"Nothing, I'm sorry to say. But I thought you might consider befriending Betsy's brother, Willie Zook. He, too, is suffering."

"Of course." He nodded slightly, then more vigorously. "Of course. It hadn't occurred to me. Certainly, Willie is suffering too. Thank you, Anna."

She smiled. "I'll be sure to let Bairn know he can expect the hardware this afternoon."

But Hans wasn't listening. He had stopped hammering and was staring at her, his eyes wide, as if he was looking through her, as if she were not there.

Oh no. Oh dear. She had an uneasy feeling that she had just stopped him from finishing the tongue for Bairn's wagon.

Stoney Ridge

Tessa was late heading home and came bursting out of the woods, clattering down a steep embankment, sending rocks and mud tumbling to the road below, startling a horse so much it reared and nearly overturned its wagon.

"Whoa!" Rumpled Martin took a while to get his horse until control.

She halted a rod away, facing him, appraising his horse management skills solemnly, while he appeared pleased at having run into her. Or rather, she nearly ran into him.

"Tessa Bauer! What are you doing, storming out of the woods like that? Is there a fire?"

"No. No fire. I'm in a hurry."

"What's your big hurry?"

"I dropped off canvas cloth for the wagon to Maria. She's sewing the seams together to cover the hoops. And she talked so long she's made me late for—" She stopped herself. "For supper." No, not just supper. She had overheard Hans promise her father that he'd be stopping by about now to deliver an important piece of wagon hardware. She couldn't believe Maria had kept her so long. And why? Just so Tessa could hear complaints that her father was consumed by the Conestoga wagon and in dire danger of neglecting the church, which, Tessa knew, translated to her father not giving Maria enough attention.

There was some truth to Maria's gripes—her father was working eighteen or more hours a day on the wagon, stopping only to sleep and eat. His temper was short, especially when Hans made him wait on needed hardware. Some church duties, other than Sunday church, had been put off until the wagon was completed. But the church was *not* neglected.

Maria couldn't see that, though. She could only see that her woodpile was growing small—something her father normally kept a close eye on and resupplied as needed. Tessa wasn't going to trouble her father with Maria's complaints. Instead, she would tell Uncle Felix. He could chop wood for Maria.

"Why don't you just cut through the cornfields? I can see your house from here."

He was right about that. The steep roof of the stone house was visible from the road, and the cornfield was the shortest route, but there was a problem. "Can't."

"Why not? As long as I've known you, you've been taking shortcuts."

What did *that* mean? She studied him warily. "Snakes." She was fairly brave about most creatures, even spiders didn't bother her, but she took exception to snakes.

He raised his chin and nodded wisely. "They do come out after a rain."

Exactly. In droves. And there had been a heavy downpour this morning. She crossed her arms behind her back, rocked left to right. If Martin would offer her a ride, it would save her quite a bit of time. She could just jump on the back of the wagon, so no one would misunderstand and think they were spending time together. She waited patiently for him to make the offer, keeping her eyes leveled at him. My, he was a scruffy-looking fellow, always in need of a haircut. And where was his hat? Unlike Hans, rumpled Martin did not seem to care a whit about how he looked.

"Any chance you're hoping to cross paths with anyone?"

"No. What makes you think that?"

"You look jumpy. Anxious. Antsy. That's it. You look like you've got ants in your pants . . . uh . . . dress."

"I'm not at all antsy," she said coolly. *Actually, I am. I want to get home to see Hans. So why don't you offer me a ride home?* "I'm just hungry. Late for supper." She took care to enunciate the word *late*. And yet, rumpled Martin did not pick up on her hint.

The silence remained tense.

"Sure you're not trying to meet anyone?"

"No. Not at all."

"Because I happened upon Hans Bauer a short time ago. He was delivering the tongue for the wagon, he said. Met him on the road going, then he passed me again as he was heading home."

Tommyrot. She'd missed her chance.

Martin glanced speculatively over at Beacon Hollow, then back at her, before picking up the reins. "Well, I better not keep you since you're in such a big hurry. So long, Tessa."

What? He didn't even offer her a ride? It was hardly out of his way. Just a mile or two.

And then he drove down the road, whistling. She watched him drive off, mystified at his lack of awareness, his lack of concern for her. She was surprised to find herself a little disappointed.

❧

Not Faxon's Farm
May 11, 1763

Catrina Müller set to educate Felix's boys and poor Willie Zook with a vengeance. For three full days now, since Monday morning, despite heavy spring rains, she arrived at eight o'clock sharp with her domineering mother Maria beside her in the pony cart, and sat the boys down at the kitchen table, next to poor Willie who was delivered by Anna. Maria plunked down in a rocking chair near the fireplace, waiting for Dorothea to rise from bed and join her.

On this gray morning, Felix gave his boys a sorrowful look, a pat on their red heads. He would be spending the day in the barn. Where his boys wanted to be. Where he needed their help to muck stalls. Where he wanted their companionship. He couldn't even look at their little round freckled faces; he felt he was letting them down. It was a terrible thing to have Catrina Müller bear down on them, stifling their joyful spirits like a fire that gets blown out before it has a chance to warm the room. "Eems Licht ausblose," he had told her. *Snuffing out their candles.*

There was plenty of time to learn to read and write, but such little time for a child to be free, to explore the natural world, to be unrestrained by adult expectations. He said as much to Catrina and she waved away his fretting as nonsense. "You sound like a man who just doesn't want to grow up."

He found that remark to be highly insulting. He was plenty grown up. He was a deacon, for goodness' sake. Did she even realize that? His job was to sniff out misbehaving church members and set them back on the straight and narrow path. And it was indeed a straight and narrow path. He was a very lax deacon, he knew, but then, Bairn was a very lax minister as well. Maria Müller threatened to leave the church on the day when Felix drew the lot, if there were only another church to flee to.

Felix would have been delighted to see the backside of meddlesome Maria Müller, and her interfering daughter too. Yet here they were, parked inside his home, torturing his poor sons under the guise of an education.

It was more than Felix could bear, watching his two active boys have to stay indoors in springtime, forced to recite their alphabet and practice sums. He tried to persuade Catrina to have lessons in the afternoon or, better still, in the evening, but she was adamant and unrelenting, unwilling to be reasoned with. "They can barely hold attention to a task as it is," she said. "Keeping their thoughts focused in the afternoon would be like trying to catch dandelion heads in the wind."

And then she told him she would be there every single day

but Sunday, including half days on Saturday, because the boys were so woefully behind in all subjects. As if it was a race! The words fell like a blow.

※

Shawnee Village, Monongahela River
June 5, 1763

For a long while, Betsy brooded over all she had lost, mulling continually over all that her family had suffered. Time, though, chipped away at her despair. As she adjusted to her new surroundings, sleeping and eating, her mind slowly quickened, her downcast spirit lifted, and she cast aside her grief for longer and longer periods. Yesterday, she found herself to be almost . . . content. One thing she had become aware of: she had found that she could endure more than she had ever thought of herself.

She knew she was fortunate. Nijlon and Numees were very kind women, good-natured, peaceable, mild in disposition, tender and gentle in how they treated her. She learned she did not need to fear them. They shared all they had with Betsy, their home and food. Betsy was becoming somewhat at ease in their mode of living, and to her surprise, she found herself growing fond of the two squaws. Numees, especially, who made her laugh. She had a talent for mimicking, and often poked fun at the villagers who came to Nijlon with their problems.

She spent most of her time with Numees. She taught Betsy how to grind corn on a stone, how to scrape a hide, how to sew and repair the woven reed mats that lined the interior of the wigwam by using a needle made from the rib of a deer. Earlier today, they went out to a small field, recently plowed, and spent the morning hours planting corn, squash, and beans. When they finished, Numees pointed to herself, to Betsy, and back to the wigwam where Nijlon remained. She held up three fingers and said, "Nesh-wonner numees."

Betsy didn't understand, so Numees tried again, and again. Then it dawned on her that she was calling the garden Three Sisters: corn, squash, and beans. And Betsy was considered the third sister.

When Numees saw that she understood her meaning, she laughed and clapped her hands, though not in a mocking way, and Betsy felt a trickle of pleasure.

Nijlon was more serious minded; she did not allow Betsy to speak English in her hearing. She was determined Betsy learn their language and adapt to their customs. Betsy was willing to learn, but she was also determined not to forget. She made a habit of repeating her prayers each day, down by the river, whenever she was sent to draw a pot of water. She wouldn't forget her father's last words of warning to her: to remember who she was, to whom she belonged, to stay vigilant so that heathen ways would not overtake her, and to keep her trust in God.

The curious thing was that Betsy had not observed heathen ways among this village. Nothing remotely close to the sacrilegious and profane behaviors she had seen among the warriors. These villagers were farmers, busying themselves with living.

Each day presented countless chores—most of which revolved around food and more specifically, corn. Corn was of great importance to the Indians. It was served at every meal in some shape or form; its very name meant life.

The food Betsy ate was entirely different food from the

kinds she'd grown up with: bowls of thin broth made of beans, onions, and squash, stewed pumpkin, fresh fish caught from the river, maize cakes sweetened with molasses. It was not an abundant diet, nothing like the rich foods eaten by her family, but it was adequate, and the villagers took great pride in sharing all that they had with each other, including Betsy. Their willingness to share was not so very different from the Schuylkill neighbors' generosity as they helped to stock the Zooks' root cellar during their first autumn in the New World.

At some point in each day, Nijlon's wigwam was filled with women whose hands were occupied with a task. Several times, Betsy had come into the wigwam to find women surrounding the fire, chattering in their language, busily stringing small white and black beads. Wampum beads. Betsy had seen wampum before; she knew it was made of shells and Indians treated it like money. Wampum strings held great significance to the Indians, for when a person held wampum strings, it meant he spoke the truth.

But it wasn't the stringing of wampum that struck Betsy as familiar, it was the women's behavior. She could have been walking into a quilting frolic at her mother's farmhouse. Perhaps that's what startled Betsy more than anything else: how ordinary the lives of Indian villagers were, how similar they seemed to people in her own church.

❧

Not Faxon's Farm
June 10, 1763

To Felix's unexpected delight, Catrina did not limit the education of his sons to books. She and the boys spent a warm

June afternoon picking plump blueberries, eating their fill in the process; the rest they sugared and dried into stiff leather. "To have a little bit of summer on a cold winter's day," she told them. She taught them how to put up butter and cheese in crocks, how to keep the crocks cold and covered with straw in the icehouse. How long had it been since they'd had butter and cheese from their own cow's milk? Dorothea gave up the tedious process long ago, and Felix had never bothered to learn. He'd just sent the boys to Anna's whenever he had a hankering for butter or cheese; she was always willing to share from Beacon Hollow's bounty. Yet he was pleased with these new skills of his boys. Secretly pleased.

The boys helped Catrina grind corn and oats from the fields to make flour and meal. Felix didn't mind those lessons either; anything that taught his boys how to stay healthy and well fed was fine with him. But when he came home one day and found his boys learning how to spin wool, he felt Catrina had crossed the line. He sent the boys outside and turned on her. "It's female work," he said.

"Don't be ridiculous, Felix," Catrina said. "Anyone who keeps sheep needs to know how to spin wool. What do you do with all that wool?"

He rubbed his neck. "Give it to Anna."

She sighed. "I'm teaching the boys skills they will need in life. You're the one who wants them to know how to survive on the western frontier."

"Not by sissifying them." He frowned. "Next you'll be teaching them to spin flax."

"In fact, I was planning to do exactly that."

"Not *my* sons!" he roared. "No self-respecting male in this valley would be caught spinning flax."

"You certainly don't mind wearing linen shirts, or sleeping under a woolen blanket on a cold winter's night. Do you think these things will magically appear for your sons when they venture west?"

They glared at each other, a standoff. Somewhere in Felix's mind came a memory of staring games with Catrina on the *Charming Nancy*. He'd always lost.

"Son, let her teach."

He turned to see his mother standing at the doorjamb.

"Thank you, Dorothea," Catrina said. She gathered her belongings and started toward the door. "I'll be back in the morning."

Now? *Now* his mother decides to get out of bed?

❧

Shawnee Village, Monongahela River
June 16, 1763

Early one morning, Betsy made her way down the bank of the river and squatted beside the water. Even before she lowered her hands into the river, she knew the icy cold would make her fingers sting. As she bent down to scoop up the water into the pot, she heard a man's voice speak in her dialect. "Do you need help?"

Betsy snapped her head up, disoriented.

That blue-eyed Indian stood beside her, pointing to the empty pot. "Do you need help filling the pot?"

At the sight of him, she faltered and nearly dropped the clay pot. "You! It's you," she said, surprised. Stunned. She had never expected to see him again. "What are you doing here? Where did you come from?"

He pointed downriver. "I have come to bring you news of your brother. He is well and strong, adapting to Indian life."

Shocked silent, she was so filled with gratitude that she dropped the bucket and grasped both his hands in hers. "Thank you, thank you!" she cried. "I rejoice to hear this news! It gives me hope that we will soon be reunited."

His eyes dropped to their joined hands. She hadn't realized she was still holding on to him. She let go and bent down to pick up the pot. Her mind started spinning with questions. "Where is he? Would you take me to him? Or bring him to me?"

"No. I have no such influence." The Indian's look grew pensive; his gaze shifted and fixed on a hawk riding the wind. The hawk banked suddenly and flew straight down to the water, snatched a fish out of the river with its sharp talons, and shot up like an arrow into the deep and empty sky. They fell quiet, listening to the wind's breath in the trees around them, the hum of activity floating down from the village.

Who was this man? She risked a gander at him. He was long and lean like other Indian men; his muscled shoulders and bare chest tapered into a hollow gut, wiry arms looked as strong relaxed as flexed. Like the other village men, he wore a breechcloth and deerskin leggings on his legs, brown moccasins on his feet. She'd never seen anyone stand so still. But no sooner had the thought formed in her mind than he spun to face her. She felt her face grow warm, embarrassed to be caught looking at him, but he seemed almost amused. She noticed a quick tightening of his mouth and a crinkling of the sun-creases that fanned from the corner of his eyes. "How is it that you speak my language?"

"My mother belonged to your people."

Betsy was shocked. "Your mother? She was Amish?"

"Mennonite. She was captured by the Iroquois and sold to another tribe. She taught me her language and her customs. And her prayers."

"You are a Christian?"

"She baptized me."

Betsy must have looked shocked at the idea of a woman having the authority to baptize because he added, "Women are not kept silent among our people, as they are in yours. You must have noticed that Nijlon is head of this village. She sits in council. Women show great wisdom as leaders."

It was an astonishing thought. She had never heard anyone express such an idea before. She had, indeed, noticed the Indian men in the village defer to Nijlon, and once she saw her speak harshly to a man. The man looked injured but not indignant, the way a child would look if his knuckles had been rapped. "So you are half German?"

He gave her a wry smile. "You have probably heard the term 'half blood.'"

"Have you thought to seek out your mother?"

"She died, many years ago." His voice remained free of emotion, but Betsy thought she saw something cold shiver across his eyes.

"What of your German relatives? Could you not go to them, seek them out?"

"Half bloods belong to no one." Then he lifted his head proudly and thumped his naked chest with his fist, once, then twice. "But I . . . I belong to the Holy One."

She was completely baffled, and the corners of his mouth lifted at her confusion. "My mother was offered as tribute, like you. And like your new sisters, the villagers who adopted

148

my mother were very kind. When the time came, I was sent out to become a man. There was a wild stallion that roamed through Pennsylvania. This horse, it is said, once belonged to William Penn, a white man who treated the natives well. With respect."

"I know of this William Penn! A Quaker man. He was given this land by the king of England."

He nodded. "My tribe believed that if the horse could be found, the people would be strong again, their reputation would be restored. But this horse was wild. He roamed free, he would not be captured. I was foolish and determined, for I had caught sight of him many times. I understood this horse. I knew where his mind would take him. I kept tracking him, far into the mountains. Too far. Iroquois warriors hunted me down and caught me, and then I was given to Shawnee." He lifted his palm in the direction of the village. "To this tribe."

It shocked Betsy to hear that Indians would capture other Indians. She had thought their evilness was directed only against white people. "How awful."

He made a dismissive sound. "It was my own foolish pride that made me think I could capture the stallion. Instead, I was captured. That is the way of all pride."

"Why haven't you gone back to your people?"

"I am slave."

"A slave? But you're not confined to this village. You seem to have the freedom to roam." But then, so did she. However, she had no idea which way to go to get home.

"A man's spirit withers if confined. Nijlon understands that." He took the pot out of her hands and squatted down by the water's edge. "Nijlon sent me to seek out news of your brother. To give you peace." He scooped water into the pot, then passed it to her. "She treats her people well. You would do well to accept your fate."

Her fate. It sounded so final, so fixed. She refused to believe that. She had to believe that she would be reunited with Johnny, returned to her people. That one hope helped her face each new day. "Tell me, what is your name?"

"Nijlon gave me the name Askuwheteau. It means 'he keeps watch.' A strong and powerful name. Names hold great meaning for Indians. A man becomes his name."

"Ask-oo-we-tow."

He winced as she mispronounced it. "My mother called me a different name. Caleb."

"There's a Caleb in the Bible who was a fine man. A man worthy of great respect. A man who never wavered. Wholehearted, God called him."

His eyes smiled. "Then you may call me Caleb."

11

Not Faxon's Farm
June 20, 1763

Felix spent a portion of each day training the young Conestoga colts to work as a team under harness, preparing them to pull the highly anticipated and talked about Conestoga wagon, if the time ever came when Bairn actually finished it and delivered it to Faxon Gingerich. That brother of his was a perfectionist of the worst sort.

Bairn said after this prototype wagon was finished, he wanted to build it again in three sizes—small, medium, and large. This first one, he told Felix, was the smallest size. He aimed for it to haul as much as two to three tons. It astonished Felix to think of horses pulling a wagon with that kind of load, yet this unique God-given breed of horses seemed suited for their role in the fast-growing New World.

As three-year-olds, the colts measured sixteen to seventeen hands at the withers and weighed nearly two thousand pounds. Their tails were short, and they had no long hair beneath their fetlocks. Another plus. The roads that led to Philadelphia were rocky paths, two ruts worn by wagon wheels and a grassy strip in the middle. In the spring or after a drenching rain, they turned into a soggy mess. Felix had brushed out enough filthy matted horsetails and fetlocks to last him a lifetime.

Best of all, this new breed displayed a remarkably gentle nature for such big beasts and took to their task surprisingly well. Gentle giants, he called them affectionately.

Felix trained two of the horses to take turns as the "wheel horse," the lead horse on the left-hand side, nearest the wagon, assuming they would be ready to lead a full team of six by the time the largest wagon was built.

He drove the team by working a single rein called the jerk line. To turn the team to the right, he yelled "Gee" and gave several short jerks of the line. To go left, he called "Haw" and pulled steadily on the line.

As he led the colts up the path toward Not Faxon's Farm, he saw Hans standing by the fenced pasture, watching the spring foals at play. He called to Hans. "Look at this!" Felix pulled out an oak board tucked under the wagon in front of the rear wheels and hopped on it to ride. "It's my resting board."

"Looks more like a lazy board."

Felix grinned. "Ah! Even better."

"Have you caught that wild stallion in the act yet?"

"No," Felix said. "He's sneaky, that horse. Jumps over the fences, does his business with the mares, jumps right back out again."

Three little foals ran past them in the pasture, kicking their hind legs as they cantered. Hans turned back to watch them run. "Just think if you caught that stallion, Felix. You'd be churning out all kinds of these creatures instead of just hoping that grand horse drops by each spring."

"Fat chance of catching him. I've never even seen him. Only Tessa."

Hans jerked his chin up. "Our Tessa?"

"Of course, our Tessa. She's seen him quite a few times. She knows his favorite spots."

"Why doesn't she throw a rope around his neck and bring him in?"

"For one thing, he's enormous. For another, she wants him to trust her. You don't win a horse's trust by lassoing its neck the first time it takes a carrot from you."

"You do if you want to breed him to your broodmares."

"That horse has a wild nature, Hans. Some animals are meant to be free. Besides, I like the arrangement we have—he asks nothing of me and I ask nothing of him. And we both get something in return."

Hans looked at him the way Felix knew he often looked at his own mother, as if he might be a little daft. "Man is meant to have dominion over this earth, Felix. To subdue it. That includes taming a wild stallion."

Felix kept his face expressionless. "Claim and tame."

"Yes. Claim it and tame it. Exactly that."

That kind of thinking irked Felix to no end. "If you want to debate the book of Genesis with your deacon, you'll have to wait for Sunday church." His tone was sharper than he felt, but it had the desired effect on Hans.

Hans spun on his heel and strode off to return to his smithy shop. Felix knew it riled Hans to have the deacon role tossed in his face, and he probably did it more often than he should. But Hans had always needed taking down a peg or two.

Beacon Hollow

The black stallion whinnied softly as Tessa approached. She wished she had thought to bring some fresh grass to offer him, then remembered she had put an apple in her pocket in case she got hungry. She held it out, palm open, and the horse's nostrils flared. She remained utterly still, giving the horse plenty of time to decide if Tessa and her offering were safe. He took a step closer, then another, and still she remained like a statue. Then he reached out and took the apple from her hand, chewed it, watching her carefully as bits of apple spewed around. She wanted to reach out and rub his flank, to stroke his neck, but she didn't dare frighten him off. When the horse had finished the apple, he stayed for a while. Little by little, Tessa moved closer to him, every so slowly. She reached out a hand and stroked his long neck, once, then twice. The horse lifted his head as if to say goodbye before trotting off into the woods, and she wanted to shout for joy; this was another momentous occasion and she couldn't wait to tell Felix.

She hurried down the trail toward Not Faxon's Farm. Her breath caught when she saw Hans riding up the path. She shouldn't be struck by the sight of him like some young adolescent, but she couldn't help it. He was so beautiful.

Even from a distance, his face looked drawn and distracted. He slowed his horse to a stop when he saw her, took his hat off his head, and rubbed his hair. When he drew close, she reached out to pat his horse's velvety nose. "I've been looking for you, Tessa. Felix said I could find you out here."

He'd been searching for her? Tessa's heart was beating too fast. She did her best to withhold a smile, though she knew her tight expression probably seemed odd looking. It didn't matter; he wasn't looking at her. "I haven't seen much of you lately. Are you well?"

"No," he snapped, stiffening his spine. "No, I'm not well." Wrong question.

His hands, spread on his knees, closed into fists and opened again. "What's most difficult is the way the world just carries on without her."

"And it's not the same world," she said softly. She couldn't imagine what Betsy's life was like now.

He jerked his head up to look at her, truly look at her. "Tessa," he whispered. "You understand. Someone finally understands my suffering."

Now it was Tessa's turn to be stunned. She thought they'd been talking about Betsy, not Hans. She could think of nothing to say that would not break the fragile moment, and she didn't want to irritate him again, so she remained silent, which he mistook as a sign of empathy.

He relaxed his stiff posture in his saddle and leaned forward, tilting his head to one side in a way she'd always found particularly charming. "Felix told me you're planning to capture the mysterious black stallion."

Tessa felt herself breathe a little easier. This was the Hans she knew. "No. Not really. Not capture, anyway. I'm trying to gain his trust. Little by little."

"I need something to distract me until Betsy's restoration." Hans donned his hat one-handed, settling it easily into place. Smile lines crinkled around his eyes, making his handsome face even more handsome. "Maybe I can help."

Tessa's heart soared.

Shawnee Village, Monongahela River
June 30, 1763

Betsy spent much of her day working side by side with Numees, and as they worked, she was taught Indian words. Slowly, little by little, they began to communicate. Betsy learned that Nijlon's husband had been killed by English troops and that was why they had gone to the gathering place to adopt a tribute. Numees asked Betsy about her life before she had been adopted. Betsy explained that she had been born on the other side of the world, beyond the Atlantic Ocean, and the thought astounded Numees. She had never seen an ocean, she said, and wondered if it was as big as the Monongahela River.

Betsy laughed and said it was much, much bigger. The amazed look on Numees's face reminded her of her brothers, Johnny and Willie, of times when she surprised them with a newly hatched chick, or a bird's nest, or a caught butterfly. Those sweet memories of her brothers brought tears to her eyes and she kept her head ducked to keep Numees from noticing. Numees, she had learned, was quite sensitive to Betsy's moods. She shared all she had with Betsy and was eager for her to be happy, to feel at home among them, and it distressed her when her countenance appeared sad. She wanted Betsy to consider herself to be Indian, to be her sister.

Betsy had indeed adopted many Indian ways. She wore a deerskin dress and moccasins, braided her hair, draped a blanket over her shoulders when she went outside at night. She had finally developed a tolerance for the smell of bear grease so that it no longer made her nauseated. She smeared it on her hands and face to protect her pale skin from getting burned by the sun. She learned how to walk silently in the woods, and how to mend her moccasins at the end of each day. She had even grown to prefer moccasins to the cumbersome shoes she had grown up with; moccasins felt like she was barefooted, though in yesterday's rain, she discovered they could be surprisingly stiff and uncomfortable when wet.

There was much that bemused her about Indian ways. Children, for example, ran freely through the village with very little supervision. Their games and laughter were not only tolerated, but the adults often stopped work to observe them at play. Clearly, they adored their children. All children. In Betsy's church, both in the New World and in Germany, children were "to be seen and not heard." Affection might spoil a child, so it was withheld. Not so for an Indian child.

Another thing that mystified her was the power that Nijlon held in this village. An Indian had reached out to touch Betsy's long blonde plait and Nijlon slapped him across his face, hard, and rattled off a rush of Indian words. He scurried off, holding his stinging cheek with both hands. Nijlon's word was law. In the world Betsy came from, a woman's word carried little weight.

Nijlon and Numees allowed Betsy a surprising amount of freedom. In the warm afternoons, the village rested and Betsy could do as she pleased. All her life, as the eldest daughter, she had worked alongside her mother from the moment she woke in the morning to the moment she went to bed at night. She was raised believing that idleness was the devil's handiwork, a sin, a temptation to resist. In this Indian village, afternoon naps were not idleness, but considered a necessity.

One such afternoon, the air in the wigwam felt stiflingly hot, so Betsy went outside. Caleb stood tending the central fire, burning out the inside of a log to make a canoe, a tedious process. He lifted a hand in greeting and she felt a ripple of pleasure by the delighted look on his face when he saw her.

"I have not seen you during the rain," he said. "I wondered if you had gone."

"Gone? Where would I go?"

He shrugged. "You might have left to find your way back to your home."

"I was warned not to escape. My father told us not to try to escape." It had never occurred to her to leave, not once, even with the freedom given to her by Nijlon.

He seemed amused. "Do you not think for yourself?"

"Yes. No. Yes. It's just that . . ." She took a few steps closer to the canoe to see the burned, hollowed-out interior.

"What?"

"I was taught obedience was pleasing to God."

"What virtue does obedience have if it is not examined and then made to be a choice?"

She'd never thought of such a thing. The way she'd been raised, obedience *was* a virtue. Not questioning, not doubting—they were all considered virtues. She couldn't imagine what kind of reaction her father might have had if she had ever questioned his decisions. He had no tolerance for dissenting opinions.

She remembered how her father's eyes burned with excitement when he announced to the family they would soon sail to the New World and leave behind the pressures and persecutions of a country that despised them. Betsy's mother was given no choice in the matter. She remembered how sullen and morose her mother had seemed, how her face was tightened with fear—a foreboding, perhaps?—even as she set about dutifully packing up their belongings.

Betsy's sister, four-year-old Mary, fell ill and died on that horrific voyage just a week or so after the ship set sail. Betsy would never forget when her little body, wrapped in a dirty white sail, was thrown over the side of the ship into the dark swirling water and the unearthly wailing sound that came from her quiet mother. Followed by the sound of her father's sharp words about the sin of grief. "Der Dod nemmt yung un alt." *Death takes young and old.*

Betsy's mind traveled to the week that the ship arrived in Port Philadelphia, and her father had news that he had purchased land in Berks County, deep in the wilderness of the frontier. Again, Betsy's mother drooped with fear, as if she had a sense of what was to come. What if her mother had felt the freedom to voice her concerns to him? Might they still be alive? Might little Mary still be with them?

She sensed Caleb's gaze on her and realized he was waiting for some response.

"Did God not give you a mind to reason with? Thoughts of your own?"

"Yes, of course. But . . ." But *what*?

"Betsy Zook, what makes your heart fill with light?"

She looked up at him, surprised. She hadn't realized he knew her name. The villagers called her Hurit. He pronounced Betsy in a unique way: Bit-SEE. "What makes my heart fill with light?" It was a lovely phrase, unexpected poetry from such a quiet man. "I suppose . . . writing. My mother gave me a journal for my tenth birthday. I wrote in it daily since then, filling it with my dreams." She smiled. "I had to keep it hidden from my younger brothers." Her smile faded and her gaze shifted to the fast-moving river. "No doubt the journal was burned during the attack."

"Perhaps it is just as well."

She glanced at him sharply.

"There is no room for new dreams while the old ones fill your mind."

"I was happy with my old dreams."

He gave her the gentlest of smiles. "There is much happiness left for you in this life."

That night, as she lay on a pile of deerskins, she thought of her old dreams. And her thoughts went straight to Hans. She hadn't let herself think of him much since the Indian attack on her home; it hurt too much.

Betsy was sixteen when she first met Hans Bauer. She had gone with her father to purchase supplies in Lancaster Town and stayed overnight at the minister's house, Bairn and Anna Bauer and their daughter, Tessa. The next day was Sunday, so Betsy and her father attended church. Afterward, she had barely walked out of the house where church was held and into the sunshine when an uncommonly attractive young man appeared in front of her. He had mesmerizing brown eyes, with auburn hair that curled over his coat collar. He told her his name was Hans Bauer, and he would like to come calling on her.

She never truly expected to see him again. But Hans had meant what he said and made frequent trips to the Zook farm. He'd brought excitement into their solemn house. He taught her family to play quoits and wisely let her father win. Even he, her overbearing father, had found little to complain about in Hans Bauer. And her sweet-natured mother adored Hans. "Die erscht Lieb roscht net," she remarked to Betsy. *First love does not rust.*

And then her father would add sourly, "Mer kann net lewe vun Lieb alee." *You can't live on love alone.* Hans visited so often that Betsy's father wondered aloud how the village of Stoney Ridge could spare their smithy, though he did not say no when Hans offered to shoe his field horses.

Love. Betsy had had no experience with love before meeting Hans. Love was something all consuming, to be sure. She felt queasy when Hans came calling, forlorn when he left. When he wrote to propose marriage, she felt thunderstruck. Surely, she was the luckiest girl in the world.

Surrender your old dreams, Caleb had advised. But that seemed ironic, she thought, because to surrender was to willingly give up. Her dreams had been stolen from her.

12

Beacon Hollow
July 5, 1763

Something had shifted between Tessa and Hans. He had started coming around Beacon Hollow on Saturday afternoons, then staying on to sup with them. He played quoits with Willie and Tessa, using old horseshoes to hit a metal marker. And after Willie went to bed, he remained in the kitchen to play checkers with Tessa. She had never been happier.

Each time Hans left Beacon Hollow to head for Not Faxon's Farm, Tessa wanted to run all the way into the deep woods behind the house and spin circles under the tall trees. Spin and spin until she fell down, dizzy with happiness. This was what love felt like, she was sure of it.

One such July afternoon, Tessa heard a knock at the door and opened it to find Martin Gingerich, the Mennonite, standing on the stoop. He looked freshly shaved and scrubbed from a bath. In fact, there was a wisp of soap bubbles left on his neck. She looked him up and down, head to toe. "Martin," she said flatly. "Why are you here?"

He held out a bouquet of wilted wildflowers. "I happened to be passing by Beacon Hollow and thought I'd drop by." He eyed Hans, standing behind Tessa. "Oh. Hello there, Hans."

Martin remained at the open door, grinning like a fool, until Tessa's mother invited him in. And in he walked, rumpled Martin.

Hans's spine stiffened and he frowned. "Martin Gingerich, why are you spending time with the Amish?"

"Amish. Mennonite." Martin shrugged. "I like to think of people as individuals."

Hans was not impressed. "Your father holds a different view, I'm sure. Wouldn't he be upset to know you are coming by an Amish girl's house?"

Tessa felt a little flutter of pleasure in her chest and ducked her head to hide her smile. Hans sounded a tiny bit jealous. But it was sinful to have such feelings, vain as well as foolish.

Tessa's father burst out with a laugh. "If that were true, then Faxon wouldn't be spending so much of his spare time in my carpentry shop, prodding and pushing me to finish his wagon."

"Besides," Martin said amiably, "the way I see it, we all come from the same stock."

"I couldn't agree more." Tessa's father gave him a broad smile. "There's far more we hold in common than what separates us."

Her mother gathered up ingredients she was making for a peach pie. "Hans and Tessa and Willie were just going out to play a game of quoits. Why don't you stay and make up a foursome? By the time you're done, this pie should be ready for eating."

Rumpled Martin couldn't have been more pleased. Tessa felt

the extreme opposite. Martin and Willie beat Hans and Tessa two out of three quoits games. Hans left for home, irritated by being bested at his own game. Martin lingered on at Beacon Hollow to eat supper with them, including two helpings of peach pie, and then played a game of checkers with Willie. His lingering frustrated Tessa, but at least he let poor Willie win.

The same thing happened the following Saturday. And the one after that. One Saturday afternoon Martin arrived at Beacon Hollow with a wooden ball and sticks with hoop nets attached. He had learned of a new game, lacrosse, and wanted to play it. He asked Tessa's parents to help make up the teams. Her mother only agreed when they promised to play the game far away from her special rose, planted close to the house. Last Saturday, poor Willie had tossed a quoit haphazardly and it landed on the rose, breaking a branch. Her mother had looked as if she might cry.

Martin explained the game and showed the sticks he'd made—*lacrosse* meant the sticks, which were fashioned with a net he called a cradle. It took a few times to catch on, but soon the ball was slinging back and forth. As Hans slung the ball at Martin, who had to dodge and dart around the yard to catch it and keep it out of the goal, Tessa's mother pulled her aside. "Look, Tessa. Look at our Willie."

Willie was laughing!

"Martin did that," her mother said, more to herself than to Tessa. "He did that for him."

"Martin looks ridiculous." Martin *was* ridiculous.

"Yes. How wonderful."

Tessa thought her mother gave Martin far too much credit.

Afterward, they plopped on the grass, spent. "Where'd you learn that game, anyway?" Hans asked, leaning on his elbows.

"I learned of it from Christy," Martin said amiably. "Over at Indiantown."

You never saw someone change so fast. Hans's face flattened, and his eyes went feral. He jumped to his feet, threw the stick on the ground, and marched to his horse, threw a leg over it, and galloped off.

Late that night, she heard her father's voice carry up the kitchen chimney flue. "You wanted our Tessa to find a suitor," she heard him say. She crouched down on her knees by the loft's hearth. "And now she has two."

Two? Two suitors? She sat back on her heels. Hans, she had a hope in her heart for. But Martin Gingerich? Why would anyone think she would find him to be someone of interest? It was a consideration to reject immediately and she would have thought her father held the same opinion. After all, Martin was a boy of low character, and he was *Mennonite*. The Amish were always fussing about the influence of the Mennonites and the Dunkers on their young folks. Their youth left to join those churches, but no one joined the Amish. If someone left the Amish, he didn't return.

So Martin Gingerich had big marks against him. Surely her father recognized that. If he were right about Martin intending to court his daughter, you'd think he would dissuade him from coming over on Saturday nights. But no! He welcomed Martin into their home as if he was . . . welcome. As if he even enjoyed his company. Maria was always complaining that Bairn Bauer was too liberal in his thinking, and perhaps she had a point.

Tessa heard her parents say something and leaned closer to the flue. "She's far too young," she heard her father say. *Tommyrot!* She wasn't too young to know her heart.

Her mother mumbled something, but she could only make out one word: Immature. Who was immature? Surely not Hans. Certainly not Tessa. Which left only rumpled Martin to be described as immature. Her head wagged in agreement.

Her father's voice sounded firm. "Nae. Y' ken how I feel."

About *what*? Tessa practically stuck her head in the fireplace, trying hard to listen. Whenever her father spoke in English, it was always worth a listen.

"He spends far too much time over there, under his thumb. I fear he is on the brink of rebellion."

Who? Where? Whose thumb? What rebellion?

Her mother said something else, but Tessa couldn't make it out. Maddening! If only her mother had a louder voice.

"He was overly indulged as a child, and I see it still."

Oh. Tessa heartily agreed. Martin *was* spoiled. She felt a sweep of relief, so happy she could hardly contain it. She could rely on her father's solid-gold judgment to shoo Martin off in another direction. And leave space wide open for Hans.

❧

Shawnee Village, Monongahela River
July 25, 1763

At some point during each day, Betsy found herself crossing paths with Caleb. He would appear at her side when she foraged for kindling to keep the fire stoked or hoisted a heavy pot of water from the river. Each time she encountered him, she felt her spirits gladden and the day lost some of its bleakness.

Early one evening, she went down near the river to forage for driftwood on the beach and found Caleb waiting for her, a pleased look on his face as she approached him.

Their gaze lingered longer than she intended and she felt her insides stirring; something she had never felt for Hans. The disloyal thought unsettled her and she quickly turned her attention elsewhere.

She pointed to the water and walked a few steps closer to it. "I've been meaning to ask you, what is the name of this river?" It was a wide, twisting river, lined with trees, and the water shown silver under the setting sun.

"Monongahela. It means River with Crumbling Banks. It is always changing, always moving. It does not want to stay in the same place for too long."

"Like you."

The corners of his mouth lifted slightly, amused. "To the Shawnee, this river is our road. Canoes"—he pointed to a row of canoes turned over on the beach—"they are our horses. You will see, come winter, when we move south."

Such a thought disturbed her, for she believed the longer she stayed in one place, the better chance she had to be reunited with Johnny. She gazed at the direction the water rushed, wondering what he meant by moving south.

Again, he seemed amused. "This river flows north, not south. It has a mind of its own."

Also like him. "Monongahela," she repeated. Betsy had learned to appreciate the importance of names to the Indians. Caleb explained that naming something held great meaning, that it represented *being*, and it made her think of Adam in the Garden of Eden, when he had been given the task of naming all the animals, plants, and trees by the Lord God. As Caleb called him, the Holy One.

But there was something else on Caleb's mind today. She could see it in his eyes; he was like a child waiting with a surprise. "Like the river, it is good to have a mind of one's own." He had been holding one hand behind his back, and now he brought it forward and held something out to Betsy. "For you," he said. It was a book.

She looked at the book but didn't touch it.

"Take it," he said. "An empty book. Waiting for your words. To be filled with new dreams."

A swirl of conflicting emotions caused her to hesitate. "I . . . can't accept it."

He frowned. "You do not want it?"

She wanted the journal, wanted it desperately, but feared what taking it might cost her. "I have no wampum to give you."

"I want nothing. It is a gift." His voice held a hint of offense.

Her reluctance had hurt him. He had never showed her the slightest disrespect, had never touched her inappropriately, not once. Even now he kept himself at a safe distance.

But where did Caleb get this book? To whom did it belong? Her first thought was that it was plunder from another raid. Perhaps it had belonged to someone just like herself.

He read her mind. "I traded a bear skin to a peddler for it." He straightened his back. "I am no warrior. I cause no one to hurt."

She took it from him and opened it. It was, indeed, a book void of words, covered in tan sheepskin, the pages a creamy parchment color, a pencil tucked inside. "I thank you," she said, glancing up to meet Caleb's eyes. "It will bring me great succor." Their eyes held, just a second too long, and she felt her cheeks grow warm. She turned away. "I must look for bits and pieces of wood."

He helped her gather kindling and driftwood; together they walked back up the path toward the central fire. Nijlon had given her the task to tend the fire tonight, but she'd been gone so long that it was reduced to nothing more than glowing coals. "Oh no," she said, picking up her pace. "I've let it go out. Nijlon will be upset with me." Nijlon was kind, but she expected her words to be carried out.

Caleb strode ahead of her and dropped his armful of wood on the ground. He picked up a stick to stir the coals, and flames soon sputtered up. He added a few pieces of kindling to feed it; wood started snapping and crackling, and the fire roared to life. Then he turned to her. "You see, do you not?" he said quietly. "The flame cannot be quenched. Light will always overcome the darkness."

From the way he was looking at her, she felt as if she were being seen, truly seen, for the first time in her life. She found it both exhilarating and disconcerting.

He turned and walked away. She watched him leave, watched how gracefully he moved, how defined the muscles in his shoulders and back were, until all she could see was his silhouette in the shadows.

❦

Beacon Hollow
July 28, 1763

Hans rode up the path from Beacon Hollow as Tessa was crossing the yard with a bucket full of steaming milk. Milking the cow twice a day was her least favorite task, and she had tried, with limited success, to persuade her mother to hand off the chore to Willie. Her mother said yes to the late-afternoon milking but not the early-morning milking, for poor Willie needed his sleep. Well, so did Tessa.

Especially now, since she had, at long last, experienced her first monthly flow. She welcomed it with her whole heart, welcomed the stomach cramps, the low backache, the mild headache, the longing to curl up and stay in bed that accompanied it. She was now, truly, *finally!*, a full-fledged woman.

Hans gave her a bright smile when he saw her and she practically swooned. It was small wonder that she acted dazed in his presence. She returned his smile, cheeks warming, dropping her gaze and fussily checking the hair at the back of her neck.

He swung a leg over his horse to dismount and walked toward Tessa, but before he reached her, her father strode out of his carpentry shop with frustration on his face. "Hans, I've been waitin' on those parts. Did y' bring them with you?"

Uh-oh. Her father was using English, a sign of emotion.

"No. I'll finish them soon."

"Nae." He shot a look of pure exasperation at Hans. "Nae, y' told me that days ago." For long moments, the two men studied each other. "And just where have y' been? Were y' off to Paxton again?"

Hans's face became suddenly hardened—an expression Tessa found oddly chilling, perhaps because his smile disappeared so completely. His words were clear and crisp, as if they froze in the air as he spoke. "I told you I'd have the parts finished soon."

"Not soon. By the end of today. Heed me, Hans. Yer holding up this wagon." With a determined grimace, he turned and moved toward the carpentry shop in long, hurried strides.

Hans glared at his receding back. "That wagon is the only thing he cares about."

"You're the best smithy in Lancaster County," Tessa said, flashing him a brief, nervous smile. "He needs your help. Truly, he does."

Hans turned toward her, as if he'd forgotten she was there. He tilted his head in a familiar gesture that made her insides go soft, and gazed at her as if he was seeing her in a new light. "So what are your plans for the day?"

"To go look for the stallion. Felix thinks he might be drawing near to his farm. Two mares are in season."

"Well, let's get Willie and go stallion hunting."

Tessa glanced uncomfortably at the carpentry shop. Her father was losing patience. "Uh, what about the parts for the wagon? You're the only one who can forge that hardware. The only one with the skills to do it."

He seemed pleased with her words. "Tessa, I could not have endured these past months had it not been for your faithful companionship." He smiled at her and she found it impossible not to return his disarming smile.

It occurred to her she might have just discovered the means to gain—and hold—Han's attention. Be his reflection, the way the sheep pond reflected her image.

❧

Not Faxon's Farm
August 2, 1763

Anna walked Willie to Not Faxon's Farm for schooling each morning and picked him up in the afternoon. She hoped a structured, normal life was a step in the right direction to help Willie mend his sorrowful spirit. She thought it best not to let him be alone on that walk, though it was safe on the well-traveled shortcut that ran through the woods between their farms. Tessa had gone back and forth between the two farms since she was younger than Willie. He was certainly safe alone on the path in the woods. More importantly, she didn't want him to feel alone.

Willie had yet to speak to Anna or Bairn, though Tessa said she had heard him say a word here and there, quietly, under his breath. That news was a great relief to Anna, for she had a nettlesome worry that his mind had become disordered. Wisely, Catrina put no pressure on him, she just scooped him into schooling in the same calm, competent way she managed Benjo and Dannie.

This teaching arrangement was a pleasant surprise. Actually, Catrina was a pleasant surprise. Anna remembered her vividly on the *Charming Nancy* as a miniature version of her mother, Maria. Catrina had appointed herself to be the town crier for the entire ship—above or below decks. She tattled on every sailor, every passenger, and thrice on the captain. She had been a thoroughly annoying little girl.

Catrina had married a young fellow from Germantown who died in a horse accident shortly after their wedding. Much to Maria's disappointment, Catrina remained in Germantown. Years later, she married a German printer, an elderly man, who promptly died of heart failure. Widowhood had seemed to radically affect Catrina's outlook, given her a sense of empathy that had been sorely lacking. She was an entirely different person than Anna remembered. A better person. Sorrow was not without its blessings.

As they walked through the woods on this warm morning, Anna looked down at Willie's little hand, tucked in hers. She didn't let herself grieve often over the little boys she had borne and buried because she believed they knew a better life than anything this world could offer. The eternal life, warm and safe, in God's glory.

But when she did let herself think of them, she mourned, especially for Bairn. She was sorry he did not have his sons beside him in the carpentry shop or down at the sawmill by the creek, the way Tessa worked beside her in the house.

Today, as she felt Willie's little hand curl around hers, she wondered what it would have been like to raise a son. To know that a soft little hand like this one would not remain soft or little for long.

They grew so fast, these children. Too fast. Tessa's monthly flow began a few days ago for the first time, and she was so happy to make that passage into womanhood that her feet had hardly touched the ground since. And all Anna could think was that she wished time would slow down. She was well aware that soon, much too soon for Anna, Tessa would marry and start a home of her own.

The passing of time had always been a comfort to Anna, slow and steady and sure. Days could flow one into the other without her even noticing. But sometime during the last year, the passing of time felt entirely different. It felt finite, difficult to grasp, like trying to hold water in her hands. Time was slipping away.

Shawnee Village, Monongahela River
August 15, 1763

It seemed as if time slowed down since Betsy had come to this Indian village. Each summer day was much like the day before and the day after. There were no markers, like the Sabbath, to create rhythm and balance for the week, and she stopped trying to keep track of days. She realized she had adjusted to her life among the Shawnee villagers, strange as it was, and she was not miserable. Nor was she happy. She was somewhere in between.

She found herself paying close attention to changes in the natural world, things that were part of her life but did not hold much meaning to her: subtle changes in the clouds that hinted at the morrow's weather, the path overhead of migrating birds, a cooling wind that skimmed the top of the river's surface before reaching the village. Until now, she had never felt anything for wilderness but dread. It was inhospitable and uninhabitable, full of dangers; its very name originated out of the word *wild*. Her father had believed that the wilderness needed to be conquered. Turned into farms.

Betsy's perspective on the wilderness had radically changed. She was no longer afraid of being alone in the woods but felt drawn to its beauty. When she ventured farther and farther out on walks, she felt a deep peace settle over her. She felt closer to God in the wilderness, though she knew that wasn't true, for God was everywhere.

A soft smile touched her lips at the memory of trying to explain to Numees that God was everywhere and in all things. Numees's big eyes grew wide as she peered around the wigwam, as if trying to locate Betsy's God. Betsy tried to make her understand God was spirit, invisible, like air. So Numees breathed in deep gulps of air until she nearly passed out, hoping to please Betsy's God.

The pagan ways of the villagers disturbed Betsy—how they worshiped several gods and believed that all of nature was linked, interrelated, from a river to a rock to a red-breasted robin.

But she also saw beauty in the lives of the Indians. To the villagers, everything was "we,"—never I, me, or mine. They were generous to a fault, sharing everything they had. And they did not have much. It was a life without creature comforts.

Each afternoon, while her sisters napped, Betsy would wander down to the river where she could write in her journal and pour out all these new insights and discoveries, trying to sift them through and come to conclusions. When she had finished writing, she would go to the place where she knew Caleb would be, tending the village's central fire, burning down the boat. His work was to hollow and shape the inside of white pine or white oak logs into a canoe.

The first step, he had explained to her, was to find the perfect tree. Burning down the boat was an all-day and all-night job, and Caleb slept by the fire. Each canoe, three, four, or five rods in length, took him one moon's turn—a month's time. Using a stone tool, he would burn and scrape the interior of the log, burn and scrape, burn and scrape, until he reached unburned wood. But the real tool, he told her, was fire.

She looked forward to their conversations. She was no longer self-conscious around him but had begun to trust him, to feel safe in his presence. His friendship was a precious gift, helping to strengthen and sustain her.

She would never have thought it possible that an Indian man and an Amish woman could become friends, but that was exactly what seemed to be happening. She had been taught to believe the Indians were her enemies, to fear and abhor them. She had witnessed their harrowing brutality. But she had also received unexpected kindness from them. Caleb, especially.

A question continued to nettle her: Was it not possible that these people were children of God? Was not the good she saw in them, the kindness, the generosity, a reflection of God's holy image? Were they not loved by God?

What would Hans say if she were to share these thoughts with him? She closed her eyes, trying to visualize him, to remember him. She could almost hear him give her stern warning: "You are facing a great trial. You must not allow yourself to be confused by heathens." Her eyes popped open. That was not Hans's voice she heard, but her father's! She squeezed her eyes shut, distressed that her mind was becoming disordered.

But the confusion in her mind wasn't all that distressed her. It was the friendship she was forging with Caleb. She was growing fonder of him than she had any right to be.

13

Not Faxon's Farm
September 9, 1763

The weather was changing. The dark, low-lying clouds, the wind kicking up, rumbles of thunder off in the distance, and Felix knew an autumn storm was rolling in. It was chilly outside but warm in the barn, and he had plenty of neglected barn chores that needed tending to. The barn smelled of straw and horses and oats and manure, a mélange of strong scents. Felix loved it.

It surprised him, how much he loved this farming life. As a boy, he was enamored with the thought of a life spent on the open sea, like his brother Bairn. When he had first met Benjamin Franklin and watched him work, carefully setting lead type, Felix discovered how letters became words, then word became thoughts, and those thoughts could affect and influence others, and he thought he might follow in the printer's footsteps.

And then, Felix found himself to be a grown man. It was time to stop dreaming about the future and make some decisions. Should he join the church? Should he leave? He felt as if he was sitting on a fence and watching himself walk by. He couldn't decide, so he didn't.

One day, Anna invited him to Beacon Hollow to welcome a new German immigrant family who happened to have a daughter named Rachel, about Felix's age. As Rachel was introduced to Felix, she had tried to say *welcome* but it came out as *fulcrum*. He never understood the expression "getting swept off your feet" until he walked into the kitchen that afternoon and heard that brown-eyed beauty mangle the word *welcome*. Meeting Rachel on that sunny October afternoon became a shifting point for him, a true fulcrum. The word had never held such promise. The course of his life path was finally set.

Rachel was the one who sparked his interest in horse breeding. She knew there would always be a need among farmers for good workhorses. Without a doubt, she was right.

A door creaked open and he peered out a barn window to see Anna leave the house with Willie. It wasn't much of a surprise when Benjo and Dannie ran down the house steps and into the barn to announce school was winding up early because a storm was coming. A moment later, Catrina walked up behind them.

"Christy passed through just a short time ago," Felix told his boys. "He was looking for you two to go fishing at Blue Lake Pond. He said fish rise to the surface in the rain so they're easier to catch."

Benjo pumped his arms and leaped up in the air. "I'm on my way," he said, halfway to the barn door.

Dannie blinked. His mind ran a little slower, but he wasn't going to be left behind. "I'm coming!" Benjo waited for him to catch up, then the brothers—similar in height, size, and pace—ran down the rest of the length of the barn to get their fishing gear.

That left Catrina and Felix, standing awkwardly in the hall of the barn. Three horses stuck their heads out of their stalls and regarded them with mild interest.

"Do you think it's wise to let the boys go fishing despite a storm coming?"

He shrugged. "A little rain never hurt anybody."

"Lightning is attracted to water."

Oh? He hadn't thought of that. His boys knew that, right? He wasn't sure. Christy would surely know, though. Wouldn't he? Felix ran a hand down the back of his head.

It dawned on him how much he counted on Christy, an Indian boy not much older than his own sons, to teach Benjo and Dannie how to make their way in this world. Was he as careless a father as Catrina made him think he was? Surely not.

She wrinkled her nose, sniffing, as she looked up at rafters. "Needs a little cleaning, don't you agree?"

He followed her eyes to see spiderwebs hugging the corners of the barn. He sniffed. He guessed it did smell a little ripe in here, but he liked the smell. Still, it would be something for the boys to do on a rainy day.

Felix led one of the yearlings from its stall down the barn and outside to the round pen. Catrina followed behind, coming to stand near the pen, leaning against it with her arms over the top rail. Felix unhooked the shank from the colt's halter and chirped to him, urging him from a jog to a lope, around and around the pen. Why was she still here? She made him nervous.

"He doesn't look so very big."

"No. I suppose not. He's average-sized."

"But Tessa said you bred big horses. Very, very big horses."

"I do, but this isn't one of them."

She opened her hands to a make a circle. "Hooves the sizes of dish plates, she said."

"Tessa is known to exaggerate." Then he glanced at her. "But I have to admit, she's right about that. Their hooves are pretty big."

"I'd like to see one of those big horses."

After a brief hesitation, he nodded. He unhooked the colt and slipped through the fence, then gestured for her to join him. They walked quite a long way before coming to another large barn, close to the woods, one Felix had built after the first year the stallion had visited Not Faxon's Farm and left behind the gift of six very large foals.

"How many barns do you have?"

"Two."

She glanced at him with surprise. "Why do you need two?"

"You'll see." He walked past the barn to a paddock. Inside the paddock, two mother horses grazed, their babies moving closely alongside. Catrina followed him to a section of fence; they stood next to each other, separated by a respectful amount of space.

"This barn here," he said, "holds my broodmares."

"Oh my," she whispered. "How old are they? About two months?"

He looked at her dubiously. She guessed correctly. He wouldn't have expected her to know much about horses. Much about anything, for that matter.

One of the foals neared. Catrina reached out her hand and the little horse bumped her hand with its nose, thinking there might be some oats in it. "I love their overly long legs and dainty little faces."

Dainty faces? That was a description he had never once considered. Now that she said it aloud, he thought she was right. The foals did have dainty faces, large eyes with long eyelashes.

She absently rubbed her palm up and down one of the foal's necks, then fiddled with a strand of mane. "Their tails look like they're made up of more fluff than substance."

"That's part of the breed. Short tails." Felix gave the baby a gentle pat on the side of its neck and it pranced away.

Thunder rumbled again, this time closer, and then something strange happened to Felix. He turned, expecting Catrina to make another snide remark about what kind of father let his boys go fishing in a thunderstorm, but she was watching the little foals with a soft look on her face. "Such sweet, sweet babies."

And he felt a lightning bolt hit him. Not literally, of course, but something about the look on her face caused a thrill to shoot straight to his vitals. Beneath her tough appearance he'd recognized a . . . what? How could he even describe it? A vulnerability in her.

Catrina Müller had never been vulnerable about anything. *Never.*

Which was very bad news for Felix, because he'd always been a sap for vulnerability.

He wondered what Catrina's life had been like over the last decade. He knew she'd been married twice, a young boy and an old graybeard. He'd even made fun of her bad luck with men, calling her a black widow spider. Not to her face, naturally. It hadn't occurred to him that she might have loved her husbands. He knew how it felt to lose someone. It shamed him now that he had been so cavalier about her feelings. He felt flooded with protectiveness, tenderness, and yes . . . desire toward her.

Desire? For Catrina Müller?! Was he *crazy*?

He was entirely unprepared for his reaction to her. How long had it been since he'd felt something for a woman? Too long.

She was watching the foals exchange hellos with their noses, a soft smile on her face. She had a pair of the nicest lips he'd ever seen, and they were downright pretty when she smiled. He fought an impulse to reach out and touch her cheek, to see if it was as soft and smooth as it looked.

Lifting her head, she caught him gawking. "What are you staring at?"

"Nothing." Guiltily, he looked up at the clouds, feeling his face heat up.

A few drops of rain began and she frowned, looking up at the sky. "I thought I could beat it home, but I'd better go wait it out and visit with Dorothea." She started toward the house, running as the drops turned to steady rain.

Felix shut himself inside the barn. Instead of getting started on the work that waited for him, he simply sat on an old wooden trunk, the very one his mother brought with her from Germany on the *Charming Nancy*. How could he be sitting here in such a normal way, in this normal place, and yet feel anything but normal? He looked down at himself, his chest, hands, legs, boots. How could he appear the same when everything inside of him suddenly felt completely different?

He'd stood next to Catrina at the fence just now and shared a conversation with her. One simple, little conversation. They'd been alone together twenty minutes at most. Maybe thirty.

But it had been long enough. Long enough to shift everything within him. He set his elbows on his knees and dropped his head into his hands. Why her? Catrina? Of all the women on earth, why had he reacted to her in this way? He felt a shocking transformation over the way he felt, as startling as the sound of thunder that rattled the barn's roof. And he was fairly confident that Catrina did not share his feelings. In fact, she seemed completely unaffected by him, hardly aware of him at all. He'd felt this kind of thunderstruck feeling only one time before. Then, too, he was sunk. Hopelessly in love. It was how he'd felt about his Rachel.

Over years of working with horses, he'd come to trust his senses. He understood horses, how to train them, how to bring out their best. He knew how a horse's mind worked. But it suddenly occurred to him that when it came to women, he had very little understanding.

He blamed the lightning.

Beacon Hollow
September 18, 1763

Sunday afternoons, according to Tessa's father, were made for napping. He was exhausted after church service and fellowship, and headed straight to bed as soon as he reached home. At her mother's encouragement, Tessa took Willie outside to play. It was a beautiful autumn afternoon, unusually warm, with leaves starting to turn shades of red and gold. Back and forth, they tossed the ball that rumpled Martin had left behind. Tessa looked up at the blue sky. "Days like these are called Indian summer, Willie." She caught the ball and tossed it back. "After we've had the first frost and then the weather turns unseasonably warm, it's supposed to signal the season for Indian attacks on settlers."

Willie dropped the ball by his feet. His face drained of color. It dawned on Tessa what she had just said without thinking. "Oh Willie, I'm so sorry."

He ran inside the house.

"What have I done?" Tessa pressed her fists against her eyes. She felt sick. When would she ever learn to think before she spoke? Willie had been doing so much better these last few weeks . . . eating and sleeping, playing with Benjo and Dannie, saying a few words . . . and she rubbed out all that good healing in one stupid sentence. Now he would be terrified that Indians would come to attack Beacon Hollow. Why, why, why did she have to say that? "I am . . . an imbecile."

"You only spoke the truth."

Tessa dropped her fists and saw Hans standing just a few rods away.

"You spoke the truth to Willie. None of us are safe, Tessa. Not even here, near Lancaster Town. The Indians are plotting attacks on all white men—everywhere in the colony."

She clutched her elbows. "That's not what my father says."

"That's because he doesn't want to accept the reality of the situation. He wants to believe that the Indians can be reasoned with, that they will respect Penn's Treaties. I don't mean to criticize your father. It's a noble thought—to judge a man by his own actions. That kind of thinking might work for some, but not for Indians. They think and act as a group."

A wind rose and lifted Tessa's capstrings, making them

dance. "But . . . so do the Amish." Same with the Mennonites and the Dunkers.

He shook his head. "It's different with us. Our nature is not violent, not corrupt. We are meant to shine brightly in this dark world. And it is a very dark world, Tessa. Look what happened to the Zooks—they did nothing wrong and yet they were brutally murdered."

Despite the heat, Tessa felt her skin prickle with chill. "My father said that the Zooks had bought property farther north than other white men. They were transgressing past the frontier."

Hans scoffed. "So it was their fault? Plowing a field and felling a tree meant they were subject to be tomahawked to death? Their bodies chopped to bits while their little boy hid in a hollow tree and watched the desecration as it occurred?"

Tessa gripped her elbows tight against her abdomen. She was sure she was going to be sick. "I . . . didn't mean that. I just meant that . . ." Her voice drizzled to a stop. She didn't know what she meant.

"Hear me, Tessa. You are young, but being young doesn't mean you must remain naïve. The Indians are on the advance, and if we don't do something soon, we will be the ones whose bodies are desecrated." Something flared in Hans's eyes. A crazed look, she thought, but when she look again, his eyes had mellowed. Maybe she was the crazed one.

He lifted up an enormous bridle he had made, crafted out of brand-new leather, including a metal bit. "I came to go stallion hunting with you." She hadn't even noticed it until now. "Think it's big enough?"

Her thoughts felt muddled; she was still furious with herself for what she'd said to Willie, and horrified by Hans's fear-inspiring predictions. She took the bridle out of his hands and examined it minutely. "Hans, it's . . . very well made." And it was. He was a remarkable craftsman. "You're very clever."

He grinned.

"But . . . you can't just slap a bridle on this horse. He's barely let me touch him."

Hans's face flattened with surprise. "Sure you can. We'll just go slow."

"It's not just that . . . it's . . . he's a wild animal. Maybe a harness might work. But a bit in his mouth—it's just not right."

"Tessa, I know how to break a horse. I've lived at Not Faxon's Farm for the last ten years. I've seen Felix break dozens of horses."

"But Felix doesn't break horses. He trains them."

A condescending look came over Hans. "Sweet Tessa, let me handle this from here."

"There'll be nothin' of the kind on this afternoon."

Tessa and Hans turned to find her father standing on the door stoop. "'Tis the Sabbath." He crossed his arms against his chest. "And where were you this morning, Hans?"

"Dorothea wasn't faring well this morning. I stayed home to be with her, so Felix and his boys could attend church. Did Felix not tell you?"

"Nae," he said. "Mayhap it slipped his mind." He lifted his chin toward Tessa. "'Tis time for the cow to be milked. Dinnae you hear her bellows?"

No, Tessa hadn't noticed. But now that her father pointed it out, she could hear woeful lows coming from the barn. She turned back to Hans to invite him to sup with them, but he had already mounted his horse and started down the path.

"The cow, Tessa. She is waitin' fer y'." Her father held the clean milk bucket out to her.

Tessa grabbed the bucket and ran to the barn. How had such a pleasant afternoon started out so sweetly and ended on such a sour note?

***

Shawnee Village, Monongahela River
September 26, 1763

The day was cool and smelled of autumn's arrival. Betsy and Numees were harvesting dried bean pods. Nijlon came to the garden with her infant in her arms and set him down on the ground near a pumpkin, fingercombing his hair before she straightened up. He was an appealing baby, large eyes black as walnuts that followed his mother everywhere, and a geyser of fine black hair that sprouted from the top of his head. He was able to sit by himself now and leaned forward to grasp the pumpkin with both hands. He thumped the orange squash with his chubby hands, like a tiny warrior pounding on a drum, and they all stopped to watch, to watch and to laugh. Unexpected pleasure stole over Betsy.

Numees lifted the basket of bean pods to show to Nijlon. She said something to her sister, and Betsy realized, startled, that she understood what she was saying.

"Many bean seeds for next year's garden," she was saying, and Nijlon nodded, pleased.

Next year.

Betsy's contentedness evaporated. *Will I still be here next year? And the year after that? Is this going to be what my life consists of?*

Not Faxon's Farm
October 4, 1763

It was a mellow day in early October. Felix balanced a log on the stump, stood back, cracked it dead center, and cleaved it with two whacks. He'd been waiting and waiting for school to let out. Anna had come to get Willie a half hour ago and was still in the house, probably talking to Dorothea. He'd already split a stack waist high, watching the house for the moment to strike. He'd chopped enough firewood to last through the winter.

Today was the perfect opportunity—Maria was over at Beacon Hollow, working with Anna and Tessa on the canvas to be stretched over the wagon hoops. It was a rare day that Maria did not spend at Not Faxon's Farm and he aimed to make the most of this chance. Finally, he saw Anna and Willie leave, and then his own boys burst out of the house and into the woods to check on their beaver traps. He let the axe fall, grabbed a rag, and wiped his face and hands. He'd been sweating like it was a summer day. He picked up an armful of wood to take to the house, and wore his most purposeful expression.

Felix slowed as he went up the steps to the house so he could catch his breath. It wouldn't do to seem too eager. His mother was resting in a chair by the fireplace and Catrina was cleaning up the table from the day's activities. He looked around the room. He hadn't noticed, but it was considerably cleaner. The clutter was gone. The room looked dusted, swept, sparkly clean. A copper pot gleamed on the mantel. Huh. He had never realized the pot was made of copper—it had been that badly tarnished, that badly in need of a polish.

Catrina stood at the end of the table, chin to her chest, riffling through a book, smiling absentmindedly at something that amused her. A stray lock of hair had slipped down and fallen against her cheek, and she tucked it behind one ear. Heaven's sake, what a smile did to Catrina Müller's face— eyes crinkling at the corners, lips softening. Gone was the stoic façade. For a moment Felix imagined Catrina belonged here, in the kitchen at Not Faxon's Farm, that she was his woman, helping to raise his boys and care for his mother. She glanced up at him, and he realized he'd been staring and became self-conscious.

"That's a lot of wood you've been chopping out there," Catrina said.

Their eyes held for several beats while he felt his face flush with color. "Well, after all, winter is coming." He dumped the wood in the box on the hearth, took his hat off, and held it against his chest, then cleared his throat. "Catrina, I wondered if perhaps you might be interested in going on a walk."

She didn't even look up as she filled her leather satchel with books she had brought with her. "A walk?"

"Yes. A walk."

She cast a glance at him. "With you?"

"Yes."

She paused and looked at Dorothea. "If you have something to discuss in private about your boys, I think your mother has fallen asleep. You can speak freely."

As if on cue, Dorothea's jaw went slack and she let out a loud snore.

"No. It's nothing like that. I just thought it would be nice to go on a walk. It's a beautiful autumn day."

She stopped packing books and gave him a puzzled look. "Felix, are you asking to court me?"

Felix swallowed. "No!" *Yes. Maybe.* "Just a walk in the woods. That's all."

"Well, thank you for your interest, but no."

"No?" No? Seriously? He backed off, rubbing his hands on his thighs self-consciously. He was never self-conscious. Never!

"No." She picked up her satchel and headed toward the door.

"Why not?"

She stopped at the door. "Does there have to be a reason?"

"No. Yes! Why aren't you interested in me?"

She put her satchel down. "You and I . . . we're complete opposites."

"But opposites are supposed to attract. Supposed to balance each other out."

She shook her head. "This is different."

"How so?"

"Please don't make me say it."

"Say what?"

She winced. "You are intellectually lazy."

"I'm what? What?" *Intellectually lazy. What does that even mean?*

"Felix, when did you last read a book?"

Felix sputtered, at a loss for words. "I . . . um . . ." The truth was . . . he couldn't remember ever finishing a book.

"If it weren't for Anna's and Dorothea's insistence, your sons would be growing up unlearned. Ignorant backwoodsmen."

190

"Ignorant? Ignorant! They can track a deer better than any man in our church!"

She lifted a finger in the air. "I will grant you that. They will not go hungry. But there is more to life than eating."

Felix was once again at a loss for words. He had never, ever been spurned by a woman. Nor had he been told he was intellectually lazy! Which he wasn't.

Maybe he was.

"Thank you, though, Felix, for your romantic ardor. It's terribly flattering." She picked up the stack of books and swept out the front door to her pony cart.

Romantic ardor? Hardly that. It was only a walk in the woods. That's all! Did Catrina Müller have any idea how many girls would be honored to go on a walk with him? Dozens! At least two that he could name.

He ran outside as she climbed into the pony cart. "Did you know, Catrina, that I'm considered the most eligible bachelor in the county?"

"A bachelor is a man who's too fast to be caught or too slow to be worth catching." She flicked the pony's reins and headed down the path.

Felix remained at the hitching post, watching the pony cart until it disappeared around the corner. He was dumbfounded. Flummoxed. And rather offended. His sons appeared at his side with curious looks on their upturned faces.

"Boys, I've made a decision. Catrina's given you a fine start at book learning. But I'm going to tell her that we won't be needing her anymore. I'll take over from here."

The boys exchanged surprised looks. Horrified looks. "Pa," Benjo said, taking the lead as was his nature, "we want to learn to read."

"Yup." Dannie lifted his hat to scratch his head. "I want to get my sums figured out too, so I can trade my skins and not get cheated."

"Of course you do. And I'll teach you."

Benjo smacked himself in the head and fell backward, sprawled on the grass. "Not this again!"

"Not what again?"

Benjo lifted his head off the ground and looked at Felix. "You say you'll teach us but you never get around to it."

Felix was flabbergasted. Kerfuffled. The world was upside down. "So let me get this straight. You *want* to learn to read."

Benjo sobered, sat up and looked at his father. "Yes."

"And you don't think I can teach you."

"Nope."

"But you think Catrina can teach you."

Benjo made his floppy hair bounce by nodding so hard. "She teaches us the stuff that matters most."

Felix started sputtering. Teaches them things that matter most? What did they think he'd been doing for the last nine years?

"Pa, she's not so bad," Benjo said.

"In fact, we like her," Dannie piped in. "And she's nice to poor Willie."

"She's nothing like you warned us she'd be," Benjo said. "All those stories you told us—like how she tricked you into getting drunk on the *Charming Nancy*, and how she was always tattling on you—she has a different version of those stories."

Dannie looked up at Felix with wide, unblinking eyes. "Maybe you have her confused in your head with someone else on the ship."

192

Felix felt his face flush as Benjo's words struck home. Catrina Müller wasn't the girl he'd remembered. Nothing like her.

❧

Beacon Hollow
October 16, 1763

On Sunday, right before church ended, Bairn stood between the benches and turned in a circle to look around at everyone, his smiling gray eyes resting on Anna. She felt a rush of feelings well up for him: love, admiration, respect.

"After our fellowship meal, I hope you will stay on for a few extra moments." Bairn pressed his hands together. "The Conestoga wagon is, at long last, completed. So many of you played a part in the making of it—all the women had a hand in spinning the linen and weaving the sturdy canvas, Anna, Tessa, and Maria waterproofed it with linseed oil and stretched it over the hoops, Hans made the hardware from his forge, Felix trained his new breed of horses to pull it, Martin Gingerich made the hemp ropes out of flax."

Bairn glanced at the men in the back row. "Many of you gave up time in your fields to work alongside me in the carpentry shop, to share a suggestion or two. Your advice and practical help shaped this wagon." He smiled, and lifted his arms wide. "Working together, we have achieved far more than we could have ever hoped. Let us take a moment to thank God for the gift of community."

So like my husband. To give praise to others for this mighty accomplishment. Over a year of his life had been consumed in the design and building of this wagon, yet he deflected all personal tribute to extend out to the church and give glory to God.

Early Monday morning, a bitter wind swept over the orchards and swirled about the house and barn, but it did not slow Faxon Gingerich from arriving before dawn to claim the wagon. Bairn had predicted as much after seeing Martin at church yesterday. "Were it not for the Sabbath, Faxon would be here today," he had told Anna as they readied for bed. "Expect him when the cock crows." Bairn had purposely waited for Sunday to declare the completion of the wagon—he wanted their little church to have the first look at it.

On this morning, Faxon brought his son Martin along, a fine young man who was smitten with Tessa, which endeared him to Anna, as did the fact that he had started to attend their church on his own church's off Sundays. Tessa was not at all endeared to him; long ago, Martin had made some kind of disparaging remark that had revealed a permanent flaw in his character, Tessa firmly decided. When her daughter made up her mind about someone, good or bad, there was no changing it. That, Anna pointed out to her, revealed a flaw in her own character. Tessa frowned and insisted her mother just didn't understand.

Anna invited Faxon and Martin into the house and out of the cold while Bairn went to prepare the wagon. She heard Tessa's footsteps above in the loft. Martin heard, too, and kept glancing up the stairs to see if Tessa might be coming down. She sighed, knowing her daughter. Tessa wouldn't dare come down as long as Martin was in the kitchen.

Anna served Faxon a cup of hot tea which he laced heavily with cream and sugar, then served him another. He sat impatiently at the table, drumming his fingers.

"I have freight to haul to Philadelphia this very morning," Faxon growled as Anna poured a third cup of tea.

Too bad, she thought, smiling sweetly. He would have to wait right there until the sun rose. She knew Bairn wanted the appearance of the horses and wagon to have the proper impact on Faxon after so many months of his haggling, nagging, and criticizing.

As the morning sun broke through the trees and lit the yard, streaming into the east-facing window and onto the wooden floorboards, she heard the sound she'd been waiting for, the signal that Bairn was ready. Faxon lifted his head and perked up, reminding Anna just a little of their dog Zeeb. It was the sound of bells.

Faxon drained his cup, ran the back of his hand across his lips, and lurched to his feet. "Well, at long last, I believe the wagon awaits."

They hurried outside. Bairn was guiding the wagon into the yard, pulled by Felix's young colts, trained to act as a team. The sight of it was magnificent and Faxon's eyes went wide with awe. Martin, who had seen the sight yesterday after church, couldn't stop grinning.

Six big and beautiful horses, two by two, with bells tinkling above their harnesses to act as warnings to anything in their way, pulled this long, boatlike wagon, with wheels as tall as a man, and canvas covering stretched tight over the bows. Bairn walked along the left side, reins in his hands.

Faxon Gingerich, for once in his life, was speechless. He walked from the front of the horses to the back of the wagon, then around the other side, dumbfounded, before he recovered his senses. "Can it float?"

"No," Bairn said, laughing. "It is not meant to act as a

boat. But it should be able to get through a creek or river without getting any supplies wet. The back end comes down, like a hatch, to make filling the wagon easier."

"What wood did you use? I'd forgotten."

"Black gum. Its grain makes it nearly unsplittable."

Faxon asked a few more questions, listened as Bairn taught him how to steer the team of horses, and then he did something unexpected. He thrust his hand out to shake Bairn's hand and said, "Thank you, Bairn Bauer."

14

Monongahela River
October 18, 1763

Along the shore of the river on a sunny afternoon, Betsy scraped dried corn kernels off cobs using the jawbone of a deer. Its sharp edge worked surprisingly well.

"That is not a new task for you."

She looked up to find Caleb standing at a distance. She hadn't been aware of his presence until he spoke, but that was not unusual. He had a way of silently appearing and disappearing. She smiled. "Yes, I've done this many times for my mother." She lifted the jawbone. "Though I've never used a bone to scrape before."

He dropped to the ground beside her, crossing his legs, and pulled out his knife to help her get through the large basket of dried corn. As they worked, they fell into an easy conversation, flowing as naturally between them as if they'd been longtime friends.

"We had no corn in Germany," Betsy said. "It was new to my family when we reached the New World, but we learned to adapt quickly. It wasn't long before it was part of every meal. Cornbread, succotash, pones, fry bread, johnnycakes."

"Johnnycakes?"

"It's a flat, thin cake, useful to carry on a day's journey. My father used to take a stack of them when he went to German-town to buy farm supplies. My brother Johnny thought they were named for him." She hadn't spoken much of her home and family to Caleb, and as she spoke, a terrible, raw longing welled up. She looked down at her lap and pinched a fold in her dress, trying to master her feelings. When she glanced up, she saw in his face not the sympathy she'd expected, but a startled recognition. "What is it?" she managed to utter.

"I was remembering," he said, in a voice as hoarse as her own, "of the time after my mother died. My father had died years earlier, of injury, and now my mother was gone, of sickness. I could not—" He stopped and shook his head. "I could not see a way out of sadness." He dropped his chin to his chest. "You do not feel at home here, do you?" He lifted his head to look at her.

She stared into his eyes a moment too long. She felt a strange seizing, deep in her heart—as if it, like the whole rest of the world, had ceased beating. "No. No, I don't."

"Can you not try?" In his eyes was a plea. "Try to accept this life?"

She shook her head, eyes stinging with tears. "I can not."

"Betsy, abandon your dream of returning," he said. "This is your home. We are now your family."

Tears streamed down her cheeks, splashing on her dress. "I still have a family. My family is my brother, Johnny. Some-day, we will be together again. I have to believe that. I don't belong here, Caleb. I never will."

He reached over and took the deer jawbone out of her hands. "But you are becoming Indian."

She shook her head. "Even if I wear Indian clothing and use Indian tools, in my heart, I belong elsewhere. My heart is elsewhere. My heart . . . belongs to someone else. My heart is pledged to another man."

Slowly, he rose, walked down to the river, and stood facing it with his arms crossed against his chest. She knew the look, the stance, well on him. Those were the moments when he seemed most alone to her, most self-contained. Not lonely, but not reachable. After several long moments, he returned to her, but didn't say another word. He bent down to brush her cheek with his hand, gently running a finger down her scar, the tenderest of gestures. He left her to finish her task and went back to tend the fire.

It was late when she returned to the wigwam. She felt weary—and grateful when Numees scooped a bowl of stew from the pot over the small fire and handed it to her. They ate in silence, side by side. She knew Numees sensed her distress, but she did not have enough command of the language to explain why, nor did she want to try.

❧

Blue Lake Pond
October 30, 1763

As long as the weather cooperated, Hans, Tessa, and Willie spent Sunday afternoons at Blue Lake Pond. Hans taught poor Willie to skim rocks, to fish, to build a fire using a flint. Too often, Martin Gingerich would appear, joining them as if invited, though he wasn't. To be fair, Blue Lake Pond was a gathering place for the handful of young people of Stoney Ridge. On this sunny afternoon, to Tessa's delight, Martin did not tag along. She had Hans all to herself. Along with poor Willie.

Tessa's feelings for Hans grew stronger each time she was with him. She had always known she loved him, but the last few weeks, she had fallen even deeper, even further; she was helplessly, hopelessly in love with him.

She knew Hans was caring of her, but she also knew that his eyes did not hold a unique ardor for her, not the way her father looked at her mother, as if she were a precious treasure. Or the way she had caught her uncle Felix gazing at Catrina during church this morning, as if he'd been struck by Cupid's arrow.

Hans *was* fond of Tessa. She did not doubt that.

And she had more than enough love in her heart for both of them. Surely, his devotion for Betsy Zook would diminish over time and there would be room enough in his heart to love Tessa.

Hans and Willie were down by the shoreline, skimming rocks on top of the water. Tessa stayed close to the fire, keeping it stoked with leaves and sticks, because the brisk wind had a bite to it. After a while, Hans left Willie to carry on and joined her, plopping on the sand beside her, elbows on his knees. For a long while, he didn't speak. He took off his hat but kept turning it around and around by the brim, as if he was collecting his thoughts and carefully choosing his words.

Then, out of the blue, he started to talk about Betsy Zook, about memories he shared with her, about their plans to marry. Tessa found herself with uncommonly little to say.

What was there *to* say? Nothing. And so she just listened to him as he described Betsy's many virtues. My oh my, she was nearly reaching sainthood! Tessa silently scolded herself. Surely a devil's spirit seized her thoughts.

Hans glanced at Tessa and his haunted expression told her plainly that he would never cease loving Betsy. Never. She turned her face from him and bowed her head.

"John Elder is convinced Betsy was killed, soon after the raid."

Tessa thought so too. Why else would they not have heard word of Betsy or Johnny Zook from someone, somewhere? Penn's Woods had many eyes and ears. "How would he know of such a thing?"

"He seems to have a unique understanding of the ways of savages. Better than most."

Tessa's father would heartily disagree. He thought John Elder was a nut.

"John Elder has admonished me to accept that Betsy Zook is part of the past and that my life must go on." There was a short silence before he added, "But there is still something to be done for her." He sat up to face Tessa, reached out and took her hands, enveloping them in his own. "You understand, don't you?" he said quietly.

She did. She understood in some vague way that his affection was not intended for her, but for Betsy Zook.

"We will form a family, you and I and poor Willie."

Tessa's heart started to pound; she was sure he could hear it.

"Tessa, when you turn sixteen, I want you to be my wife."

Her stomach did cartwheels and color surged to her face. She counted the months, the years, she'd been waiting for this moment. *This* moment! It was as if her tongue had vanished from her head and she was unable to express any words, but as she looked at him, her heart spoke for her. It shouted out an ear-splitting *Yes!*

Monongahela River
November 1, 1763

The days had grown short and the sun had become distant. When the corn was harvested and seed was scored from the dried cobs, some of the village men loaded it into canoes, the very ones that Caleb had fashioned from hollowed logs, and proceeded upriver. Those who remained, mostly women, packed all they could carry and prepared to break camp in the morrow.

Caleb had told Betsy to expect this. This Shawnee tribe had winter quarters in the south; next spring, they would return to the same wigwams and fields. She had asked if her brother Johnny's tribe would do the same, and he said it would depend on their food supplies for the winter. "They are Munsee," he had said, as if that explained everything. She must have looked confused because he added, "Hunters, not farmers."

On the first day, the villagers walked along the river for hours, feet crunching through half-frozen mud, then turned inland and climbed a bank to reach a trail. When the sun dropped below the horizon, they stopped to eat and sleep under the stars, and then they were on the trail again early the next morning.

Numees had taught Betsy how to tell directions from the

sun, and so Betsy calculated that they were heading southeast. At times she felt as if the last few months of safety in the village was a dream, and in truth she was back among the warriors, marching aimlessly toward a bleak and unknown future. She knew she appeared sad, as Numees often tried to cheer her up, pointing out migrating birds in the sky or pressing extra food on her to eat. She seemed worried about her. Numees lightened Betsy's heavy basket by taking out a reed mat and adding it to her own burden.

Betsy tried to assure her she was fine, that all was well, but it wasn't. She wasn't. Her moroseness covered her like a heavy fog.

On the third day, she caught sight of Caleb as he walked with another man. Though he did not look in her direction, she knew he had seen her. He had not sought her out since the day they spent scoring corncobs, when she had told him about Hans, about longing to be reunited with him. She thought she had hurt their friendship beyond repair by telling him the truth.

The next afternoon, the trail grew narrow and steep and twisting as it wound through a thickly wooded forest. Betsy was last in line, struggling with the weight of the heavy basket on her back. Caleb slipped back, helping others cross over a creek, until just the two of them remained. He took her elbow and they continued walking. When the others went round a bend and down a hill, he pulled her off the trail and into a thicket. At first she was frightened. This behavior was so unlike Caleb, and she struggled to break free from his grasp.

"Hush." He put a finger to her lips. "I am taking you to your people."

15

Beacon Hollow
November 13, 1763

On the night that Hans had proposed marriage to Tessa, he had told her he would seek out an opportunity to speak to her father at his earliest convenience. Nearly two weeks had passed and he still hadn't found time for that important conversation. Nor had he kissed Tessa yet. She had hoped he would, had dreamed of the moment, for it was custom when a couple pledged to marry. Instead, Hans only took her hands and gently squeezed them whenever he said good night to her.

Tonight, as her family returned from a visit to Not Faxon's Farm to check on her perpetually ailing grandmother, Tessa felt wave upon wave of disappointment. She had felt confident that Hans would speak to her father tonight. Alas, Hans wasn't even at home!

Felix shrugged when she asked him where he was. "Paxton, most likely. He's been gone all day. He skipped out on church again."

And her father scowled at that piece of information. "He's becoming a pig in the python."

She expected her mother to give him a warning look, but she seemed to agree with his assessment.

This engagement wasn't proceeding very swiftly.

She hoped her parents would have no objection to their betrothal. After all, getting married would keep Hans settled, in the church, turn his attention away from John Elder and his cronies in Paxton. And she would remain in Stoney Ridge. What more could they want?

A future son-in-law who would actually reveal his plans to marry their daughter, for one.

She spent the rest of the bumpy trip home comforting herself with the thought that Hans would speak to her father tomorrow. Surely, tomorrow he would ride over to Beacon Hollow. Ask her father, get his blessing, set the date. And then she and her mother could begin to plan for the wedding. She could hardly wait to see the pleased look on her mother's face when she and Hans told their news. Tessa had already planned the wedding meal in her mind.

As the wagon turned up the lane to Beacon Hollow, old Zeeb pricked his ears and let out a bark. Tessa's father squinted his eyes and peered at the house. "Somebody is on the stoop."

"Who?" Tessa asked. Her heart started banging around inside. Maybe it was Hans! He had come to speak to her father.

"I can't see who. It's too dark," her father said. Zeeb growled, crouched, ready to bound out of the wagon, until her father's deep voice ordered him to stay put.

The moon was in hiding. Somewhere far away an owl

hooted, and chills shot up Tessa's back. She strained to see, but all she could make out was the shape of a small person sitting on the stoop.

"It's probably a Conestoga needing a meal," her mother said.

Such an occurrence happened frequently, especially in the wintertime, but if the stranger were a Conestoga, it would be two or three together as they seldom traveled alone.

Her father pulled the horse to a stop and jumped off the wagon. "Can we help you some way?" he asked.

Tessa kept a warning hand on Zeeb's head.

Slowly, the person on the stoop rose. At first Tessa thought it was a child, a girl, but then the voice belonged to a woman, though timid sounding, almost afraid. She wore Indian clothing. "Are you Bairn Bauer? The minister?"

"I am."

"You might not remember me. My name is Betsy Zook."

Willie's breath exploded out of him. "It *is* her! It's Betsy!" he shouted. He jumped off the wagon, pushed past her father to run toward his sister. As she realized it was her brother who was running toward her in the twilight, she opened her arms wide and suddenly they were hugging fiercely.

❧

If Anna hadn't heard Betsy Zook identify herself, she would never have recognized her, for she had changed that much. It wasn't just her clothing, though she wore animal skins for dress and shoes and leggings, and wrapped a blanket around her shoulders the way the Conestoga wore their blankets. Her skin was tanned, her blonde hair hung in a long thick plait. And so thin! She didn't look like a girl anymore.

Despite her joy at encountering her brother, Betsy seemed almost reluctant to come inside the house. Anna noticed that her eyes kept spanning the darkness as if there was someone outside with her. Zeeb sensed someone or something, too, and remained poised on alert, even his drooping tail was pointed, until Bairn whistled to him to follow him and Tessa to the barn with the horse.

Willie was the one who coaxed Betsy inside, tugging her hand until she crossed the threshold. Anna lit the candle on the table as Willie stoked the coals and added kindling to get the blaze started. As the candle flame flickered, it threw shadows across Betsy's face. She was so terribly thin.

Soon the wood caught and flared, and Anna hung a kettle of water over it to boil. The room quickly warmed. Willie dragged his chair right beside Betsy and the two clutched hands as if they would never let each other go. He kept patting her arm, as if to affirm she was real, that she was here at last.

Anna made a cup of weak tea for Betsy and handed it to her. "How did you get here?"

Betsy took her time answering. "I waited for the right opportunity to escape. We've . . . I've been walking for days."

Anna heard echoes of the girl's voice she remembered, but at the same time it was new to her. "Oh, dear child. You must be so hungry." She put together a simple meal of bread and milk and served it to Betsy. "I fear your stomach will be tender for some time," Anna said. "Best to eat slow until you get used to decent food again."

"The food they gave me . . . it was decent. Mostly." Betsy

smiled, but her eyes had a shielded look, as if she had woken from a dream and wasn't sure where she was. She seemed . . . bewildered.

Anna sat across from Betsy, unsure of whether to ask questions or let her story unfold when she was ready to tell it. Willie filled in the silence, his words were practically tripping over each other, so eager was he to share his life in Stoney Ridge. He told her about the Conestoga horses, the mighty wagon, the English he was learning, the boys he sat with at the table.

Anna's heart swelled; he would not be considered poor Willie any longer.

While Betsy finished the bread and milk, he rubbed the sleeve of her deerskin dress. "You look just like an Indian."

"Come," Anna said, rising from her chair. "Let's find something for you to wear."

Willie tried to follow them into Anna and Bairn's room, but Anna stopped him. "We won't be long, Willie, and Bairn and Tessa will wonder what's happened to us. They should be back from the barn any minute." They were taking an extraordinarily long time putting the horse away.

Willie's small face fell.

Betsy put an arm around his shoulder. "When I return, I will look more like the sister you remember." And that seemed to satisfy him.

Within minutes, Anna had found a flaxen dress, a new shift, an apron, a pair of shoes, and a prayer cap and laid them on the bed. Betsy rose from the chair, curious to see the clothes. She fingered the prayer cap, gossamer thin, and tears filled her eyes. Anna wondered what was running through her mind. Would she ever truly be the sister Willie remembered?

For a brief moment, Anna wasn't sure if Betsy wanted to abandon her Indian clothing. She rubbed her sleeves, as if committing it to memory, then suddenly yanked and slipped off the deerskin dress. She reached for the shift and covered herself, then pulled the flaxen dress over her head. A moment later Anna was pinning a fresh apron around her. A faint whiff of lavender rose from the cloth and Betsy lifted it to her face and inhaled, letting out a sigh of pleasure.

Anna stepped back and studied her. "Your hair."

Betsy nodded.

Anna found her wooden comb and began to unbraid and comb out Betsy's hair. It reminded her of those intimate moments between a mother and a daughter, when Tessa was little and she would comb out her long hair after a Saturday wash.

It took some time before Anna was satisfied with pinning Betsy's hair. Then she arranged the prayer cap over Betsy's head.

"How does that feel?"

"It feels strange," Betsy said. "Strange yet familiar." She glanced down and smoothed out the wrinkles in her brown dress. "Do I look Amish?"

Anna cupped her face in her hands. "You always did. That hasn't changed."

A smile bloomed on Betsy's face.

Tessa walked the horse down the aisle of the barn and led it into the stall, taking her time as she filled the water bucket and gave the horse a scoop of oats. She carried out the chores slowly, her thoughts felt sluggish and foggy, as if smoke had filled her mind.

Her father appeared at the stall door.

"Tessa, darlin'," her father said. "I've saddled a riding horse. Y' must go fetch Hans."

She turned to look at her father. His gray eyes were full of compassion.

"Now, darlin'. Straightaway. Hopefully, he's returned from Paxton by now. He needs to be told Betsy Zook has returned."

"Can't you go?"

"Nae. It needs t' be you. He needs t' hear it from you. And y' need t' tell him."

It was one of the hardest things Tessa ever had to do. She went to the horse and climbed astride, then slowly went through the woods toward Not Faxon's Farm. The horse trotted along easily, without urging or direction. By the time she arrived at Not Faxon's Farm, Hans had returned from wherever he'd been all day. He opened the door to her knock with a welcoming smile, inviting her to come in, but she refused. She stood on the porch and told him that less than an hour ago, Betsy Zook had shown up at their doorstep. For a moment, Hans seemed puzzled, as if he couldn't discern her words. Then the news sunk in and he grabbed his hat and coat off the peg, bolted past Tessa, jumped on the horse, and galloped off toward Beacon Hollow. On Tessa's horse.

She walked home through the woods, though by now it was dark. Her eyes kept filling with tears, splashing down her cheeks, and she felt so ashamed of herself. At war within her: she was glad Betsy had returned; she was sad Betsy had returned.

Why now? Why not six months from now?

She knew that God would guide her through this situation,

would want her to trust in His sovereignty completely, but why now? She must not be doing something right.

She picked up her pace and broke into a run, then slowed as she caught sight of the stallion moving through the trees toward Not Faxon's Farm. His ears were pricked forward, nostrils flaring as he sniffed the air. She wondered if any of Felix's broodmares could be in season, if the stallion had picked up a scent and was heading for a visit. Felix would be happy. At least someone would be happy tonight.

Besides Hans and Betsy. They'd be plenty happy.

Then she stopped short. She thought she saw a shadow on the far side of the stallion, a man, moving stealthily toward it. Tessa let out a bloodcurdling scream to warn the horse; startled, it galloped away and disappeared. She squinted her eyes to see who had been trying to capture the horse, but saw no one. A shudder went through her; she was certain she had seen someone. She turned and ran as fast as she could toward Beacon Hollow.

She burst in the door, puffing and panting, only to find Hans, weeping, dropped on his knees in front of Betsy. She was gazing down at him and stroking his forehead in a gesture so tender that Tessa's heart twisted to witness it.

She removed her bonnet and set it wearily on the peg by the door.

"Praise God! You are alive! I knew it. In my heart I knew it," Hans said over and over again. His voice was raw, hoarse, almost a sob. When he finally recovered his composure, he rose to his feet and held her face in his hands. And then he drew back, his eyes wide in alarm. "Your face. Oh my dearest Betsy. What in God's name did those savages do to your beautiful face?"

Beacon Hollow
November 17, 1763

Betsy had never told Caleb goodbye. Not goodbye, nor even a thank-you for all he'd done for her, at tremendous personal risk.

After nearly two weeks of walking on foot, over one hundred miles, somehow he had delivered her right to the doorstep of Beacon Hollow. Days spent walking, yes, but also days spent talking. Each night he built a fire to keep them warm, to roast the rabbit or turkey or quail he had caught while she scrounged the forest floor for nuts and wild plants, and then they would talk until the moon rose high in the night sky. They talked about their past, their fond childhood memories—hers of growing up in Germany, his of being raised as a tribute child. But they never once spoke of the future.

When they had finally arrived at Beacon Hollow and realized no one was at home, he told her to wait on the stoop and he would search for food. She assured him that the Bauers would not mind if they waited in the unlocked house, or if they helped themselves to an egg from the henhouse. That was the frontier way, an open hospitality.

Caleb's mouth took on that grim look of his, his lips formed almost a straight line. "You may do as you see fit," he told her, "but I have seen half bloods hung for much less than the stealing of a chicken's egg."

His words startled her. Not only had it not occurred to her to think of food as belonging to anyone—the Indians viewed it as belonging to all—but she was also faced with the realization that they had crossed into the white man's world.

She sat on the stoop of Beacon Hollow while Caleb hunted for a rabbit or wild turkey, providing for them as he had done on a daily basis for the last ten days. But before he had returned, a wagon came rumbling up the path. She recognized Bairn Bauer at once by his tall posture on the wagon seat. The Bauers were coming home and she had no idea where Caleb had gone, or if she would ever see him again. She knew he wouldn't appear at Beacon Hollow; he was convinced that half bloods were not welcome in the white man's world. He couldn't return to the village, for helping her escape had put him in great danger. He was a slave. As kindhearted as the villagers could be, it was no small thing to betray them, and he had done that in two ways: by leaving, and by taking Betsy with him.

Caleb was never far from her thoughts, and as the days passed, she came to realize the enormous effect he'd had on her. He had changed the way she saw the world, the way she understood life to be. Even the life she wanted for herself. When she was with the Indian village, she longed to be reunited with her brothers, with Hans, with her own people.

But now that she was restored, she found herself worrying about Nijlon and Numees, concerned they might still be searching for her, frantic with fear. She had grown to care for them. She missed them. She missed Caleb. She couldn't help herself—it hurt a little that he had so readily left her at Beacon Hollow and had not sought her out since.

She did not share her swirl of confusion with Hans, though he was eager, almost obsessively eager, to hear every detail about her captivity. She felt a strange reluctance to speak of it with him. She did not want to relive those first few weeks after the raid, the terror, and the violence, and yet he did not want to hear about the peaceful village by the river. Two days ago, for the first time, she mentioned the two sisters who had treated her so kindly and he looked at her as if she had spoken nonsense.

She quickly recognized the look on him, the one that overcame him when she spoke of any pleasant memories among the Indians. She knew the stance, the arms crossed tightly against his chest, the clenched set of his jaw, the furrowed brow. That was when she knew to change the subject.

Hans was desperate for her to feel at home in Stoney Ridge, to be the girl he had remembered her to be. He was sweetly attentive, stopping by Beacon Hollow once or twice each day, encouraging her to eat more to regain her health. Her health was quite strong, she thought, but he believed her to be too thin. "Did you sleep well?" he would inquire each time he saw her, studying her face with concern.

"Of course," she said with a smile, though it was a lie. The truth was, she had not slept soundly since her return. Night after night she was awakened by a strange and recurring medley of dreams—Johnny ahead of her in the long line of captives, getting farther and farther away from her. Her mother's panicked words to her, as the warriors circled their home, to watch over her brothers. And somewhere in each dream would be Caleb, wandering alone in the wilderness, without a home to return to. Without anyone to belong to. She would startle awake, gasping for air, and sit upright. As she listened to Tessa's soft breathing next to her, and to Willie's whiffling snore on the cot, her heart would slow its forceful pounding. She would lie back down and try to sleep, or at least to rest, until she heard sounds of Anna and Bairn stirring below in the kitchen. Then she would rise and start the day, grateful to silence her dreams.

Betsy had been so determined to get back to the world she belonged in that it had never once occurred to her she might not belong to it any longer.

16

Tessa was on her hands and knees in the fenced garden near the house, sifting through the carrot patch with a trowel, searching for any buried and overlooked carrots. The stallion's fondness for carrots was not unlike Maria Müller's sweet tooth—unquenchable. This fall, the horse had become so trusting of Tessa that she no longer had to wait for him to find her in the woods. She would whistle for him, then wait to hear a nicker in response. Soon, he would emerge, eager for carrots. Gaining the horse's trust had become a solace to her, her only succor, and she used every excuse she could to escape to the woods.

"You make a lovely picture," said an achingly familiar deep voice.

Tessa stilled, wiping her hands on her apron. She'd not been aware Hans was nearby until he spoke, and felt instantly frazzled by his presence.

Hans had come to Beacon Hollow each day since Betsy had been restored to them, but he had not sought Tessa out.

The uncertainty of what lay unspoken between them felt like a heavy weight. To her, anyway. He seemed unaware of her heartache.

He unhitched the garden gate and came in, then sat gingerly on the ground next to her. He raked a hand through the soil she had overturned, as if studying its dark contents. She turned her face from him, for looking at him would only dazzle and scatter her thoughts. He didn't say anything for the longest time, and she had to keep telling herself, *Do not cry. Do not cry.*

In a somber tone, he said, "Betsy and I will be married soon, just as we originally had planned, before the massacre." He was silent for a long moment, then reached for her chin and tipped her head up so she would look at him. "You understand, don't you, Tessa?" He gave her a sweet, sad smile, the one that could make her forgive him almost anything. "You've always been so understanding. So supportive."

She thought he was going to say more, but he did not continue. He dropped his hand and turned his attention back to the soil, sifting it through his fingers.

She took a moment to find words for her thoughts. She would *not* cry. "Of course. Of course I do," she said, feeling a sting of guilt as the lie passed her lips.

"That's my girl." He leaned over and gave her a kiss on the top of her head before rising to his feet.

She watched him as he went through the garden gate, carefully latched it behind him, and strolled to the house. All she could think was, *But I'm not a girl. Don't you see? Haven't you noticed? I'm* not *a girl.*

As soon as he went into the house, she threw the trowel

in the ground and ran from the garden, ran far away from the house that held Betsy and Hans and all their big fat love and happiness. She ran and ran and ran, until she reached the sheep pond and could go no farther.

She dropped to the ground, panting, and stared at her reflection in the sheep pond. Her face looked white and bleak. With sudden, stabbing intensity, she faced what she'd known all along—that Hans had never loved her at all. The dreams she'd had for them were hopelessly one-sided. Even if Betsy had not been restored when she did, even if Tessa and Hans had married, he would never have loved her, not the way she wanted to be loved. She squeezed her eyes shut and pressed her fists against her eyes. Soon sobs wracked her body and tears streamed down her face. She cried and cried, until she had emptied herself.

When she had no more tears to cry, she sucked in some deep breaths, splashed her hands in the cold water, and rinsed her face. When she lifted her head, she saw someone across the pond. A man was watching her. An Indian.

She jumped to her feet, prepared to run, but he lifted his hands to show he had no weapon and meant no harm.

He walked around the sheep pond until he stood a few rods away. "You are not well?"

"I am well," she said, still poised to flee, and then it dawned on her that he was speaking in her dialect. Not English.

"You received a death message?"

"No."

"Then your mind is unhinged?"

"My mind? No! My mind is fine."

"When I saw you first, you screamed. And now, you wail like someone is dead."

She gasped. "You! It was you! I knew I saw someone in the woods. The night Betsy Zook was restored to us. You tried to capture the black stallion."

He shook his head. "You cannot capture such a horse."

She relaxed, ever so slightly, though she watched him carefully. "No. No one can." *Wait.* She did a double take. This Indian had blue eyes. She'd never seen an Indian with anything but dark brown eyes, nearly black. Everything else about him looked Indian—straight dark hair that draped over his shoulders, prominent cheekbones, high forehead, beardless, tall and muscular. But those blue eyes—they were the color of a tropical sea, though she'd never actually seen an ocean.

"Betsy Zook. She is well?"

Betsy Zook. He pronounced the consonants with precision, almost emphasizing them. Bet-See Zok. As if he had said the name many times, had his own way of saying it. Something clicked over in Tessa's mind. "Did you . . . did you help Betsy Zook escape from the savages?"

He looked away. "She called us savages?"

Tessa frowned. "No. No, she didn't." It was a phrase Tessa had picked up from Hans, and she felt a sudden shame. Clearly, this Indian was no savage. Just the opposite. There was a courtliness about him that reminded her of Will Sock.

"And so she is well?"

Of course. More than well. Tessa bit her lip. "She has everything she ever wanted."

The Indian narrowed his eyes, tipping his head slightly as if he could read her mind. "You are not glad she has returned."

Tessa stiffened. "It wouldn't be Christian to not be glad for such a . . . miracle."

"Perhaps not," the Indian said, eyes crinkling almost as if he were amused with her, "but it would be honest." He took a step closer. "What can you tell me of this horse?"

"The black stallion? Quite a lot, actually." It was her favorite subject, in fact. The blue-eyed Indian seemed riveted to her every word as she started to explain what history she knew of the horse. She told him the background of the stallion breaking into her uncle's broodmare pasture one year, and from that a new breed had developed—the Conestoga breed.

Usually, this was the point where she bored others, but the Indian was listening so carefully that she was encouraged to keep talking. She told him that her uncle trained the first- and second-year foals to work the wagon her father had designed and built. She surprised herself with how much she knew about the horse, about his habits. She even told him that the horse was learning to trust her. "I probably set things back with the horse when I screamed at him the other night. I thought you were a danger to him."

"I am no danger. Not to the horse. Not to anyone."

Tessa could sense as much. There was humanity in those blue eyes. "Do you want me to take you to Betsy? I'm sure she'd like to see you."

He gave a slight shake of his head.

"You could come to Beacon Hollow. Other Indians stay with us, especially when the weather gets cold."

His eyebrows lifted in surprise. "Other Indians?"

"The Conestogas. I figured you might be staying with them. They're peaceful people. Indiantown isn't far from here."

He went still. "Which direction?"

She pointed to a ridge of tall pointed trees, off in the distance. "It's not far. Ten miles or so, just beyond those trees. It's a small village near the Susquehanna River. There aren't many Conestogas left anymore, not after the great sickness last year. It nearly wiped them out. I'm sure they would welcome you." She wasn't sure, actually. She should seek out her father; he would know. "May I ask your name?"

"Askuwheteau. An Indian becomes his name. My name means 'to keep watch.'"

"My name is Tessa. And I don't know what it means."

He tipped his head. "Perhaps it means Little Girl with Big Feelings." He lifted his hands high in the air as he spoke.

She was *not* a girl. Why did everyone think she was? She was a full-fledged woman, complete with a full-blown broken heart.

"My Christian name is Caleb."

His *Christian* name? "Did Betsy have an Indian name?"

"Yes. Hurit. It means 'beautiful girl.'"

Of course it did. "Shall I tell Betsy I saw you?"

"No." He kept his eyes fixed on a spot on the ground. "You said she has everything she wants."

"Not everything, I suppose," Tessa said. "She talks often about her missing brother, Johnny. He's still with the sava— the Indians." Her voice became gentle. "I've heard her cry in the night for him when she thinks I'm asleep."

He lifted his head and their eyes met. Something flickered through the Indian's eyes, a feeling that Tessa recognized at once. This Indian worked hard to keep the expression out of his face, but she saw it, all the same.

He loved her. This Indian loved Betsy Zook.

Not Faxon's Home
November 19, 1763

Felix read and reread the same passage in the book a dozen times, and he still didn't understand it. When Tessa stopped by to drop off some jars of freshly made apple butter for Dorothea, he thrust the book in her hands. "Read that. Explain it to me."

She looked at the cover. "*Othello*? By William Shakespeare? Who's that?"

"I don't know. I've never heard of him."

"Where'd you get the book?"

"From Martin Gingerich."

Tessa looked so stunned that he frowned at her. "Is it so surprising to see me reading a book?"

"It's the first time I've ever seen you with a book other than when you read the Bible verses at church. Plus . . . I didn't know Martin could read."

Felix rolled his eyes. "Of course he can read, Tessa."

"Why did he loan you a book?"

"Because last week at church I happened to mention to him that someone considered me to be intellectually lazy."

A laugh burst out of Tessa. "Someone like Catrina!"

He scowled, then glanced at her. "Think she's right?"

He saw her bite her lower lip in a feeble attempt to keep from smiling.

"Fine," he said, knowing he sounded testy. "Then explain that passage to me." He pointed to a paragraph.

"'O beware, my lord, of jealousy. It is the green-eyed monster, which doth mock the meat it feeds on.'" She read it again and again. Then she handed it back to him. "I have no idea what it means. What's the story about?"

He rubbed his jaw. "This fellow Othello loves Desdemonda but thinks she is cheating on him with Cassio."

"So who's the monster? Cassio?"

"No, no. The monster isn't a person. It's jealousy." He took the book back from her. "Othello is getting a warning to avoid the green-eyed monster." Yes! Yes, that was it. *Now* he understood the passage. He read it again, just to be sure. He looked up at Tessa but she was gone.

❧

Beacon Hollow
November 20, 1763

On Sunday, Betsy woke to the first real snowfall of winter. There had been dustings of snow all week, but it melted away as the sun rose. Not today. By midday, when Hans arrived at Beacon Hollow, the snow was six inches deep and still falling.

Hans's eyes were dancing. In his arms was a large bundle wrapped in a flour sack. He marched straight inside, laughing, encouraging everyone in the house—which consisted of Tessa, Betsy, and Willie—to draw near to see what he had brought to show them.

Betsy saw Tessa grab her shawl and slip outside. Though she and Tessa shared a bed like sisters, they did not act like sisters. Tessa was polite to Betsy but not warm, not the way she was with Willie. Betsy had tried to befriend her, but to no avail. Tessa would answer Betsy's questions with a *yes* or a *no* or *ask my mother*.

Hans didn't notice the departure of Tessa; he stood by

the fire with the bundle in his arms, a broad grin on his face. Hanging from the rafter above his head were bundles of dried herbs—lavender, thyme, rosemary—that added a sweet pungency to the air.

Whatever was in the sack made a loud thump when he set it on the tabletop. "I'd nearly forgotten. Look. Look at this!" He reached in and pulled out a large, thick Bible. "It was one of the few things that did not perish in the attack. It was found in the cellar."

Betsy clapped her hands around her mouth to cover a gasp. *This* Bible. Her father's prized Froschauer Bible, kept in his family for generations, brought over on the ship from Germany. How her father had treasured this Bible! He had refused to let his sons touch it for fear they would smudge it with dirty hands.

The last time she had seen this Bible was on the night of the raid. When the first sounds of war whoops had rent the air, her mother bundled a tablecloth with their meager family valuables—this Bible and a purse of gold coins—and shoved it in Betsy's hands. "Go to the cellar and stay there," her mother said. "Keep watch over your brothers." She put one hand on Betsy's head. At the time, Betsy had thought of it as a prayer, but now she realized it was a benediction. A goodbye blessing. "Pray to God, Betsy. He will not fail you."

Betsy and Johnny hurried down to the cellar and hid themselves, terrified, listening to the sounds of the attack above them, but Willie never came down. It was only when she arrived at Beacon Hollow that she learned he had escaped by running from the house and hiding in the hollow tree.

Betsy didn't think she could ever touch this Bible again without her mind traveling right back to that awful night.

She glanced at Willie. He was staring at the Bible, eyes wide, then his small face crumpled. He turned and bolted up the stairs to the loft. She looked at Hans. "I think perhaps it's . . . too soon."

Disappointed, Hans put the Bible back into the flour sack. "My apologies. I meant well."

"Of course," she said, trying to smile, though she knew she radiated a false brightness. "Of course you meant well."

He picked up the sack and gave her a solemn look. "Do not fear, Betsy. They will not go unpunished for their atrocities. The devils will get their due." He held the Bible against his chest. "Soon, all Indians will be subdued and contained."

She felt her stomach clench. What did he mean by that? "Surely not all. Some are guilty, but not all. Many Indians were very kind to me."

He shook his head forcefully. "None can be trusted. They are pagans, like the Canaanites who had to be removed from the Promised Land. God commanded Moses to rid the land of all heathen inhabitants. All of them."

Betsy felt a shiver down her spine as if he had put a handful of snow down her back. "That was long ago, Hans. Those words from God were for a different time, meant for a different world."

"The world has not changed. Evil is still among us." Then the fierce expression on Hans's face shifted to one that was immeasurably sad. He touched his finger to the scar on her cheek, as if he wished he could rub it away. "My beautiful, beautiful Betsy." Sweetness and compassion permeated his voice. "It's no wonder you are overwrought. We will talk about this another time."

As she gently closed the door behind him, she realized

why she felt such caution to discuss her captivity with him. He did not want the truth.

✢

Tessa waited inside the warm barn until she saw Hans leave the house. She couldn't tolerate being in the same room as he and Betsy, not the way he gazed so tenderly at her, oblivious to Tessa's aching heart. She watched him mount his horse and ride off in the opposite direction of Not Faxon's Farm. The opposite of Lancaster Town. Where could he be going in this snowstorm?

Why did it matter? Obviously, Hans cared not a whit for her. He only cared for Betsy. She knew that, and she also knew, deep down, it wasn't Betsy's fault that Hans loved her so. Betsy was a lovable person—kind and gentle and annoyingly beautiful. So why couldn't Tessa be more charitable toward Betsy Zook? Why couldn't she muster up some kind of empathy for her? As she slid shut the barn door, she said aloud, "I must be the worst person in the world."

"Surely not the worst."

She spun around to face Martin Gingerich—of all people— looking as if he'd been tossed about in the air and dropped down into the yard of Beacon Hollow like a rag doll, his hair disheveled and his cheeks wind-stung red. And where was his hat? Why could this man-child never, ever remember a hat?

She scowled at him. "What are you doing, sneaking up on me like that?"

"I did nothing of the sort," he said with his customary cheer, oblivious to the dusting of snowflakes on his head and shoulders. "I stopped by to see if you might like to go sledding down Dead Man's Hill."

Sledding? With him? Where others might see them together? "Martin, you can't be . . . surely you don't think I could ever . . . take you seriously. I mean, you're a Mennonite. I'm Amish. And that's only part of the problem."

"So you're blinkered. Most are. Not me, of course. I'm quite open-minded."

Blinkered? Me? Hardly! Ridiculous.

Not to be fobbed off so easily, he asked, "So what's the other part?"

Fine. He asked. "You told everybody that giants ran in our family."

"Oh Tessa. That was years ago! Back when you were a foot taller than me. Than most every fellow. I was embarrassed to be so short next to such a fine-looking woman."

Fine-looking? Woman? Did he just call her a fine-looking woman? She felt herself soften just a wee bit.

"Don't tell me you hold grudges over such a small thing."

Yes. She was a dedicated grudge holder.

"So what's left?"

It pained her to say it, but he left her no choice. "You're . . . you."

Any other young man would be mortified by what she had just said. To be truthful, she was mortified at her own candor, but she had spoken the truth. That was how she felt about rumpled Martin. He was him.

And would you believe that rumpled Martin seemed almost pleased, as if she had just paid him the biggest compliment of his life? "That's exactly right, Tessa. I'm me. Irresistible. Incomparable."

"Conceited."

He lifted a finger in the air. "That, too."

She was tempted to keep flinging out insulting adjectives, but that would not be merciful. "Martin, why me?" she said with a thump at her chest. "Why are you so persistent about me? Of all the girls in Lancaster County, why me? Why not a Mennonite girl? There's plenty of them! Your church is always stealing from other churches."

"The girls in my church act shy and withdrawn. In all my years, I've never had a girl look me directly in the eye. Not even my own mother. They're all afraid of men."

"That's only because all the men in your church are like Faxon the Saxon."

Martin's eyes went wide and she gasped and covered her mouth. She couldn't believe she had called his father that name, right to his face. She winced, squeezing her eyes shut.

A laugh burst out of Martin, then another, and soon he was doubled over, guffawing. The kind of belly laugh when your eyes tear up and you can't catch your breath. Tessa watched him, perplexed. It took him a full minute to pull himself together.

"Oh Tessa, you are a pearl of great price." He wiped his eyes with his fists, still chuckling. "See what I mean? You're different from most girls. You say what you think and what you feel. You speak your mind."

She was vexed to feel herself blushing. Those were the very complaints most everyone, particularly Maria Müller, leveled at her.

"So, will you come with me to Dead Man's Hill?"

She sighed. Rumpled Martin might be the most persistent person she'd ever met. But sledding with Martin was better than being stuck inside the house with Betsy. "Can Willie come too?"

He flashed a relieved smile, hooked one thumb in his waistband, and backed off boyishly. "Of course. Anything you want."

Discovering that Martin had been more nervous than he let on made Tessa's chilly feelings toward him warm another degree or two. Ever so slightly. But it would never do to let Martin know. She lifted one shoulder in a reluctant shrug. "I'll go get Willie."

His face broke into a dazzled, jubilant hosanna of a smile. "I'll wait outside for you." As she passed by him, he softly added, "Sweetheart."

She whirled around and jabbed a finger at his chest. "I am *not* your sweetheart." Her face felt beet red.

Martin's eyes took on a glow. "Maybe not yet. But one day."

Fat chance of that. She sailed toward the house, muttering to herself. Who did he think he was?! She didn't want him visiting her, she wasn't at all nice to him, and besides, he was a Mennonite. A *Mennonite*.

Not Faxon's Farm
November 21, 1763

One of Felix's favorite horses, a chestnut mare, lay on the ground, quiet except for her contracting belly. As Felix knelt in the straw beside her, the mare looked over at him with such serene eyes, despite the hard shudders that emanated like waves through her middle.

"Is something wrong?"

He looked up to see Catrina peering over the ledge. Was

school already over with? It must be later in the day than he thought. Much, much later, for he just now realized how dark the barn had grown. "Her water broke a long time ago. She's having some trouble." He got up to light the lanterns. Earlier, anticipating the mare's condition, he had hung a few lanterns on nails he'd hammered around the stall. He went around to light them now, yellow light spilling over the mare.

"The boys told me you were in the barn with a suffering horse. Anna brought over a potpie, so I fed it to the boys and Dorothea."

"Oh. Well, thanks." He hadn't given any thought to dinner.

"Can I help?"

"Actually, yes," Felix said, rolling up his sleeves. "Over on that trunk, I prepared a few supplies. Fetch me that bucket of water and a piece of baling twine." As she disappeared, he called out, "And lye soap. It's near the bucket."

When she returned with the bucket and twine, he assumed she would set them down and promptly leave. The day was drawing to an end and soon it would be dark. But she surprised him by squatting down alongside him. "It's uncommon to have a foal at this time of year, isn't it?"

"It sure is. Usually nature makes sure babies arrive before winter comes." He plunged his arms into the cold water, scrubbing hard with the lye soap. "But this girl, she's a maiden mare."

"A maiden mare?"

"An amateur. Everything's a little off-kilter."

A sound burst out of Catrina, and Felix looked up in alarm to find her giggling, covering her mouth with girlish shyness. He hadn't thought her to have a sense of humor.

A hard contraction rolled over the mare. Her neck stretched, her whole body strained, her eyes bulged, her upper lip peeled back. As they waited, kneeling side by side, watching the horse labor, Felix felt very aware of Catrina. Of the way her hand rubbed and massaged the belly of the mare, the calm and soothing way she spoke to her. "With life comes suffering, sweet girl," she whispered to the horse.

Such small, white hands Catrina had. Small hands with tapered fingers. Hands that moved tenderly, almost lovingly over the mare's neck. And then he shook that thought right out of his head and busied himself with unraveling the twine. What was the matter with him, anyway? This was hardly the time to notice a woman's hands.

"Isn't there something you can do to help her?"

He stole a glance at her. From the troubled look in her eyes, she appeared to be suffering right alongside the mare. "There is something I'm planning to do, but you might not want to stick around for it. It'll shock you."

"I don't shock easy."

He glanced at her. "Suit yourself." He washed his hands thoroughly with the lye soap, rinsed them in the bucket, then pushed a hand inside the horse's womb. The foal was positioned backward, with one hind leg aiming to get out and the other hind leg bent forward. The horse stretched her neck forward and rolled her head as a fierce contraction shook her body. The squeezing muscles bore down hard, crushing Felix's hand between the foal's leg and the horse's pelvic bone. The crushing pain was so intense that he nearly howled.

When the contraction finally ended, Felix slid his hand out, slimy with birth mucus. "The foal's legs are twisted around all funny, and my hand's too big. I can't get it up there far enough."

"Let me try."

"No. Absolutely not. When a contraction hits . . . it's powerful. It's hurts like . . . the dickens." Slowly, he stretched out his aching fingers.

"At least let me try."

He held his hand against his chest, wondering if it was broken, and barely glanced at her. "No."

She straightened her shoulders. "It's not the first time I've helped with a foaling. I have small hands, Felix Bauer, and a sturdy countenance. I can do it. At least let me have a go at it."

He dropped his hand and looked straight at her. She was determined, that's for sure. "It will hurt, even if your hand is dainty." *Dainty.* Did he really use that word?

"I know."

He cleared his throat. "The trick is going to be to get your fingers around two hind hooves—knowing which leg belongs up front or in the back—and ease them until they're pointed right. You can't let go, even when it hurts."

"All right, then." Catrina's breath eased out in a sigh. She rolled up her dress sleeves and scrubbed her hands with the astringent lye soap.

She had to crouch down on the straw bed, practically flat on her belly, to push her hand inside the mare. With every one of the mare's contractions, tears filled her eyes and spilled down her cheeks, but she never cried out and she never gave up. She found the two hind hooves and held on to them; each time the mare labored, the legs eased down the birth canal an inch or two. Then, finally, the mare gave one last shuddering strain and the foal slid out, bloody and glistening and gleaming, onto the yellow straw.

Felix tore the membrane that enveloped the foal, peeling it away from the tiny dark face, and rubbed its nose. "Breathe, baby. Breathe, breathe!" The foal let out a gasp and lifted its head, peering around the stall with an amazed look. Its long ears dropped and its spindly legs sprawled out. It kept shaking its head, stunned, as if to clear its head.

Catrina sat on her knees, staring at the foal, wearing a wide-eyed look of pure wonderment. When the foal sneezed once, then twice, she laughed.

He picked up a burlap sack and handed it to Catrina. "Hold on. Our work isn't done yet. Here, rub it down." In a sudden graceful movement, the mare had risen to her feet, membrane still hanging from her. Deftly, he knotted the membrane so that she wouldn't step on it before her body released it with a few more shudders.

The mare touched noses with her baby, a tender way to say hello, then nudged it to get it up on its four wobbly legs. Felix and Catrina sat with their backs against the stall wall, watching mother and foal. After many starts and stops, the foal managed to rise up and then balance on all four legs. The mare leaned close so its baby could start to nurse.

"There. That's a sight that never fails to pull at my heart," he whispered, more to himself than to Catrina.

Now, the work was done. All was well. His chest ached with the joy that always came with a birth.

He was so caught up in watching the foal that it took him a moment to realize that Catrina was staring at him. He turned away when he found her eyes on him.

"You're good at this."

Felix sighed and stretched, feeling loose-jointed with weariness. "I've been doing it a while."

"I have a confession to make. I've never helped with foaling."

What? Catrina had told a fib? He didn't think it was possible. But then he realized that she had wanted to be here with him, had wanted to help him. His heart did a stutter step, and suddenly he felt boyish, a little awkward, a little uncertain. He liked the feeling. He scooted closer to her. "Since you're finally realizing what a wonderful man I truly am, why not reconsider letting me court you."

She looked down at her apron and twirled the edges. "Felix, I've loved two men and I've buried both of them. The thought of loving again . . . it's too hard. I can't go through another loss."

The funny thing was that he understood. After Rachel's death, there were many mornings when he didn't have the gumption to face the day. But he had two little yowling infants who wouldn't let him off the hook. They needed him, and it turned out that he needed them. If he hadn't had those baby boys, he wasn't sure what grief would have been like for him. Catrina didn't have anyone nipping at her heels to get back in the game of life. Other than her mother, Maria, who nipped at everybody's heels.

He leaned against her, shoulder to shoulder. "Do you know what's even harder?"

She glanced at him out of the corners of her eyes.

"Not loving again. That's far worse than losing someone." For a moment neither of them moved. They sat rooted by surprise, as if seeing each other in an entirely new light. He nudged her gently, and slowly, the corners of her lips tugged

234

into a smile. He smiled in return, and they sat there like two foolish adolescents, gazing and grinning at each other, until a creaky sliding door noise broke their reverie. Felix rose, stretching his back, to see who had come into the barn. Through the cracks in the barn, the night was beginning to soften into dawn. Had they really been in this stall all night long? Hours had flown like minutes.

Hans emerged from the shadows, leading his horse into its stall.

"Hans! Where've you been?"

Hans stopped abruptly. "What are you doing up?"

Felix pointed his chin toward the mare's stall. "Foaling. Where have you been?"

Hans continued down the barn aisle. "Mind your own concerns, Felix."

"You were in Paxton, weren't you?"

Hans didn't bother to look at him.

"Hear me, brother. If you were in Paxton meeting with John Elder, that is my business. Bairn's, too."

Hans closed the stall door behind the horse. "You are *not* my brother. Neither is Bairn." And he strode down the hall and out of the barn.

Felix stayed in the aisle, hands on his hips, perplexed by Hans's hostility. What was driving such anger? He had felt sympathy for him prior to Betsy's restoration, but no longer. If anything, Hans seemed even more belligerent now.

Catrina came up behind him. "Like father, like son."

"What's that?"

"Hans's birth father was Peter Mast, was he not?"

"Yes," Felix said. "He left our church years ago. Almost the day after his father Isaac was buried."

"I remember. And I remember my mother saying that Peter Mast was always shaking his fists at God."

As she tied her cloak, Felix thought she had just summed up Hans's hostility. He was shaking his fists at God. A dangerous thing to do.

17

Beacon Hollow
December 9, 1763

As the weeks passed, Anna was pleased to see that Betsy grew stronger. She seemed less bewildered by her circumstances and more at home among them. Though she rarely spoke of her time with the Indians, it was obvious that she'd been strongly affected by her time among them. She'd even adopted some mannerisms that reminded Anna of the Conestogas. Hans had noticed, too, and was not shy to voice his disapproval.

For one thing, Betsy had acquired a habit of peeping under her eyebrows with her chin tucked low. She moved through a room silently, so quietly that Anna didn't even realize she was nearby. She preferred to be outside, even if the weather was poor. More than a few times, Anna found Betsy studying the sky, eyes fixed on birds as they flew over the farm, as if she were part of their migration. The other day she had used the term *moon* to signify a month's time and Hans snapped at her. "You are not with the savages any longer," he said in a cold voice.

Cold was just the word to describe Hans. Distant, too. Anna would have thought that Betsy's restoration would have brought Hans back to the fold, to correct that rebellious spirit he had. The Lord God had answered his prayers of protection for Betsy—all of their prayers—in such a miraculous way. How could anyone not feel his faith expand? How could anyone not want to fall on his knees in worship and thanksgiving of the Lord God who brought Betsy back to him?

Instead, the opposite occurred. At times, when the talk turned to Indians as it often did, Anna thought she detected a strange flash in Hans's eyes. He seemed overly focused on the abuse Betsy had received. How many times had Anna seen him run a finger gently down her scar, as if trying to erase it? He'd even bought her an expensive white powder, pearl dust, from Lancaster Town, to use on the scar. Betsy had rubbed the powder between her fingers and looked up at him.

"But the cut has healed," she said, not understanding, lifting her hand to her cheek. "It's no longer infected."

"Not for infection," Hans said, tenderly cupping her hand over her cheek. "For covering it."

The sting in Betsy's eyes could be felt across the room to where Anna sat at the spinning wheel. Anna had cringed at Hans's thoughtlessness.

Maybe that was the source of Hans's internal conflicts, right there. He wanted to expunge her time in captivity, but the scar would not allow him to do so.

Betsy's return had caused a rift between Hans and Tessa too. Her daughter would not confide in her the specifics, but Anna could guess. In a way, she blamed herself. She was the one who had encouraged Hans to pay some attention to Willie, for Betsy's sake, and he did just that. She hadn't expected him to scoop Tessa into that circle. Her daughter was naïve enough, and in love enough, to believe that he cared for her. Since Betsy's restoration, he had barely acknowledged Tessa, and it hurt Anna to see her daughter cast aside so carelessly.

Tessa certainly needed maturing before she was ready to love and be loved, but she didn't need to have her spirit broken, as it seemed to be now. Hans didn't even notice what damage he had inflicted. Tessa seemed quiet, withdrawn, morose—so unlike her—and made use of every opportunity to leave the house as often as she could, as if just being near Betsy brought discomfort to her. Anna knew that Betsy sensed Tessa's standoffishness, but she had no idea how to bring her daughter out of it.

Frankly, there was a part of Anna that was relieved Hans's attention had turned away from Tessa. Hans would not be Anna's choice as a husband for her passionate daughter. He could not appreciate her lively spirit, her wholehearted endeavors. He would have tried to subdue her, the way he did Betsy. The way he had tried, as a boy, to do when he kept the butterfly in the crock. No air, no light.

Anna woke well before dawn one morning and heard sounds in the kitchen. Bairn was still sleeping, so she pulled a shawl around her shoulders and tiptoed to the kitchen to find Betsy at work, pounding bread dough that had been rising throughout the night. The fire had been started for the day, the water kettle was heating.

Betsy peeped up at her in that way she had with her chin tucked low, a gesture that had become a part of her. "Did I wake you?"

Anna smiled. "Well worth it. What a lovely sight on this cold morning. You've done half my chores." Betsy went back to pushing and pulling the dough, but Anna could see that something was troubling her. "Did you not sleep well?"

"Well enough." She kept her head down as she formed the dough into a ball.

Anna noticed that Betsy's hands were quivering. "Betsy." Anna placed her hand on her wrist, so that she had to stop working the dough. "If you have need to talk about anything that may be troubling you, I hope you will feel at ease to talk with me."

Betsy put the dough in the dough box and covered it with a cloth for its second rise. She wiped her hands on the coarse fabric of her apron, then curled one hand into a fist and wrapped it up in her apron. "Last night, Hans remarked that all Indians are devils. I do not think all Indians are devils."

"Nor do I."

"When I objected, he said he feared my mind has become disordered." She looked at Anna with worried eyes. "Please be truthful with me. Does my mind seem disordered to you? There are times when I wonder myself . . ."

Anna reached out and put a consoling hand on her shoulder. "Not in the least disordered. Just the opposite. I think you have great clarity." The relief flooding Betsy's eyes tugged at her heart.

"Anna," Betsy started, then hesitated, as if gathering her thoughts. "Is the scar so terrible? As I was walking past the sheep's pond the other day, I stopped for a moment to peer at my reflection." She glanced at the fire. "It did not seem to be as disfiguring as Hans suggests."

If Hans were in the kitchen right now, Anna would smack

him. How dare he make this lovely young woman feel less than
. . . lovely. "Hear me, Betsy. The scar is hardly noticeable."

She snapped her head around. "Truly?"

"Truly. In fact, it has faded in color since you arrived. I
think Hans has made the scar more than it is, though I don't
know why."

"Nor do I." Betsy closed her eyes and sank to a chair. "I
don't understand the source of such darkness within him. I
don't know if it has always been there and I did not recognize
it, or if it is a newly acquired part of him. A response to the
attack on my family."

Anna digested those questions. Perhaps it wasn't either
one but both. Perhaps the darkness had been within Hans all
along and the right circumstances brought it to the surface.
*But then, isn't that true for each one of us? Don't we all have
a darkness within?*

Betsy covered her eyes with her hands, as if her head hurt.
"I fear he is straying beyond the bounds of reason."

"Your captivity caused Hans great distress. He has been
influenced by outsiders to exact revenge."

Betsy dropped her hands and opened her eyes. "But the
captivity was not the same thing as the attack. They weren't
the same kind of people as the warriors." She sank back in
the chair. "The sisters who adopted me, they treated me like
one of their own. They were good to me, kind and tender.
We even had a garden called the Three Sisters."

"Beans, corn, squash." Betty Sock had taught Anna that
gardening trick soon after she had married Bairn. The beans
fed the soil for the corn, and the squash vines provided shade
for the roots of the corn. "I don't think we would have survived that first year without the gift of Three Sisters."

"Yes! That's exactly right."

Anna sat down in the chair beside Betsy. She hoped Bairn would remain asleep awhile longer, as this was the most Betsy had volunteered about her time in the village and she wanted to give her all the time she needed.

Words were tripping out over each other as if they'd been pent up in a bottle. "At first, after I was separated from Johnny, I wanted to die. Little by little, I grew accustomed to the ways of the village. I grew fond of my Indian sisters. I know it sounds hard to believe, but I loved them."

"But still you escaped. You managed to get here alone."

"I was not alone." She glanced at Anna. "I didn't mean to mislead you about my escape. It seemed best not to say more than I needed to." She was silent for a moment. "There was a young man in the village, a half-breed. He spoke our dialect. He understood the longing I felt to be reunited with my brothers. He was the one who helped me escape. He risked his life to bring me here." Her eyes filled with tears and she wiped them away with the corner of her apron. "I am fearful for him. I don't know what has become of him. If he is found by other Indians, he will be slain for his betrayal. But if he is found by people like those friends of Hans, the ones who seek to subdue the Indians, he will surely be killed. Just for the crime of being an Indian."

"How in the world would he have learned our dialect?" It was a peasant language that came from Germany, known only by those who lived in Palatine.

"From his mother. She was a Mennonite, stolen as a young girl during an Indian raid, and then offered as tribute to another tribe. Just like I had been. She taught him the language. She taught him about the Bible."

"He is not a heathen, this Indian?"

"No! He is a Christian. His mother baptized him before she died."

"It was just as we prayed," Anna whispered. "For God to keep watch over you."

Betsy's eyes lit with a soft glow. "His Indian name means 'he keeps watch.' His Christian name is Caleb. He was very good to me, Anna. He helped me with chores around the village, he explained Indian customs to me, taught me some of the language. But more than that, he gave me a sense of purpose."

"Did Caleb give you any details about his mother's people?"

"No. He was young when she died."

Vaguely, Anna recalled a story of a frontier Mennonite family that had been attacked, years ago, and a daughter taken captive. No one ever knew what had happened to her. She'd have to ask Bairn for more details, but she wondered if there might be a connection to this young man. "The Conestogas are a peaceful tribe who live nearby. Perhaps your friend sought shelter with them."

Hope filled Betsy's face. "Is there any way to find out?"

"Bairn might be able to find out."

Then the brightness illuminating Betsy's face disappeared, like a candle that was snuffed out. "But Hans must not know of Caleb. I cannot speak of this to him."

"No," Anna said softly. "You cannot."

"I don't know what he would do, were he to find him." Her voice faded and tears filled her eyes.

All Anna could do was to take Betsy in her arms as if she were a small child. "Go ahead, have a good cry. You deserve it."

Later that day, Anna sought out a private moment with

Bairn when she saw him stride across the yard from the sawmill and head into the carpentry shop. As their household had grown, she was finding it difficult to have important conversations with him. She had thought Tessa was the worst eavesdropper until Willie moved in. More than once, she had found him hiding under the kitchen table while they talked. He claimed he was trying to learn English, but she was not fooled. He was as nosy as Tessa.

Bairn looked up and smiled when she came in. "Did you see those geese fly overhead? They were in a hurry to get south. A sign that cold weather is coming, I fear."

Anna leaned against a cabinet to tell Bairn all that Betsy had shared with her. "Do you think you could plan a trip to Indiantown soon and see if this Caleb might be with them?"

With a broad axe, Bairn was hewing a round tree trunk into a square beam, bit by bit. He had stopped working as she spoke and listened with a thoughtful expression on his face. "It'll have to wait until after Sunday, but I'll get over there as soon as I can."

"Bairn, do you recall any details about a frontier Mennonite family that had been attacked by Indians, years and years ago? About the time we were new to Stoney Ridge."

His hand fell and the heavy iron axe made a clunking sound on the floor. "I do. They were newly off the ship and were sold land by an agent in the hottest part of the frontier. The attack happened within days of their arrival." He set the broad axe down on the floor. "If my memory serves me correctly, I believe it was Faxon Gingerich's sister who was stolen."

Anna snapped her head up.

"Aye, lass," he said, switching to English as his eyebrows lifted. "I ken what is runnin' through yer mind. There's a chance that this bloke Caleb might be Faxon's nephew."

❧

Beacon Hollow
December 11, 1763

Saturday's snowfall dumped a thick layer of snow over Stoney Ridge. Cold and icy, just the conditions for excellent sledding. Tessa would be loath to tell rumpled Martin, but she had a wonderful time sledding down Dead Man's Hill a few weeks back. So did Willie. They flew down the hill, tumbling off the sled at the bottom of the hill after each turn, laughing so hard their eyes stung with tears. Then they jumped to their feet and climbed the hill again, again and again, until they finally ran out of energy. Martin followed them home like a stray dog. Her mother had taken pity on him and invited him to stay for supper at Beacon Hollow with the family, as if he were one of them. Which he wasn't.

Tessa hoped rumpled Martin wouldn't be at church this morning. To her mind, he should just stay home on his off Sundays and keep everybody happy, especially Faxon the Saxon, who must be bothered to think of his son spending time with the Amish. She asked him once why he came to their church and he said, smiling with that big goofy grin of his, that the preaching was better. How could she disown that remark? The preacher was her father.

And right now, her father and Willie were bringing the horse and wagon to the front of the house. She reached for her black bonnet and turned to Betsy. "Let's go."

Betsy looked at her curiously. "Your cap, Tessa. It's missing a string."

Tessa felt for the strings but only touched one. She looked around the room for the missing capstring. "I knew it was loose. I should have stitched it last night." She shrugged. "Oh well."

Betsy seemed astonished at the thought. "You can't go to church with a missing capstring! Someone will notice. Your mother gave me two caps. She set the extra on top of the cupboard upstairs."

As Tessa climbed the stairs, she wondered about the kind of church Betsy had been part of in Berks County. She didn't think anyone in her church would have even thought twice about it, other than Maria Müller, who stuck her long nose in Tessa's business.

She looked on top of the cupboard drawer but couldn't locate the prayer cap. She opened the cupboard drawer and her eyes landed on a little sheepskin-bound book, its cover smooth and its edges worn.

Curious, Tessa picked it up and opened it. Betsy's fine penmanship filled the pages and her eyes lingered on a telling line:

> *How is it possible to love such a man? Yet my soul is bound to him in a way I've never known before.*

Tessa snapped the book shut, stunned by the strong feelings of the words within, knowing it was not meant for her eyes. She heard light footsteps come up the stairs and quickly put the book back and shut the cupboard drawer.

Betsy appeared at the top of the stairs. "I just remembered I had set it on the bedpost so its shape would stay round."

Thoughts swirling, Tessa turned from the cupboard to the bedpost and reached out to grab the cap. She pulled the pins out of the cap she was wearing and quickly replaced it with Betsy's cap. As she pinned the cap in place, she asked, "Is it crooked?"

Betsy hesitated for only an instant, and Tessa sensed she was studying her, looking for some sign written on her face. Was she wondering if Tessa had opened her book? Opened and read it? Tessa felt her face grow warm. She was just about to confess her crime when her mother's voice called up to them. "Girls, we must be off. Maria wanted us to arrive early."

Still at the top of the stairs, Betsy turned and started down. "Straight and stiff and starched," she said, looking back to give her a smile. "No one could find fault."

Before Tessa went down the stairs, she tiptoed back to the cupboard, took the little book, and slipped it in her pocket.

❧

Not Faxon's Farm

It was the first time Betsy had attended church in Stoney Ridge. It was held at Not Faxon's Farm, and she did not want to face Hans's disapproval if she were to beg off another Sunday. It took only minutes for her to regret that decision. All morning long, she felt eyes around the room glance curiously at her when they should have been attentive to the minister. She told herself she was imagining things, but not a moment after Bairn offered the benediction, a cluster of women surrounded her. Panic rose within her as the circle drew closer. She felt like she was about to be trapped and suffocated, and had to force herself to smile at them. The women spoke to her soothingly, as if she had been on death's doorstep and made a recent recovery. They kept making sympathetic clucking sounds that only increased her discomfort.

She thought she recognized one or two of them from the time she and her father had come to Stoney Ridge, but could not recall any names other than Maria Müller. She remembered Maria as a particularly prying woman, and she confirmed that impression when she pushed her way through the women to ask Betsy if she had been defiled by the Indians. Betsy was astounded by the question; she couldn't even bring herself to respond. Her silence was so heavy that the thin, gray-haired woman briefly looked away.

"I was not mistreated," Betsy said in a cold voice.

Anna, bless her, noticed and came to her rescue, pulling her away from the clump of women and into the kitchen. Feigning exhaustion, Betsy asked Anna if she could be excused to go to Beacon Hollow and rest.

"I had a concern that it was too soon," Anna said. "I'm so sorry, Betsy. What Maria asked of you—that was appalling. I'll get Tessa to accompany you."

"If you don't mind, I'll walk. I'd like a little time to myself. I know the shortcut by now. Just follow the trail through the woods."

Anna hesitated, then gave a quick nod. "It's a straight path."

Betsy waited until she knew Hans was preoccupied with settling Dorothea into her chair by the fire, then she slipped out of the house, around the back, and into the woods, hurrying her steps as she cut through the snow. She didn't slow until she was halfway to Beacon Hollow. A bright red cardinal sang in a leafless tree above her head and she stopped to listen. Would she have even heard its sweet and lilting song before her time with the Indians? She felt as if her hearing had sharpened during her time with them, as if she had grown more aware of nature's gifts, sweet moments waiting to be noticed. The world had changed in so many ways since she went to live in the Shawnee village by the Monongahela River. No—the world hadn't changed. She was the one who had changed.

Something startled the red cardinal and he flew off in a hurry. She saw a tall figure, a man, coming toward her through the trees. She couldn't make out who he was and felt a momentary stab of fear. The thought flashed through her mind that she should flee, return to the house, seek safety. But before she could put her feet in motion, his voice, calling her name, cut through the trees. *Caleb.* It was Caleb's voice!

18

Not Faxon's Farm
December 11, 1763

All during the sermon, Tessa had been unable to stop think-ing about the little diary she'd found in Betsy's cupboard. About that two lines her eyes happened upon:

> *How is it possible to love such a man? Yet my soul is bound to him in a way I've never known before.*

Was Betsy describing her feelings about Hans? But if she were describing Hans, why would Betsy sound so distressed? No, this mystery man couldn't be Hans, she was sure of it. Betsy Zook loved another man.

And then, as her father was giving the benediction, a face popped into Tessa's mind and she realized *whom* Betsy was writing about—the blue-eyed Indian. Of *course.*

Colliding thoughts filled her mind—what would happen if Hans were to find out about him? Yet it wasn't her busi-ness. And it was wrong of her to read the diary. She should stay out of it. Yet on the other hand, it wasn't right for Betsy to keep this from him. He should know! And how could he know if Tessa didn't tell him?

Her mother had a saying: Thoughts might come for a visit, but you need not invite them in for a meal.

But Tessa did just that. That awful thought floated through her mind and she invited it in for a long stay, long enough to spin a scheme, a terrible scheme. During the fellowship meal, she slipped Betsy's diary into Hans's coat pocket. No sooner had the meal ended—and it was a bitter meal to swallow because Maria had burned the bean soup—but regret stabbed Tessa's conscience, and she hurried to retrieve it. Both Hans and his jacket were nowhere to be found.

She went to find her mother in the kitchen with the other women. "Where's Hans? Where did he go?"

"Betsy left for Beacon Hollow before the meal was served. He left to catch up with her as soon as he finished eating."

Maria looked up from washing dishes in a hot kettle. "You'd best redirect your heart elsewhere, Tessa."

Tessa snapped her mouth shut and felt her face turn a half-dozen shades of red.

Maria puckered her mouth. "Oh, don't look so found out. You've never been able to hide your feelings for Hans Bauer." She pointed a soapy finger at her. "Mind you, Betsy and Hans are destined for each other. No doubt we'll be planning a wedding before long." She was suddenly in front of Tessa, peering at her. "What's wrong? You look like you've swallowed snakeroot."

Tessa was hardly aware of Maria's scrutiny. What had she done? What had she done to Betsy out of jealousy? Out of spite? Suddenly, she was desperate to be outside, someplace where she could draw cold air into her lungs. "Your burned soup. The smell is making me sick. I need some fresh air." She grabbed her cloak out of the pile and rushed out the door to avoid Maria's indignant sputtering.

Snow had started to fall again, in large, wet disks. She pulled up her hood and walked toward the woods, taking in great swallows of icy air. What kind of person was she becoming? She had just made one of the gravest mistakes in her life. Betsy Zook had done nothing to her. It wasn't Betsy's fault that Hans was devoted to her. Tessa's stomach churned in a way that she thought she might actually get sick, and it had nothing to do with Maria's awful burned soup.

"Tessa?"

She spun around to see Martin Gingerich walking toward her. "What are you doing here?"

"I attended your church today."

He did? She hadn't even noticed. That was more than a little embarrassing to admit because it was a very small church. Besides, her mind was muddled. *She* was muddled. No . . . muddied was a better word. She had muddied her soul with sin.

"I saw you slip out the door. You're not ill, are you?" He came closer. She could see his face—the kind smile, the sparkling eyes. Although Martin was in no way handsome, this was not the first time she'd noticed his eyes. Why was he always so happy? And where was his hat!

"No." She shook her head and tried to smile back, a weak attempt, but she doubted he could see her face beneath her hood. "I needed fresh air. Maria burned the soup badly and . . . the smoke seemed to fill my mind."

He nodded. "I wondered why it tasted funny." He grinned

and looked up at the sky. "Being outdoors always helps clear my mind too. Helps me focus."

She didn't need her mind focused. She was far too focused as it was. She glanced at him and found him watching her with concern. "I'm all right," she assured him.

He was silent for a moment, studying her intently, as if his eyes could read her mind. But when he spoke, it had nothing to do with what she was thinking. It came out of the blue. "I'm considering getting baptized in your church."

Tessa's eyes went wide. "I would think your father would heartily object."

Martin lifted a shoulder in a shrug. "His bark is worse than his bite."

"But why would you want to leave your church?"

"It's not so much leaving my church. It's joining yours."

"Mine?" Oh. *Mine.* Now she understood.

Something caught at Tessa's chest. "Martin—"

"I'm not worthy of you, I know that. I've always known that."

Not worthy of *her*? That would mean he was pretty low on the worthy scale, because right now she considered herself the lowest human being on earth.

"Would it make a difference to you? If I joined your church?"

She felt a wave of shame. "Martin . . ."

"You used to call me Marty. Back when you hated me. I sort of liked it."

She sighed. "Marty . . . this may shock you to hear me say this"—it shocked her to say it—"but you deserve so much better than me."

Marty stared at her, an odd expression on his face that Tessa couldn't discern. "That is just *not* possible."

Tessa's eyes filled with tears. That wasn't at all what she expected him to say. Not at all. She expected him to agree with her. Couldn't he see how depraved she was? How deceitful and underhanded?

She wasn't sure how she felt about rumpled Marty—he didn't tease her the way he used to, and she didn't feel quite as annoyed with him as she usually did, plus he was surprisingly easy to talk to. His blue eyes—they were quite nice blue eyes. But her feelings were nothing like the ones she had for Hans. Not even close. "Marty, what do you do when you've made a mistake?"

"A mistake?"

"Yes. A terrible, terrible mistake." She kept her eyes fixed on her shoes.

"How terrible?"

"Sinfully terrible. It was a sin. A dark, horrible sin." There. That should shock him senseless. His feelings for her would melt and dissolve like the snowflakes that were landing on his hatless head.

"I see. I happen to have plenty of experience in that particular area."

She glanced up and was surprised to see a big grin on his face.

"So here's what I do." He leaned close to whisper to her. "Repent. Confess. Then make it right."

❧

Near Beacon Hollow

Caleb stood a rod away, watching Betsy. For a moment neither of them moved. She felt an overpowering impulse to reach out and lean against his chest, to feel his arms around her, to breathe deeply of his scent, to touch him and make sure he was real. She wondered if he felt the same longing for her. She might never have known until she took a step or two closer, and at that very moment he held out his hand to prevent her from coming closer. Why would he resist her touch if it had no effect on him?

"I thought you'd left Stoney Ridge," she said. "I thought you'd gone away without saying goodbye."

"I left, but only for a short time. I came back to bring you a present. A goodbye gift."

She couldn't bear the thought of not seeing him again. "Where will you go?"

He smiled, but it did not reach his eyes. "I am Indian. No Indian can be in one place for too long."

Now she was the one to plead with him, the way he once pled with her to remain among the villagers on the Monongahela River. "Couldn't you try to stay in Stoney Ridge? For my sake?"

"We belong to different worlds, you and I."

"You're wrong, Caleb. We're not so very different. You are half white. I have become half Indian."

He laughed at that. "Go. To your house. The gift is waiting for you." He started to move past her, but she touched his arm.

"Come with me. The Bauers will be home soon. Please, Caleb. I want them to meet you. Please. They're not like others."

He hesitated, uncertainty in his eyes, before giving a brief nod. She walked ahead of him on the narrow trail, feeling his gaze on her back. She wished that she could think of something fitting to say, but no words came to mind. She slowly realized that no words were necessary with Caleb—that somehow he always knew and understood her heart.

When they came to the clearing, she saw a huddled figure sitting on the stoop.

She stopped so abruptly that Caleb nearly bumped into her. "Who—" she gasped, and it was a gasp, for she could hardly breathe. Her heart started to pound. She spun around and looked at Caleb, eyes wide, as if she had seen a ghost.

Johnny!

She broke into a run. Flat-out, arms and feet spinning like a windmill. Her bonnet fell off, her cloak came loose, and still she raced toward the house. Her brother stood when he saw her coming and met her in the yard, arms opened wide. She threw herself at him, embracing him shamelessly, saying his name over and over. When she finally released him, she took his shoulders to look into his eyes, pressing her fingers deep into the blanket that wrapped around his shoulders. Tears ran down her face and dripped off her chin. He was thin, so thin, and taller than she remembered. His face was filthy with grime and soot and who knows what else, but he was smiling.

She turned to Caleb, astonished. "So this is where you have been these last few weeks? You went to get Johnny and bring him to me." She turned to Johnny. "To *us*! For our brother Willie is *here*."

Johnny's eyes went wide. "He did not perish?"

"No!" Didn't Caleb tell him? But then . . . how would he know? "Willie escaped—the night of the attack. He's been here, with the Bauers, for months and months. Safe and sound." There were a thousand things she wanted to ask

Johnny, to say to him, but talk could wait. She couldn't stop smiling, nor could she stop touching her brother—sliding the palm of her hand down his cheek, patting his shoulder, fussing with his hair, reassuring herself it was truly him. "Caleb, Johnny, come inside. I'll fix you something to eat as we wait for the Bauers to return from church."

Her heart overflowed in a way she had not thought possible.

Beacon Hollow

Tessa had promised Felix she would help clean up after church, but as soon as the last cup was rinsed, she left Not Faxon's Farm to head home to Beacon Hollow. Willie wanted to stay and play with Benjo and Dannie, so her parents remained to visit with Dorothea.

As Tessa crossed the yard to the house, she saw smoke rising from the chimney. Betsy was home, which meant Hans would be there too. She took a deep breath as she pulled the latchstring and went into the kitchen. She was startled by the sight of a young white boy in Indian clothes who sat at the table. He was strongly in need of a bath.

Betsy was glowing, fairly dancing around the room in her excitement. "Look, Tessa! Look whom God has returned to us. My brother, Johnny!" Standing behind him, she put her hands on his shoulders, as if to pin him down. "I feel . . . aflame with wonder!"

Tessa felt aflame too . . . first with amazement and then with shame as soon as she realized Hans sat at the far end of the table, arms folded against his chest. She tried to recover her composure quickly. "Welcome, Johnny. You might not remember me, but my name is Tessa." There was no doubt he was Betsy's brother. He had the same thick curly blond hair as hers, the same beautiful eyes.

Tessa hung her cloak on the wall peg, her mind spinning. Hans's coat was hanging on a peg too. Perhaps he hadn't noticed the book in his pocket. Perhaps it wasn't too late and he hadn't read it yet. She felt her spirits lighten. Surely she could wait for a moment when everyone was distracted and quietly retrieve the book. She let her hands drop down along Hans's coat, hoping for a bump to know which coat pocket the book was in. She felt nothing. "I see Betsy has given you bread and milk. My parents will soon be here."

"And Willie," Betsy said. "He'll be here soon. He'll be overjoyed to see you, Johnny."

"I am still unclear how Johnny has been restored to us," Hans said.

Johnny looked up from mopping his bread in milk. "Caleb came to the village in the night and helped me escape. I couldn't have survived without him. He brought me all the way here, just like he did for Betsy."

"Caleb?" Tessa's voice was a squeak. The blue-eyed Indian?

Johnny pointed to the stairs. Tessa spun around and saw Caleb sitting on the bottom step, long legs stretched in front of him. He sat in the shadows, so silently she hadn't even noticed he was in the room. She hadn't even *noticed*.

Caleb's eyes searched hers, and she realized he was going to let her decide if she was going to acknowledge that they had previously met.

Tessa chanced a look at Hans. His back was as straight as

a plank. There was a tautness, a tension inside of him that almost seemed to hum with vibration. "And tell me again, who is Caleb?" he said. He spoke as if Caleb were not in the same room.

Betsy turned and lifted a palm toward Caleb. "He was in my village. I told you."

"Today is the first I have heard of him. You had not mentioned that he had helped you to escape." Hans's tone surprised everyone with its force. Even Johnny stopped eating to look between Betsy and Hans. "How well did you know this . . . half blood?"

Betsy's happiness dimmed. "Caleb has shown me great kindness, Hans. He has been a good friend. He is responsible for bringing Johnny and me, both of us, to Beacon Hollow."

"Shown you kindness," Hans repeated.

"Yes. Many, many times."

There was a long and heavy silence. Then Hans's gaze shifted toward Caleb, bright with suspicion.

He'd found it. He'd read it. Surely Hans had read Betsy's diary.

❧

Beacon Hollow

The snow that began on Sunday morning did not let up. The temperature continued dropping as Anna and Bairn and Willie returned home in the wagon, late in the day. Bairn had told Anna he would drop them off at Beacon Hollow and then head over to Faxon Gingerich's. He would try to find out more information about the sister who had been taken captive by the Indians so long ago, but he cautioned Anna to not assume this young man was Faxon's nephew—and to not let Betsy know—not until they had more information.

But if it were true . . . what a wonder! Only God could have orchestrated such a miracle of restoration. Anna was eager to meet this young man, eager to tell him that he had family nearby.

"Keep in mind," Bairn warned her in English so that Willie would not realize what was being said, "there's no guarantee that Faxon would consider the Indian to be kin."

"Surely, he would," Anna said. "His own sister's son? To have a legacy left from her? Surely he would welcome him into his home and regard him with affection."

"Nae, darlin'. 'Tis a lovely thought, but nae certain at all." Bairn shook his head. "I ken nae what Faxon will think."

"Just because this young man was reared among Indians doesn't mean he isn't a child of God. Are we not all bound together as one family in the sight of God?"

"I believe so. You believe so. But that dinnae mean others do."

Bairn pulled the horse and wagon as close to the front door of the house as possible, so that Anna and Willie could hurry in.

No sooner had Anna crossed the threshold into the warm kitchen than she realized they had a visitor. Her first thought was the stranger who sat at the kitchen table must be the Indian who had rescued Betsy—he was dressed in animal skins, his long hair was gathered in a queue, but it was . . . light-colored hair. And then she saw his face and there was no mistaking who this boy was—he was a slightly older edition of Willie, a male version of Betsy.

Coming around Anna at the door, Willie skidded to a

dead stop. His eyes grew wide and his shoulders hunched. Then he screamed "Johnny!" and charged across the room to greet his long-lost brother, nearly toppling him over. Zeeb barked at the two boys, locked in a tight embrace, until Betsy shushed him and wrapped her arms around her brothers. A circle, completed at last.

Laughing, Anna watched the family reunion, soaking up the merriment, tears prickling her eyes. All three Zook children shared similar physical traits—large and trusting bright eyes, flushed cheeks, thick blond hair, all three small in stature with delicate facial features. They sat together at one end of the table, taking turns listening to each other. Despite his ordeal, Johnny's health seemed good, his spirits were cheerful, his mind was not disordered. Unlike Betsy on her first day back, he did not seem bewildered. Instantly, he engaged with Willie the way brothers teased and laughed with each other, even standing back-to-back to see who was taller.

Like Betsy, Johnny was quite thin. Tonight he would receive a hot bath and a change of clothes.

Clothes! She would have to send Tessa over to Not Faxon's Farm to borrow shirts and trousers from Felix's twins. To-morrow, first thing, she would sew new clothes for this boy. She had noticed Willie was already outgrowing his shirts—he would need new clothes soon too.

She was filled with awe. She had never thought she would be sewing clothes for little boys. Was there any limit to the wonders of God's providence?

Across the room, something moved, catching Anna's eye. Not some*thing*—some*one*. An Indian. She hadn't even seen him until now. He was leaning against the roughly hewn boards of the wall, hidden in the shadows of the slanting sun. From his gentle demeanor, Anna discerned his identity immediately. She walked toward him and held out her hand. "So you must be Caleb."

His chiseled face softened as he gripped her hand. "And you are Anna."

Oh my, she thought with a smile. *Oh my. He has Faxon Gingerich's blue eyes.*

When Tessa's father walked through the door to learn the news of Johnny's restoration, he looked as astounded as her mother did. He held his hand out to Johnny. "Welcome to our home, son," he said, in a voice as reverent as a prayer. And her mother started dabbing at her eyes with the corner of her apron all over again.

At length they roused from their absorption, and Tessa waited for a lull in conversation to excuse herself and go upstairs. Her mother asked if she wasn't feeling well, and she said yes, which was true in a way, but she didn't tell her why. It was because of what happened before her parents returned home. It was because of the way Hans had snatched his hat off the wall hook and stomped out of the house just after Betsy asked Caleb to stay for supper.

Conscience-torn, Tessa plopped on her bed and stared at the ceiling rafters. The door slammed and she heard Willie and Johnny outside. She went to the small loft window and saw them dash off to the barn like puppies after a ball, milk buckets clanging, stopping now and then to toss snowballs at each other, the way brothers did on a normal day.

But it wasn't a normal day. It was a hugely significant day.

For Johnny, for Willie, in a good way. For Betsy, Caleb, Hans, Tessa . . . it was a messy day.

If only she could turn back the clock and start the day all over again. She would have left Betsy's diary in the cupboard. She should have.

But she hadn't. She had taken it and given it to Hans.

What had she done? She pressed her fists against her eyes. Why had she done it?

She knew why. *Jealousy*. Envy. The green-eyed monster. She was consumed by it.

Her father's deep voice floated up the chimney flue. She heard the name Gingerich and jumped off the bed. She crouched as close to the fireplace as she could without getting burned. Whatever he was talking about sounded serious.

"Caleb," he said, "before the boys return from milking the cow, there's something you should know. There's reason to believe that your mother's brother is our neighbor. His name is Faxon Gingerich."

"Oh Caleb!" Betsy said. "Wouldn't that be wonderful?"

Tessa heard Caleb mumble something in reply, but his voice was too low, too soft-spoken for her to understand it.

Tommyrot! She wished she had her grandmother's ear trumpet. She crept to the top of the stairs and bent down. She could clearly see the four of them, seated around the table like a checkerboard: her father's thick gray-brown hair, her mother's black prayer cap, Betsy's white prayer cap, Caleb's shiny coal-black hair.

"Nae, Betsy, I'm sorry to say that Caleb guessed correctly," her father said. "Faxon does not want to acknowledge him."

"Surely Faxon will have a change of heart," her mother said, her voice tinged with upset. "It must have been a shock to discover that he has a nephew from a sister he presumed dead."

"I am half-blood," Caleb said, almost sounding sad. "He will not want a nephew with Indian blood."

Something inside Tessa twisted hard.

"But you belong to them!" Betsy looked up at him, her eyes wide. "They're your family."

The breath eased out of Caleb in an odd sigh. "Do not pity me. I belong to the Holy One."

"Aye, and to the family of God," her father said. "And that means you always have a place with us, Caleb. And I insist you stay here until this storm lets up. It is growing worse out there."

A knock came at the door and Tessa assumed the boys had finished milking the cow. Her mother was closest to the door and hurried to open it. Tessa could feel the draft of cold come in and sweep right up the stairs.

"Martin! Come in, come in, get by the fire," her mother said, closing the door behind him.

Martin?!

Rumpled Marty stepped near the fire, extended his palms, and rubbed them together. His coat and hatless head were covered in snowflakes.

He swung around to face everyone. "I wanted to meet Caleb," he said, and Tessa noticed that his eyes landed on Caleb. "I can't speak for my father, but he can't speak for me either. I wanted to meet my cousin." And then he grinned that big goofy grin of his—so bright and cheerful it could light a room—and came forward with hand extended to Caleb.

19

Beacon Hollow
December 14, 1763

Tessa woke in that quiet time just before dawn when the whole earth seemed to be holding its breath, waiting for the sun to rise. She hadn't been sleeping well the last few nights due to the extreme cold, and to her extremely guilty conscience. On top of that, she worried about the black stallion.

She knew it was a ridiculous thought. That horse, and his father, and his grandfather, had survived the elements for decades. Lately though, the only thing that distracted her from dwelling on her own flawed character was when she filled her mind with thoughts of the horse. About how he had grown to trust her when she felt so very untrustworthy.

Whenever her mind circled back to Hans and Betsy, her stomach lifted to her throat. For the last few days, Betsy had searched high and low around the loft for her diary. Did Tessa admit that she had taken it? Given it to Hans? Betrayed her? *No.* The words she should have spoken stayed locked in her heart. Tessa remained stone silent.

Rumpled Marty had given her excellent advice: Repent. Confess. Make it right.

Tessa definitely repented. She was highly motivated to make it right. It was the *confession* piece. That one had her stymied.

She'd seen plenty of others sit on the confession bench in church, seen the shame that covered them. She wondered if confessing to Betsy alone might be enough. She decided to run the scenario past Marty—glossing over specifics, of course—and get his opinion. Until then, she carefully avoided being in proximity of Betsy. And that was not an easy thing to do in a snug house during a snowstorm.

She slipped out of bed and dressed, tiptoed downstairs, grabbed her cloak off the peg by the door, and left the house as quietly as she could. Yesterday, Tessa's father, Willie, and Johnny had shoveled a path to the root cellar so they could get potatoes for supper. She swung the cellar door open, lifted the lantern high to light the path down the icy steps, and carefully made her way into the cold, dark room. Cold, yes, but well insulated, without the sharp bite in the air that made it hard to breathe. Here, she could breathe in deeply, filling her lungs with the scents of Beacon Hollow's harvest: pungent apple cider, barrels filled with onions—kept far away from apples, her mother insisted, or you'd be eating an apple that tasted of onion—potatoes, beets, cabbages, carrots, turnips, and walnuts, all mingling with the smokiness of hams hanging from the rafters. She heard a mouse or two scurry behind the barrels and shuddered. She despised mice. *Hated* them.

She hung the lantern on the wall hook and lifted one lid barrel to rummage through sawdust. She grabbed what felt like a carrot and held it up to the lantern. Turnip. The stallion hated turnips. So did she. She shut the lid on turnips and tried another barrel. Carrots! She filled her apron with all she could find.

"Tessa?"

She whirled around to find her mother standing on the bottom step of the cellar stairs, her woolen shawl wrapped tightly around her shoulders.

"Are you not well?"

"I'm well. I'm quite well, in fact." Tessa fit the wooden lid back on the barrel. "I woke early and thought I'd take some carrots out to the stallion."

Her mother took a few steps into the cellar to study her, concern in her eyes. "You've been so quiet, lately. So withdrawn. It's not like you. You're not feeling . . . left out, are you?"

"Left out?"

"Betsy, Willie, and Johnny. They seem very close. I just wondered if you felt left out. I know you've always yearned for a sister. For brothers. They'll soon feel more at home, and include you in their circle."

Nothing could have been further from Tessa's mind than feeling excluded by Betsy and her brothers. She wanted to avoid them! She took great pains to avoid them.

But how could she tell her mother what she'd done to Betsy? Her mother believed the best in her. How could she disappoint her? "Mem, I'm fine. Truly."

Her mother knew better, but she didn't press Tessa. "At least put the carrots in a sack so your hands can stay covered." She held out an empty flour sack and opened it so Tessa could dump the carrots in her apron into it.

"I'll be back soon. I'm just going out to see if the stallion might be nearby. I'm worried he hasn't been able to find food during the snowstorm."

"But the snow is so deep."

"Not so deep in the woods. It's probably barely reached the forest floor. And if I get hungry" —she lifted the sack— "I'll just eat a carrot."

Her mother gave her a relenting smile. Tessa handed the lantern to her and closed the heavy cellar door. She waved to her and cut through the fresh snow with long strides, heading for the hill behind the big stone house. She was right about one thing: once under the thick canopy of trees, there was very little snow to trudge through. She stuck to the trail, calling to the stallion but didn't see any sign of him. She was thinking of turning back home when she caught sight of a man riding toward her on a horse, his shoulders hunched forward and his head bowed low. Though he was quite a distance away, she recognized him immediately. Hans. Her heart betrayed her and started pounding. Hans hadn't come around Beacon Hollow since Sunday, when Johnny was restored to them. "Hans! Hello there! I'm out looking for the stallion." She took a carrot out of the sack and fed it to his horse when he approached her.

Hans raised his head and looked at her. He wore a strange, haunted expression, and gazed at her in a way that produced a terribly uncomfortable feeling—as if he did not recognize her. He seemed to be struggling for words, an adversity Tessa had not thought him capable of.

"What's wrong?" She caught a whiff of smoke in his clothing. "Where have you been?"

"It was just meant to be a warning . . ."

"Hans, did you fall off your horse?" Hit his head? She

268

reached out to put a hand on his knee, but he flinched, shaking off her hand as well as her concern.

"It's all my fault." His voice scratched the air.

"Your fault?" She gaped at him, wondering if he might be intoxicated. She'd seen a drunken man once or twice in Lancaster Town. They spoke nonsensically, just as he was doing. Then she noticed a hatchet tied to his saddle. It was covered in blood. She pointed to it. "Did you go hunting?"

His eyes momentarily met Tessa's and she felt the shock of his despair. "I . . . I . . . Yes, yes. I went hunting. Caught a rabbit." He hesitated, then said, "I must go."

She watched him ride away until he was out of sight, wondering if she should follow him home to ensure his safe arrival. She decided not to, as he was only a mile or so from the path to Not Faxon's Farm and the horse knew its way to the barn. Besides, for the first time, she felt frightened by Hans. She knew that he could be moody and sharp tongued, but she had never seen him so distraught. She had no idea what triggered a mood like this, but he looked and acted like he'd seen a ghost.

The sun was painting the tops of the trees, her stomach was rumbling, and she knew she'd better get home before her mother sent someone to fetch her. Someone like Betsy Zook.

As she went around a bend in the trail, she heard a familiar nicker. She yanked her hood off her head and listened for the direction the sound was coming from. She cut off the trail and started to run through the trees. Then she stopped.

There, high on a rocky ledge, was the mighty black stallion, with the morning sky lit behind him.

Tessa blew out a startled breath. She wasn't sure what she'd expected . . . but this sight? This beat everything.

For the last three nights, Betsy had slept soundly and woke rested. Both of her brothers were sleeping nearby in the loft and Caleb—Caleb!—slept below near the hearth. It made her so happy to know that he was willing to go to Indiantown with Bairn when the weather improved, to be welcomed in by the Conestogas. Perhaps he might even stay there. She hoped for it. She prayed for it.

For the first time in a very, very long time, Betsy had no worries on her mind other than Hans's tetchiness on Sunday afternoon, the day when Johnny was returned to them. Certainly, Hans was pleased to see Johnny, but learning of Caleb's existence stole the joy of the happy reunion. A dark mood descended over Hans, a side of him that was showing up with greater frequency, a side that disturbed Betsy. And Hans hadn't been back to Beacon Hollow since, though to be fair, the weather had been fierce.

She was grateful the storm came through Stoney Ridge when it did—it gave her an abundance of time with her brothers, sitting close to the fireplace. There was so much to talk about, to share, to grieve about. Betsy felt as if she was finally able to move the heavy rock of grief for her parents, to come to terms with their deaths. Obviously, they had no funeral for their parents; in an unexpected way, the storm drew them together and served that purpose.

She lay in bed and pondered such thoughts when she was startled by a mighty racket, as if someone was trying to break the front door down. She sat up in bed and heard a flurry of upset voices coming from the kitchen. She swung her bare feet to the icy floor and dressed quickly to see what had transpired. By the time she hurried down the stairs, Caleb alone remained. He leaned with his back against the front door as if waiting for her, a wooden look on his face, arms crossed against his chest, and she had a growing dread that what he was going to say would change everything. Another before-and-after moment. She halted on the last stair step, not wanting to know anything, to hear anything he might tell her.

Through the east-facing window, she saw Bairn harness a horse to a wagon. A boy sat huddled on the wagon seat, head bowed, wrapped in a quilt. She saw Anna wrap another quilt around the boy, then brush the bangs off his forehead the way a mother did as she said goodbye to her child.

"Betsy?" It came out softly, falling from Caleb's lips as sweetly as an endearment. She turned her head to face him and he pushed off from the door and walked toward her, speaking in a low, flat voice as he approached. "There was a massacre last night at Indiantown. Six Conestogas were killed. One boy named Christy escaped and came here." He stopped in front of her and dropped his chin to his chest.

"No!" Betsy cried, barely able to speak. "But why? They've done nothing wrong!"

He raised his head to look at her. In those blue eyes she read heavy sadness, utter defeat. "They were born Indian." He said it as if this was what he had been seasoned by life to expect.

She saw the horse and wagon rumble down the path, saw Anna watch the wagon go, standing in the cold with just a shawl to protect her from the cold. "Where are they going?"

"Bairn Bauer is taking the boy to Lancaster Town for safekeeping."

Caleb turned to leave, but she stepped forward without hesitation to reach out and grasp his arms. "Caleb, where are you going?"

"To Indiantown. To bury the dead."

"Oh no. Please go to Lancaster Town with Bairn. *Please*." She bit her lips and felt unshed tears swell as the fear of helplessness began to take hold.

But Caleb was already turning away, moving beyond her reach, and she knew there was little point in arguing with him. At the door, he spun around. Their eyes locked and held. She knew hers were entreating, desperate. His were haunted, defeated. Abruptly, he reached for the latch. The cold wind swept in as he swept out.

Betsy stared at the closed door after he'd left. She hadn't even realized her brothers stood at the top of the stairs.

"Betsy, all is well?" Johnny asked, worry in his voice.

She turned and looked up at the two of them on the stair steps, at their sleepy faces, their pale blue eyes, their blond hair that looked like rooster tails standing straight up from the tops of their heads. They were here, they were safe. God was sovereign over all. Over *all*. "All is well, Johnny," she said, giving him a reassuring smile. "Hurry and get ready for school. I think the snow has finally stopped."

Four hours later, Bairn returned from Lancaster Town, his face ashen. He couldn't sit still; he paced the room as he provided scant details to Anna and Betsy: six Conestoga Indians had been brutally murdered during the night, and all the homes had been burned down.

"What of Will Sock?" Anna said, white-faced. "What of his family?"

"Nae. They are safe. But Captain John was killed."

"What happened to the others?"

"It was such a bitter-cold night that most of the others had taken shelter elsewhere, like Will Sock and his family."

"A small blessing, I suppose," Anna said.

"I'm not so sure," Bairn said, running a hand through his hair. "I suspect those responsible for the massacre will try to complete what they set out to do."

Anna winced.

"I'm hopeful that it will not be public knowledge that Christy escaped," Bairn said. "I fear that if they know there's a witness, they will try to silence him."

"Did Christy recognize anyone?"

Bairn shook his head. "He said he did not see any faces." He hunkered before the fire, elbows to knees, then rose, ambling around the room again.

Up to this point, Betsy had remained quiet, but she had many questions. "What kind of monster would do such a thing?"

"Christy said it was the work of several men." Bairn wrapped his arms tightly across his chest. "He said they fired their guns into the huts, then burst inside with tomahawks to kill the survivors before setting the little village afire." He shuddered. "Somehow, he escaped in the chaos and ran all the way to Beacon Hollow. Barefoot." In English he added, "The poor laddie's feet were bleedin' from the cold."

"It was the Paxton Boys," Anna said quietly.

"We ken nae for certain," Bairn said, but the look on his face said otherwise.

Betsy tipped her head. "Boys?"

"No, not boys. Not boys at all." Anna's shoulders sagged. "That's just what they call themselves. They're men from

Paxton who believe that all Indians are dangerous and to be feared."

"To be annihilated," Bairn murmured. "That's what they want."

Betsy looked from one to the other. "Hans has mentioned Paxton."

Bairn and Anna exchanged another glance. "He has become friendly with a preacher named John Elder, who fires everyone up with his rhetoric."

"And you think John Elder led the Paxton Boys to commit this . . . atrocity?"

Bairn frowned. "I cannae and should nae say, nae without any evidence. But I pray truth will prevail. And at least the remaining Conestoga are safe in Lancaster Town in the workhouse until the offenders are caught. The sheriff said he would ask Governor Penn to issue bounties for arrests."

Betsy jerked her head up. "What's a workhouse?"

"'Tis a . . . gaol."

She still didn't know the meaning of the words so Anna stepped in to translate. "A jail."

Betsy tried to imagine Indians confined in a jail, but all that came to her mind was a memory of Caleb at the central fire of the village, patiently burning the inside of a log to form a canoe. Of proud Nijlon, sitting cross-legged in the wigwam, quietly nursing her little wide-eyed baby. Of lighthearted Numees, laughing, always laughing, playing chase with little children through the village. "They can't be locked up. Their spirit . . . Indians suffer when confined."

Bairn gave her a kind, paternal smile. "I understand your worries, Betsy, but this is only for a short time. Only until the perpetrators are dealt with." He folded his long frame in his chair and Betsy thought he was finally calming down, but then she saw that he had clasped his hands so tightly that the knuckles had bled white. "Christy brought the original treaty William Penn had made with the local Indians in 1701. Will Sock's mother had kept it safe, all those years. A worn, thin paper of great value to them." He rubbed his forehead. "A tragic irony."

Betsy kept her eyes down. "I want Caleb to go to this workhouse. I fear he has put himself in needless danger today by going to Indiantown."

"The sheriff and undertaker are heading out there this afternoon," Bairn said. "Perhaps they will persuade him to return with them."

Anna set a cup of hot tea in front of her husband. "Caleb struck me as a young man who feels an unusual sense of responsibility toward others."

"He does," Betsy said, startled by Anna's keen insight. "He watches over others. It's what his Indian name means. To the Indians, a person is meant to become the name."

Anna tilted her head. "That's true in the Bible too. God called Gideon a mighty hero when he was hiding out in a wine press. Christ called Simon Peter the Rock, though his temperament was mercurial."

Betsy regarded Anna thoughtfully until Bairn broke into her thoughts. "She's the real preacher in this household."

The latch on the door opened and Tessa burst in, cheeks flushed with cold, spirits oozing with joy.

"Tessa, where have you been?" Anna said. "You said you'd only be out for a few hours. It's nearly noon."

"You'll never believe it! I rode on the horse's back. I really did! Not for long, but he let me climb on his back. He's remarkably gentle, once he trusts you." Abruptly, she stopped talking and looked, confused, from Bairn, to Anna, to Betsy and back to Bairn. "Is something wrong? You all look as if you've lost your best friend."

In a strange way, Betsy realized with a start, without intending to, Tessa had just sized up exactly what she feared most.

🌱

When Tessa heard about Conestoga Indiantown, her delight over making such a significant stride forward in gaining the horse's trust popped like a soap bubble. It had been such a wonderful morning—alone in the snowy woods with the black stallion for company—while just a few miles away, a tragic event had so recently occurred. Her father spared them details, but she could tell by the wilt of his shoulders that the carnage was horrific.

And then a new thought chilled her. It came out of the blue and there was no basis to it, no reason to think it, no purpose in believing it. Still, it was like a popcorn kernel stuck between her molars. She couldn't dismiss it.

Earlier this morning, where had Hans been coming from?

20

Beacon Hollow
December 22, 1763

Anna was astounded by the conditions of the workhouse in Lancaster Town. The jail was in a stone building on North Prince Street, a cobblestoned road that ran through the center of the town. It was dirty and overcrowded and woefully lacking in simple provisions for the remaining Conestoga Indians who had willingly gone there under promise of safety by the sheriff. Anna and Betsy and Tessa went to town nearly every day, bringing food and blankets. Bairn supplied barrels of raw materials from the sawmill so the Conestogas could continue their work. To do something while they waited in the dimly lit, bone-chilling cold cells. Waiting and waiting for the perpetrators of the Indiantown massacre to be arrested.

The Indians seemed relatively content despite their troubling situation. During the days, they sat in small groups to make brooms and weave baskets. Anna was surprised to hear one or two of them tease and laugh as they worked; they seemed almost oblivious, as if they were unaware of their own troubles.

Caleb stayed nights in the workhouse despite Bairn's standing invitation to sleep at Beacon Hollow. He spent his days hunting game for the Conestoga to eat, as the provisions by the government were appallingly paltry.

A few days before Christmas, Anna sought out Bairn in the barn and asked him to appeal again to Faxon Gingerich, to ask him to meet Caleb. "This is his sister's son. Her *son*. Faxon may be strong minded, but he is a fair man."

Bairn wagged his head. "'Tis not the right time. If Faxon were to take in Caleb as a relative, he could be targeted for attack. There are bloodlusters in town, Anna. They need no excuse to go after anyone who shows sympathy to the Indians. The atmosphere is highly charged right now. 'Tis best to wait until arrests are made."

Their gazes collided, each thinking the same thought. *If.* If arrests were ever made. The provincial governor had created a warrant for the arrest of any and all assailants, but he offered no bounty. It had been a week since the attack on Indiantown, and no arrests had been made. No witnesses, no evidence, no leads came forth to identify the perpetrators.

Anna agreed that everyone was on edge after the attack. On edge . . . and on one side of the story or the other. The attack was strangely polarizing. It was disheartening to hear so many express a high regard for the attackers. She overheard the baker's wife in Lancaster Town say the attackers should be thanked for "cleaning house." "Bairn, could Caleb be putting himself in danger when he leaves the workhouse to hunt?"

"Aye, but it's what he has chosen. He wants to help provide for the others."

"To watch over them."

"Aye. To watch over them."

"The town will calm down. Surely tensions will ease soon."

"I dinnae. There is growing anger toward Will Sock." Bairn raked a hand through his hair. "I fear I am t' blame."

"You? How could that be?"

"I was the one who asked Will Sock t' seek out information about Betsy Zook's whereabouts. He was observed up north, speakin' to hostile Indians, ones who bore weapons. A rumor took shape that he has collaborated with them."

"Do you think that's the reason the Conestogas were attacked? Because of that rumor?"

He lifted his shoulders in a shrug and let them down with a sigh. "Ever since Pontiac's Rebellion last spring, there has been a growing animosity toward the Indians. All Indians."

"Stirred up by John Elder and his Paxton Boys."

"'Tis not our place to judge," he said, sounding more like a minister than a husband.

Anna had no trouble placing blame where it belonged—at the feet of the Paxton Boys. Annoyed, she spun around and left him in the barn to preach to the horses.

With Christmas coming, Anna planned to make it a special day for the Zooks. She had knitted mittens and scarves for Johnny and Willie, and stayed up late to make special cookies to surprise them. She hoped Tessa would do something nice for the Zooks—she seemed far more interested in that black stallion than in Betsy, Johnny, and Willie. She did her chores as quickly as she could, and slipped off to the woods to tame the horse at every possible opportunity. After Christmas, Anna would address Tessa's remoteness. For now, there were enough other concerns to deal with.

But the following afternoon, Bairn and Felix returned from

Lancaster Town with solemn looks on their faces. "Anna," Bairn said. "Where are Betsy and Tessa?"

"Betsy went to get the boys at Not Faxon's Farm. Tessa went to seek out the horse."

Felix looked at Bairn. "I'll be right back."

Anna knew something distressing had happened. Felix had never come and left Beacon Hollow without a joke, a light word. He looked like he had seen a ghost.

She looked to Bairn for an explanation.

He read her mind. "He's gone to fetch Hans at the forge."

Something had happened. "Shall I leave you three alone?"

"Nae. You need to hear this."

Not much later, Felix returned with Hans, still with his leather apron on. "Where's the fire?" Hans said, smiling. Then his smile faded as he took in the grave look on Bairn's face. "Something wrong?"

"Yes, there is," Bairn said. "Sit down, Hans."

They all sat around the table: Bairn, Anna, Felix, and Hans. Bairn cleared his throat before he began, steady gray eyes fixed on Hans. "We've just come from the workhouse in Lancaster Town. The sheriff told us disturbing news. It seems that John Elder has implicated you in the massacre on Indiantown."

Implicated Hans in the massacre? Anna glanced sharply at Hans.

Hans's lips pressed together in a tight line and a muscle ticked in his jaw, but he stared back at Bairn without flinching. "That's rubbish. Elder is lying." There was a protracted silence before he added, in a frosty voice, "But it appears you do not believe me."

"I'm askin' you for the truth, Hans," Bairn said, his tone crisp. "I cannae help you if I dinnae ken the truth."

There was a short silence before Hans said, "And that is what I'm giving you."

Felix jumped in. "John Elder is telling others you have been an Indian hater for a long time. He said you were the one who delivered blankets infected with smallpox to the Conestogas last year. That you volunteered for the task because you'd had it."

"He's lying!" But his eyes widened in alarm. "I . . . I did deliver those blankets, but I did not know they were infected. I did *not* know."

"Hans," Felix said, "where were you during the night of the massacre? I know you weren't at home."

Hans reeled to his feet, as if he was suddenly in a hurry to leave. "I was caught in the storm. I took refuge."

"Sit down!" Bairn barked, and Hans slowly sank to his chair. Anna could feel the tension rising in the room. "Have you any proof of where you spent the night?"

"Isn't my word enough?"

"Not if the sheriff comes to arrest you."

Hans eased himself back in the chair. "But that's . . . they've got it all wrong! All wrong."

Bairn crossed his arms against his chest. "Hans, I'm going to ask you again. Were you involved *in any way* with the massacre at Indiantown?"

"No."

"But that's not true."

Everyone turned to see Tessa, halfway down the stairs.

Anna inhaled a sharp breath. "I thought you'd gone out."

Tessa shook her head. "I was sewing in the loft." She came down the stairs and stood on the bottom step, as if hesitating to come any closer. "I was out in the woods early on the morning of the massacre. I happened upon Hans as he rode through the woods toward Not Faxon's Farm. He stopped when we met up, I gave his horse a carrot, we talked for a few minutes. He seemed . . . disoriented. Like he'd hit his head and was confused. He wasn't making any sense. I thought, maybe he'd been drinking. Maybe he was drunk."

Anna held a moan behind her pressed lips. What had become of this boy she once knew?

"He had a hatchet tied to his saddle." Tessa blew out a puff of breath and looked at her feet. "The axe . . . it was covered with blood. Fresh blood."

Hans slapped his hands down on the table so hard the dishes rattled. "You'd take the word of a silly girl over me? A girl with nothing more on her mind but chasing after a wild horse?" He glared at Bairn. "I did not *do* anything!"

The injured look on Tessa's face when Hans called her a silly girl crushed Anna. She looked at Hans, mystified, as if she didn't recognize him anymore. Images of him as a child filled her mind: running in and out of the house, trying to keep up with Felix. Hans had always been a charming rascal, with a lazy smile and teasing ways. Dorothea had certainly spoiled him, but Anna had seen such potential in him. What had soured him to this extent? Betsy's captivity seemed to have caused greater harm to Hans than to her.

Hans stared coldly at Tessa, as if trying to impale her. Anna wondered if he was trying to intimidate her. If so, she was pleased to see that her daughter didn't cower or back down. She returned his gaze, steady and confident. "I know what I saw," she said in a quiet but firm tone.

"Then your vivid imagination has drawn a picture that isn't accurate."

"I'm not accusing you of anything, Hans. I'm just telling what I saw."

Bairn leaned across the table to look straight into Hans's face. "What did Tessa see, Hans? Where were you coming from? Where had you been that night?"

Hans swallowed and took his time answering, rubbing his finger over a dent in the tabletop. He shifted in his seat to face Bairn. "I admit I went to Paxton to speak with John Elder." The words came out low and recalcitrant.

"Why did you need to speak to him on a bitter, snowy night? What was so urgent?"

"Because . . . of Betsy, of course. I couldn't stop thinking of what they'd done to her. Each time I saw her face, that hideous scar—I couldn't forget. That's why he did it, that warrior. He sliced her face, her beautiful face, so we could never forget. And then I found her diary in my coat pocket— she described such terrible atrocities. Her mother's scalp . . . Bairn, the savage played with the scalp right in front of Betsy, taunting her with it . . . like it was a toy! Her *mother's* scalp! Someone had to pay for what they'd done. Someone had to do something." His shoulders sagged. "So I decided to show the diary to John Elder."

"You didn't," Tessa said in dull surprise. "Please tell me you didn't do that."

Anna felt anxiety begin at the back of her knees and crawl upward—sharp needles of creeping heat.

Hans ignored Tessa. "John Elder read the diary. He decided to send some men over to Indiantown to give them a warning. To *send* a warning. To all the Indians."

Bairn's brows knit together in a frown. "What was the warning?"

"That their rebellion would be subdued."

"So you joined in on their rampage?"

Hans dipped his head.

"Why? Why would you have joined the Paxton Boys on a rampage?"

He looked at Bairn, and for a brief moment, Anna saw the boy within. "It was just meant to scare them. Just a strategy of fear, he said." His voice broke. "But once we rode into Indian-town, things got carried away. Someone shot off his rifle, then another . . . and it quickly got out of hand. One thing led to another." He squeezed his fists. "I did not hurt anyone, Bairn. I didn't kill anyone, I didn't burn anything. I promise you that."

"Nor did you stop it."

"No. Nor did I stop it." His voice grew hoarse. "I don't even remember seeing Tessa when I came through the woods. My mind was like scattered buckshot." He sighed, spent of words and emotion, and rubbed his face with both hands. "Should I go to the sheriff? Tell him what I know?"

"It can wait until after Christmas," Bairn said. "Lancaster Town is a tinderbox right now, just waiting for a flint to hit the rock and set the fire."

"The Paxton Boys are all over Lancaster Town," Felix added. "Who knows what might happen if you showed your face in town. The mob might hang you. The sheriff can't control them."

Hans's shoulders slumped down by degrees.

"Surely Christmas will remind everyone of peace," Anna said, hoping it would be true. "The town will calm down after Christmas and second Christmas."

Bairn leaned forward on the table. "Hans, so long as you're telling the truth—"

Hans looked at him with a glimmer of hope. "And I am."

"So long as you are, then you've nothing to fear. You're not guilty of the crime John Elder accused you of. But you must not accuse the Paxton Boys of involvement."

"Because you fear they'll retaliate against me?"

Bairn looked at him in disbelief. "Because our church believes that no man has the right to accuse another."

"But I know the names of the men who committed those crimes. I can identify them."

"Even then. It's the way of our church. How can we accuse another and stand before God? We are all sinners in his eyes."

A silence covered the kitchen.

"Hans, did you not think to confess your involvement?" Bairn asked.

"I did not." Hans lifted his head, his eyes sagging with regret. "I did not know where to begin."

Tessa turned and ran up the stairs.

❧

Beacon Hollow
Christmas Day 1763

Tessa tried to be cheerful on Christmas Day, for the sake of the boys, for Betsy, mostly for her mother. She knew she'd been difficult lately, moody and distant. Her spirits lifted when Felix arrived, bringing Benjo and Dannie, Hans, of course, and Dorothea—her first venture away from home in a few months. And then Catrina and Maria arrived. After the bounteous meal, Catrina and the boys—all four—surprised everyone with a performance. They sang songs and recited poems, short stories, and Scripture verses. And then, the boys lined up along the hearth and recited in unison this ending, in English:

> We're glad it isn't size and weight
> And age that counts today,
> 'Cause then we might not have the chance
> To stand up here and say . . .
> "Happy Christmas!"

Catrina beamed as everyone clapped. "Anna, this is credited to you. You insisted that Felix and I learn to read, write, and speak English on the *Charming Nancy*."

Tessa's father reached out and squeezed her mother's hand. "How well I remember! Down in the lower deck, near the pigs."

Felix grinned. "We brought to the New World the most well-educated pigs known to man."

They laughed at that, but soon Felix's smile faded and his face grew solemn. He rose to his feet. "I have an announcement." He cleared his throat and his cheeks, Tessa noticed, had turned a curious shade of red. "Somehow, I have persuaded Catrina to be my wife and the mother of those two imps I call my sons."

There was a stunned silence, and then, an explosion of happy sounds. Benjo and Dannie whooped with joy, Bairn clapped Felix on the back so hard it made him cough, Maria started crying—hopefully, for joy, though Tessa wasn't quite sure. Maria had always been sharply critical of Felix, but then, of whom wasn't she critical? Her mother hugged Catrina and welcomed her to the family.

And with that, a knock came to the door. Tessa opened it

to find rumpled Martin on the stoop with a squirming puppy in his arms. The wind had painted Marty's nose bright red, his hair looked like a gale force had arranged it, and his face was lit with a grin. "Happy Christmas, Tessa!"

After everyone had left for home and before the darkness of evening folded in, Betsy crossed the yard, the frost crunching under her feet as she passed through the deep shadow cast by the barn. It was her Christmas gift to Tessa—a week of milking the cow. Once in the warm barn, she took her heavy cloak off and tossed it on top of a barrel. Something slipped out of her cloak pocket and clunked on the floor. She bent down to pick it up, astounded. It was her lost journal. She was sure she had left it upstairs, sure she had kept it in the cupboard; she'd turned the loft upside down looking for it. She couldn't remember putting it in her cloak pocket, but perhaps she had. Regardless, she had found it. And on Christmas Day!

She skimmed through it, satisfied that it was intact, and slipped it back in her cloak pocket. The sun had dropped below the horizon and shadows cast eerie light against the barn walls. She scooped up hay from a stack and dropped it on the ground in front of the cow. She plucked the milk pail off the wall peg, and the stool, and sat beside the cow, leaning her forehead against its warm, sweet body. She had nearly finished when she realized she wasn't alone.

Caleb.

She blew out a startled breath. He stood a few rods away, watching her with a soft look on his face. She pulled the pail away from the cow so she wouldn't kick it over and spoil all that good milk. She rose to her feet, and approached Caleb slowly. "I was hoping to see you today. I wanted to wish you a happy Christmas."

"My mother was the last person who wished me a happy Christmas."

"Where have you been?"

"Hunting game for the prisoners."

"They're not prisoners, Caleb. It won't be much longer. They'll be free to live where they want to, as they want to."

He gave her a sad smile. "This . . . massacre. It's the first of more to come. The white people are hungry for land. And there are many more of them than Indians."

She dropped her head. Without warning, tears stung Betsy's eyes. The realization of why he had sought her out this afternoon lay like a stone on her heart. "You've come to say goodbye. That's why you're here, on Christmas Day." *Tell me I'm wrong. Oh Caleb, don't be considering such a thing.* But she knew he was, and they need not discuss it further for Betsy to know *why* he was leaving. Even still, she lifted her eyes to him for an explanation.

"I am Indian. I cannot stay in one place for long."

"You're only part Indian, Caleb. You belong here. We are your people too." She knew her tone sounded both urgent and injured, but she was desperate to make him stay.

He lifted his chin. "Soon, you will marry the blacksmith."

She looked up at him, and despite the dim lighting, she could detect great sadness in his face. "Before the attack on my family, Hans and I were planning to wed."

"And you long to return to that time." He stroked her cheek with the back of his fingers, the cheek with the scar running down it, and his gentle gesture nearly undid her.

288

Tears began to spill down her face. "But it can't be done," she whispered. "That attack changed everything. The time in the village changed me." She looked up at him. "I don't know who I am anymore. I don't know where I belong."

"Yes, Betsy. Yes you do. You belong to the Holy One. That will never change." He took her in his arms and she clung to him as he held her, stroking her back. He rested his chin on the pleats of her prayer cap and held her closer. Then he pushed out a sigh that sounded as if it hurt, and he released her, stepping back slightly. His palms clasped her face and she reached up to cover his hands with hers. She wanted him to stay. His somber expression twisted toward a smile.

"Be happy, Betsy Zook." He kissed her scarred cheek and quietly left her, walking silently down the hallway of the barn and into the darkness.

She stared at the door as it shut behind him, and her eyes burned with tears.

The cow shuffled impatiently and Betsy wiped her face, before reaching to pick up the milk pail. As she bent down, she caught a flicker of something moving in the far corner of the barn. She jerked, and the pail splashed milk over her apron. "Who's there?" she called, feeling a chill crawl down her back.

Hans stepped out of the darkness.

"Hans! I thought you'd left for home."

His hat cast his face in shadow, with the brim hiding his eyes. "Dorothea picked up the wrong bonnet. She wanted me to return it, so I went to the house. Anna told me you were in the barn." He took a step closer to her. "It's him. I read in the diary about a man you loved—but I assumed it was me." He scraped a hand over his chin; he seemed dumbfounded.

"Your soul was bound to him, you wrote. I thought you had written of me. But it's . . . him."

"You read my journal? How did you get it? So you . . . did you put it in my cloak pocket?" She paused while she tried to compose her thoughts into a sensible order. How long had he been there? How much had he heard?

Hans thumbed his hat back, frowning, and she saw something flit through his eyes—a strange and urgent light, that crazed look in his eyes before. The look that made her fear him. "You love *him*. The half blood."

"Hans," she said gently, in as calm a tone as she could muster. "Caleb is my friend. He has been good to me."

"You seemed distant, distracted, since your restoration, but I thought it was because of the grief you suffered for your parents." His eyes fastened on her. "It never occurred to me it was because you'd fallen in love with a . . . half blood."

The silence in the barn grew oppressive, even the cow stilled from chewing her feed and turned her big head to watch them.

"Hans, Caleb is my friend," she repeated. "He risked his life to bring me to Beacon Hollow. To the Bauers." She reached out a hand to him. "To you."

"Don't lie to me, Betsy," he whispered. "Please, don't lie to me." He backed away from her, one step, then another, and left the barn the way he'd come in.

21

Beacon Hollow
Second Christmas 1763

Throughout the next day, Tessa kept the puppy by her side. Despite the giver of the gift, Tessa found herself charmed by him. Marty said he gave her the puppy because he realized old Zeeb had switched loyalties to the Zook brothers, and he thought she needed a dog of her own. She laughed as she watched the puppy tear around the kitchen, its tail whirling in a circle. When she went to the loft to work on her sewing, she brought the puppy along and let him curl up on her bed. She decided to name him Rumple.

Betsy came upstairs and sat on the edge of the bed, patting the sleeping puppy. In her other hand was her diary.

Tessa stilled. Her heart started pounding. "So you found it."

Betsy's face held a pensiveness, her pale features seemed strained. "Tessa, by any chance . . . did you give Hans my journal?"

"Your journal?" Her insides felt shaky.

Betsy held it up. "Yes. This journal. Did you give it to Hans?"

A wave of shame and remorse rose and crashed over her, and as it crested, her eyes filled with tears. *Confess, repent, make it right.* Rumpled Marty's words echoed and echoed in Tessa's head. She pulled her eyes from Betsy's to answer. "Yes," she whispered. With a sob, she dropped her forehead to her knees and circled her legs with her arms. She felt sickened by her action, and ashamed. So very ashamed. A hand gently patted her shoulder. *Oh no. No, no, no. Don't be nice, Betsy. Yell or scream or cry or call me names, but please don't be nice.*

"Why?" Betsy said softly. "What could make you do such a thing?"

Tessa winced. Her heart sank lower and lower. "The green-eyed monster."

"What? What's that?"

Tessa chanced a look at her. "Jealousy." She slid off the bed and sank down onto a stool by the fireplace, then dropped her head on her knees again.

"You're jealous of me?"

"Of you. Of Hans. Of Hans and you, together." She lifted her head. "I've loved Hans for as long as I can remember. I was born loving him."

Betsy sank to the ground and leaned against the bed frame, directly across from Tessa. "So *that's* why you've disliked me so."

"Yes. I'm sorry, Betsy. I'm so sorry." She let out a big sigh. "He's never loved me, if that helps. He's only loved you."

Betsy gave her a sad smile. "I've always been jealous of you."

"Of me? Of me." Tessa blinked. "Why?" Why in the world would anyone, *ever*, be jealous of *her*?

"You've always been free to speak your mind. Free to be yourself."

"It's my worst fault. I'm far too outspoken."

"Assured. Confident."

"Maria calls me bold-minded."

"Plucky."

"And I've heard the three stout sisters call me brazen."

"I prefer . . . spirited." Betsy smiled. "There are worse things."

"Like what?"

Betsy's gaze shifted to the window. "Like feeling trapped in a cage when you're meant to fly free." She tipped her head. "Tessa, what made you love Hans?"

"He is so beautiful, I suppose."

"He is, indeed. The comeliest man in all of Pennsylvania. But the strength of his character does not match the strength of his physique. That is a mistake we both made, you and I." Betsy rose and went to the window. "I fear Hans has gone to Lancaster Town. I don't know what he might do, given his state of mind."

"What do you mean?"

"I heard your father say that the Paxton Boys are all over Lancaster Town, drinking and carousing. Hans is angry and hurt. He can be . . . vengeful." She put a hand against the cold window. "And I don't know how to warn Caleb." She touched her forehead against the window. "If he has gone to Lancaster Town, I fear for his life. And there's nothing I can do, not for Caleb, not for Hans. They could not be more different, those two, but they are both very stubborn."

Tessa moved across the floor to sit in front of Betsy, folding her legs under her. "Tell me more about Caleb. Tell me more about the time you spent in the village by the river. I've never asked. I'm sorry I've never asked."

Betsy looked at her for a long while, as if trying to gauge her sincerity. Then she slipped down to the floor beside Tessa and started from the beginning, the night of the raid on her parents' farm. She told Tessa everything, and Tessa told her all she knew too—even the parts that were hard to tell. Hans taking the infected blankets to the Conestogas. Meeting Hans the morning after the raid on Indiantown. They talked until the boys came home from school and supper needed tending and the puppy woke and needed to be taken outside, fast.

That night, Tessa barely slept. She had no idea all that Betsy had endured. Nor did she realize what kind of man Caleb was, or the background of his mother's captivity. Being raised as a tribute child, then going on his journey to become a man and ending up as a slave. Becoming the one who kept watch over others. Like the way he had watched over Tessa when he found her in tears by the sheep pond.

Caleb the Watchman.

Confess. Repent. Make it right.

Make it *right*.

As soon as the cock crowed, Tessa slipped out of bed, dressed, and tiptoed to the stairs.

Betsy rose and leaned on her elbow on the bed. "Where are you going?" she whispered.

"There's something I need to do," Tessa whispered back. "To try and make one thing right."

Stoney Ridge
December 27, 1763

Tessa searched for the stallion all morning long. It was like looking for a needle in a haystack—melting snow hid all the usual telltale tracks. But she knew he would be hungry, and she knew there were only a few places where he could find enough food to satisfy. She tried each place she had seen him feed, and finally decided to check out one last spot.

Despite her fear of rodents, she crossed Faxon Gingerich's cornfield of short stalks, past his big barn and behind his large silo, and headed to a small section of the silo that had rotting wood. Oblivious to Faxon, his harvested corn poured out of the hole. Tessa had seen deer at the corn hole, raccoons, mice, moles, squirrels, all kinds of birds, and one time, she had seen the stallion here. It was like all the wildlife of Stoney Ridge knew of this feeding spot, all except for Faxon the Saxon.

And there was the stallion, just as she had hoped. His long neck was stretched out, his big head was *in* the silo. He was helping himself to a winter meal, thanks to Faxon Gingerich.

She tiptoed close, then clucked her tongue to let him know she was near. He pulled his head out of the silo, big mouth full of corn, and kept chewing as he watched her. She lifted a halter and let him sniff it, then gently wrapped it around his giant head and buckled it. "I think there's someone who needs to meet you."

He let her climb on his back. With one hand on the reins and one hand on his mane, they went toward Lancaster Town.

295

Beacon Hollow

Betsy was filling the bucket with water from the well, wind whipping her capstrings, when Felix came galloping down the lane from the road.

"Where's Bairn?" he shouted, throwing himself off the horse. "Bairn!" He seemed frantic.

Bairn bolted out of his carpentry shop. "What's happened?"

"A mob broke into the workhouse in Lancaster Town. They're dead, Bairn. All dead. Will Sock, his wife, his son." Felix choked on the words.

White-faced, Bairn reached for the horse's bridle. "What of Christy? Of Betty Sock?"

"Dead." Felix seemed wild-eyed with disbelief. "Murdered in cold blood. In broad daylight. I heard the sheriff just . . . stepped aside."

Betsy stared, trying to make sense of it all. She listened to Felix with a growing dread. For a moment all sounds ceased, or seemed to, as if she were underwater. She heard nothing beyond the frantic thumping of her own heart. She didn't want to acknowledge the fear this news had set in her heart. But it came anyway, along with an overwhelming panic.

"Caleb?" she whispered, her eyes wide, her throat hot and tight. "Was he among them?"

"I don't . . . know. The bodies . . . they were . . ." Felix bent to grasp his knees, as if he was going to get sick. "They'd been chopped to pieces. The bodies." Head bowed almost to the ground, he let out a sob. "Our friends' bodies . . ." He breathed in and out, trying to hold himself together.

For a moment Betsy closed her eyes, gulping, unable to

swallow the lump of fear in her throat. Was it possible? Could Caleb be dead? The awful reality hit her full force. Tears filled her frightened eyes, and she pressed a fist to her lips.

Bairn stood ramrod straight, stiffly, woodenly, as if he might snap in two. He spoke in an urgent tone. "Did they make any arrests?"

"No." Felix drew in a deep, unsteady breath and straightened up. "No arrests have been made." Still breathing hard, his eyes were fixed on his older brother. "And our Hans didn't come home last night."

❧

Tessa took a shortcut through the woods to Lancaster Town when she saw a lone figure standing, waiting, through the thick trees. Or rather, he saw her and seemed to be waiting for her. Caleb.

He had a knack for seeing someone before that someone saw him.

She slipped down off the stallion and led him by the halter to approach Caleb. He looked exhausted, covered by a weariness that went bone-deep. "So you have tamed the mighty stallion." He let the horse sniff him, and then the horse did something that surprised Tessa. Surprised, and yet didn't surprise her. The stallion took a step forward and nuzzled Caleb with his nose, a greeting of sorts. On some level, in some part of his memory, this horse knew Caleb, Tessa was sure of it.

She smiled. This felt right. It was the first deep-down-done-something-right feeling she'd had in weeks and weeks. Months, perhaps. "Yes. Or maybe you could say, we tamed each other."

He regarded her thoughtfully, while sliding a hand down the horse's long neck. "You have heard of the massacre?"

Her gaze snapped to his face. "Heard what?"

"In Lancaster Town. In the workhouse. White men burst in and started a rampage."

Tessa struggled to absorb his words. "You were not there?"

"I was there." Caleb kept his eyes on the horse. "But someone pushed me out the door just as the fighting began."

"You escaped." *Thank God.*

A gust of wind circled them. Caleb's long coal-black hair flickered through the air, slapping his shoulders and partially covering his face. He was not looking at Tessa, but at the horse. "I did. Others did not, I fear. I do not know."

Tessa pressed her hand over her mouth and stared at Caleb as he told her what he had seen; she tried to absorb this information, what it meant. Will Sock. Betty and Molly. Had they been killed? She squeezed her eyes shut. She had to get home.

"Caleb, this horse, he's meant for you. And you for him. You need each other." She handed him the lead and he accepted it willingly, which made her glad.

"I will treat him well."

"I know you will. But . . . won't you consider staying in Stoney Ridge? You're welcomed here. You're *wanted* here."

He made a grunting sound that could have meant anything. "Not by everyone."

"But if you leave, Betsy might marry Hans."

"She will definitely marry Hans."

"Why would you let that happen? She loves you."

Caleb crossed his arms and stood spraddle-footed. "Hans loves her. She will forgive him, and learn to love him again."

"Hans doesn't deserve her. You do."

"Life is not that simple." He looked at her with such intensity in his blue eyes that they almost burned Tessa. "Hans Bauer was the one who pushed me out of the workhouse. He tried to dissuade the attackers. He was not successful, but he did try."

Caleb mounted the black stallion, and when he sat on top of that horse, Tessa knew she had done the best thing she could have done by bringing the two together. He looked . . . regal . . . on that black stallion. They belonged together, those two lonely beings.

"Farewell, Little Girl with Big Feelings. May your God bless you for helping me. May He grant you a happy life."

She didn't mind the name so much, not the way he said it. "Goodbye, Caleb. God be with you."

Confess. Repent. Make it right.

❧

All morning, as Betsy pounded and kneaded bread, she stood at the far end of the table so she could keep an eye on the east-facing window, watching for Felix to return with more news from Lancaster Town.

Anna sat near the window, carding wool with two hand carders. She, too, kept nervously glancing outside. At one point, she stopped carding and gave Betsy a sad smile. "That bread is getting such a pounding, I think it will be the lightest, airiest bread we have yet to eat." She looked down at her lap. "And I suspect there will never be finer yarn." She had been carding the same bundle of sheep's wool, over and over.

Betsy sighed and lifted the bread. It was smooth and elastic, silky to the touch. She set it in the dough box for one more rise before baking it. "Waiting for news to arrive . . . it's awful."

Another hour passed before she heard the galloping hooves of a horse come up the lane to Beacon Hollow. She ran to the window and saw Felix picket his horse and march straight down to the sawmill to seek out Bairn. She wanted to run outside, to stop Felix and ask him—beg him—to tell her what he knew of Caleb, but her feet didn't move. Couldn't move. She didn't want the answer.

Anna came up behind her and put a hand on her shoulder. "Betsy," she said softly. "God is sovereign over everything."

"Even this?" Betsy said, leaning her forehead on the cold windowpane. "Even *this* kind of evil?"

Anna didn't answer for a long moment. "He promises to bring good out of all things to those who love Him. All things. Even this."

Not much later, Felix and Bairn came out of the sawmill, somber looks on their faces. Felix mounted his horse and slowly headed, shoulders slumped and head ducked, to the shortcut in the woods that led to Not Faxon's Farm.

Betsy and Anna sat at the table to hear what news Felix had brought of the workhouse massacre. "Felix has just come from town," Bairn started, then stopped and swallowed. "Most of the news, you've already heard. All the Conestoga Indians were slaughtered. Not one survived. Not one." Bairn exchanged a look with Anna—a look that was terribly discomfiting to Betsy. She braced herself, waiting to hear news of Caleb.

The door latch opened and Tessa came in. Her cheeks were bright pink from the cold. Her eyes were red and swollen from crying. The puppy bounded out of its basket and over to her.

"I heard," she said, bending down to pick up the puppy and hold it close to her. "I heard about the workhouse."

"How did you hear?" Anna asked.

"I met Caleb in the woods."

"Oh, thank God!" Betsy clapped her hands over her mouth and started crying. Her heart felt full to bursting. Caleb was alive! "Thank God he wasn't in the workhouse." She felt overwhelming relief, quickly followed by a sweep of shame. While she did not know these Indians, she empathized with the Bauers' sorrow.

"Caleb had been there." Tears slid down Tessa's face. "He escaped from the massacre. He's gone now, heading to the Ohio Valley. On the black stallion."

"Tessa, sit down, please, there's more . . . ," Bairn started, then stopped. "Hans . . . our Hans . . . he *was* in the workhouse."

Tessa saw the shock that riffled across Betsy's face. "It's not what you think," she quickly said.

But Betsy wasn't sure what to think. Thoughts went spinning out of control and her heart thundered. Hans was in the workhouse, part of the mob. How could it be possible? Feelings collided within her—she felt incensed at Hans, she felt guilty that the contents of her journal might have driven him to this. *This.*

Bairn broke into her thoughts. "Tessa, how did you know Hans was there?"

She sat at the table, the puppy on her lap. "Caleb told me."

"What did he say?"

She wiped away tears, swallowed once, then twice. "Caleb said that Hans pushed him out of the workhouse and told him to run for his life. To leave town and not turn back.

He said that Hans was trying to stop the mob." She looked around at each person. "Where is Hans?"

Bairn took a deep breath and reached out to cover Anna's hand. "Felix said Hans was found dead in the workhouse. Not mutilated, not like the Indians were. A stray bullet, most likely." He swiped at his eyes with a sleeve. "Felix has gone to tell Dorothea the news."

For several long seconds, no one moved, no one breathed. They just stared at Bairn, whose eyes were fixed on his hand covering his wife's. An odd feeling came over Betsy as she sat very still. She became aware of the hiss of the fire in the hearth and the sweet yeasty smell of the bread as it baked in the kettle. A kettle Hans had made in his forge. Anna had told her so this very morning as she hooked it on the trammel. A gust of wind shuddered against the windows. The puppy licked at a spot on the table where some food must have been missed. Anna reached across the table to clasp her hand, Tessa put an arm around Betsy's shoulder, but she was barely conscious of them.

Hans was dead. Caleb was alive. Both were gone.

The sound of bells ringing in the air broke the silence, then the earth started rumbling, ever so slightly, just enough to rattle the salt crock on the mantel. Anna crossed the room to peer out the window. Her breath fogged the glass and she had to wipe it clear. She turned back to them with wide eyes. "Oh my. You should all see this." They crowded around her to see Martin Gingerich walk alongside the Conestoga wagon, reins in hand, leading six enormous horses to Beacon Hollow. When he reached the house, he called to the horses to halt.

Bairn went outside to speak to Martin. When he returned to the house, he had an odd look on his face, as if he was trying very hard not to cry. "Martin thought this large a wagon would be needed to bring the bodies back from Lancaster Town. To bury them properly, Martin said—" his voice breaking—"he thought using the Conestoga wagon would be a way to honor them." He drew in a deep breath of air. "Evil will *not* have the last word. It will *not*."

22

Beacon Hollow
January 10, 1764

Early one morning, a messenger arrived at Beacon Hollow with a note for Bairn. Anna heard the rider gallop up the lane and was the first to meet him. The young boy was dressed like the English, he and his lathered-up horse looked like they'd ridden all night. "I was told this was where Bairn Bauer lived."

Anna spun toward the barn and saw Bairn already striding over, Felix beside him. "Here he comes now." She turned back to the rider. "Would you come in to get warm? Take some nourishment?"

"Not until I give this letter to Bairn Bauer."

"What news are y' bringin', laddie?"

Bairn's eyebrows drew together in a slight frown as he opened the envelope and read the letter, but Anna felt the seriousness of its contents deep in the pit of her belly. He glanced up at her. "The Paxton Boys are gatherin' t' march on Philadelphia. Over 250 of them. They want t' overthrow the provincial government. Benjamin Franklin has asked me to come to Germantown and try to reason with them. He's agreed to listen to their grievances."

Felix's eyes narrowed. "What grievances could they possibly have?"

"The same grievances that have spurred them on to do evil. They believe the government has not protected the settlers from Indians."

Felix snorted. "The government has not protected the Indians from the Paxton Boys."

"Mr. Franklin told me to wait for a message from you," the boy said.

"Y' can tell him that I will nae come to Germantown," Bairn said. "I dinnae think my role is t' interfere with the government."

Anna spoke up. "Your role is to strive for peace, Bairn. They will listen to you."

"You think me t' have too much influence, Anna."

"John Elder will listen to you. Use your strongest brogue, roll your *r*'s like you were born in Edinburgh, and he will listen."

"I'll go with you, Bairn," Felix said. "We'll both go."

"You'll both go, and you'll take the Conestoga wagon," Anna said, surprising them all with the force of her words. The wagon was still at Beacon Hollow after being used to carry the bodies of the Conestoga to Indiantown to be buried. "Ride in on the wagon. Ride in with Felix's big horses. They will notice. They will listen."

❧

Beacon Hollow
February 2, 1764

Bairn and Felix had been gone to Germantown for over three weeks. Catrina stayed at Not Faxon's Farm to care for Benjo and Dannie and Dorothea. Without being asked, Martin Gingerich stepped in and managed the daily upkeep of Felix's horses. His father was annoyed with him, but Martin didn't shirk his own responsibilities, and as he often said, his father didn't do his thinking for him. "He'd like to, though," Martin said, grinning.

Anna found herself growing very fond of Martin Gingerich. She had a hunch that Tessa's opinion was softening too. Her eyes sparkled whenever Martin stopped by Beacon Hollow, which was becoming quite a regular thing. This friendship, Anna could see, had substance to it. Something to grow on.

She looked over at Betsy, spinning flax in the corner of the room, head bent down as she examined the distaff. The sun was streaming down on her head, giving her an almost angelic appearance. Her delicate features gave the impression that she was as fragile as a porcelain teacup, yet her spirit was remarkably solid. Sturdy. Resilient. There was a strength to Betsy that had emerged out of the losses she had faced. It was not apparent to others, but Anna saw it and felt it, especially evident after Hans's tragic death.

In a way, Hans gave Betsy a great gift in his sacrificial death. She was free to be her.

Surely, God is sovereign over all things. All things.

Bells pealed in the air. Anna dropped the bread dough she was kneading in the bowl and rushed to the door, not even stopping to grab her shawl. There, coming up the lane, was the enormous Conestoga wagon, with Bairn walking alongside the team of horses. Felix sat on the lazy board, waving to her. She ran down the lane and right into her husband's open arms, not even caring of witnesses. She had felt more frightened about this encounter with the Paxton Boys than even she had realized.

She pulled back and looked at Bairn's gray eyes. "How did it go?"

"Violence was averted," he said, eyes smiling.

"Just by a cat's whisker," Felix said. "Hundreds, some say thousands—"

"A gross exaggeration by my wee brother."

"—of Paxton Boys were there, coming from north, east, south, west, all riled up. To quote John Elder"—and here Felix lowered his voice to a baritone and added a horrible Scottish accent—"'The storm that has been so long gatherin' has finally exploded.'" Felix jumped off the lazy board. "Anna, you should have been there. Our Bairn, alongside Benjamin Franklin—"

"And many others."

"—patiently responding to those hotheaded Scots. Could've gone down a different path, a very violent one, were it not for the forbearance of your husband."

"Again," Bairn said, "credit goes to many others." He pushed the lazy board back against the wagon. "The corner was turned when Benjamin Franklin agreed to read the Paxton Boys' long list of grievances to the government. That seemed to satisfy them and cool their tempers. And it was agreed that those who caused such harm in the Lancaster workhouse would be sought out."

"Sought, yes," Felix said, disgust on his face, "but no bounty on heads was offered."

"It's a start," Anna said.

"Aye, lassie, 'tis a start," Bairn said, turning his gray eyes directly on her. "So what is new in our little town of Stoney Ridge?"

"Well, for one thing, some youth have been waiting for you and Felix to return. For baptisms."

Bairn laughed. "Truly? Well, that *is* fine news. And just who will be bending at the knee?"

"Your daughter, for one. Betsy Zook for another. And . . . believe it or not, a fine young man named Martin Gingerich."

Bairn and Felix exchanged a glance. "Faxon will be outraged," Felix said, looking much too pleased.

"We will fill you in over dinner," Anna said. "You both must be famished."

"That we are. Cold, too. The warmth of the kitchen beckons." Bairn snapped the reins and started the horses toward the barn. First things first. He and Felix would care for the horses before they cared for themselves. That was the way of the farmer.

Anna went back to the house to finish kneading the bread, stopping by the door to examine her rose. Soon, spring would come and the rose would bloom again. That rose. How she loved it. Brought all the way from Ixheim, Germany. How many times had it been dug up? Twice in Germany, twice in the New World. And somehow, it pushed roots down deep into the ground and sent its branches and leaves upward, and it kept on growing, year after year after year. As if it refused to give up.

She knew Maria would call it blasphemous, but she held a belief that the rose's ability to survive despite the unlikeliest of circumstances—not just survive, but thrive—was a sign from Above that all would be well.

She put the bread in the bake kettle, the one that Hans had forged. Soon the house would be filled with a heavenly smell. As she set the table for supper, a new thought occurred to her and her heart was suddenly too full for words. Their table was full. It was *full*.

Surely God's providence knew no bounds.

Beacon Hollow
March 26, 1764

On a sunny Monday morning in March, Betsy, Anna, and Tessa began the weeklong process of serious-minded spring cleaning. Church would be held at Beacon Hollow on Sunday, as well as Felix and Catrina's wedding, and everything was to be scrubbed spotless. Not a single spider was to be left on the property, Anna insisted, not when a wedding was going to be held in her home. Betsy laughed and rolled up her sleeves.

Before the boys left for school at Not Faxon's Farm, they helped Bairn carry the furniture outside and sweep out the ashes in the fireplace. Bairn filled the barrel in the yard with hot water, and the three women spent the morning washing linens and hanging them on a clothesline to dry in the sun. As Anna and Tessa wiped down the inside walls for a new layer of whitewash, Betsy scrubbed the floor with sand until it shone. As she scrubbed, she thought of all the feet that had walked through this kitchen in the six months since she had first come to Beacon Hollow and were now gone—Hans and his stiff leather boots, Caleb in his soft, silent moccasins. Christy, the Conestoga Indian boy, who had arrived bloody and barefoot in the middle of December, bearing news of the Indiantown massacre. She knew it seemed silly, but she was a little sorry to scrub away all evidence that they had once been here.

But they weren't forgotten. She would never forget them. This had been the most important year of her life. She had come to think of it as her pivoting point, in which everything else shifted. She was only seventeen years old, but she had discovered that she could endure much more than she had ever imagined. She knew who she was, and who she wanted to be for the rest of her life. She knew whom she belonged to.

As she went out to the stoop to dump the bucket of dirty water under Anna's rose, she heard a horse gallop out of the woods and into the yard.

"Tessa!" Felix shouted. "Tessa! I saw him! The stallion!"

Tessa ran outside as Felix pulled his galloping horse up hard. "Just a short time ago, I saw him leap over the gate to my broodmare's pasture, like it was nothing more than a log in the road." He was beaming, positively beaming. "Tessa, you were absolutely right. He is a magnificent beast."

"I knew he'd be back," Tessa said. "Deep in my soul, I knew he'd be back."

"Me too. I knew he couldn't stay away from my girls."

"Is he there now?" Tessa asked.

"He was when I left."

That was all Tessa needed. She dropped her brush in the whitewash bucket. Felix reached down a hand and hoisted her up on the horse.

Tessa suddenly remembered Betsy. "Do you want to come? Come with us and see this mighty horse."

She smiled. "No. You go on without me. I think I'll stay here and finish up." She watched them canter off until they disappeared into the woods through the shortcut. Then she lifted her head and let her gaze roam lovingly over the farm: over the lofty barn built tall and square, the neat carpentry shop, the large stone house with Anna's rose planted by the stoop. She smiled at Anna's delight, earlier this morning, when she saw the bud of the first spring rose. Betsy looked toward the wooded hills behind the house, blurred by the haze of spring. Her heart felt full to the point of overflowing.

Somewhere out there, she knew Caleb was nearby. She could feel his nearness. She had known he would return, could sense it in her heart the way Tessa knew the stallion would return. When Caleb was ready—ready to be a part of them, ready to belong—then he would show himself. Until then, she knew he would be keeping watch. Until then, that would be enough.

SNEAK PEEK AT THE FIRST NOVEL
IN SUZANNE'S NEW SERIES!

Phoebe's Light

1

8th day of the ninth month in the year 1767

Phoebe Starbuck flung back the worn quilt, leaped out of bed, and hurried to the window. She swung open the sash of the window and took in a deep breath of the brisk island air, tinged with a musky scent of the flats at low tide. It was how she started each morning, elbows on the windowsills, scanning the water to see which, if any, whaling ships might have returned to port in the night. It was how most every Nantucket woman greeted the day.

Drat! She couldn't see the flags among the jumble of bobbing masts.

Phoebe grabbed the spyglass off the candle stand and peered through it, frantically focusing and refocusing at each mast that dotted the harbor, counting each one. And then her heart stopped when she saw its flag: *The Fortuna*, captained by Phineas Foulger, the foremost, most admired man on all the island, in her opinion. And the ship sat low in the water—signs of a greasy voyage, not a broken one.

Today Phoebe was eighteen years old, a woman by all

rights. Would the captain notice the vast changes in her? She felt but a girl when he sailed away two years ago, though her heart had felt differently. What a day, what a day!

"Make haste, Phoebe dear," her father called up the stairs. "Something special awaits thee."

The morning light lit the room as Phoebe scooped up her clothes. She tugged on a brown homespun dress and combed her hair until it crackled. She wound her thick hair into a flattering topknot, pinned it against the back of her head, then covered it with a lace cap. She gave her bedroom a quick tidy-up, plumping a goose-feather pillow and smoothing the last wrinkle from the bed.

Downstairs, Phoebe smiled as she entered the warm keeping-room, its fire crackling. Father, the old dear, a small and gentle man, sat at the head of the table with a wrapped bundle in his hands and a cat-that-swallowed-the-canary look on his weathered face, seamed with lines.

"There she is, my daughter, my one and only. Happy birthday, Phoebe." He rose and held the seat out for her. When he stood, she noticed the patches on his overcoat, the sheen at the elbows, the fraying threads at his sleeve cuffs. *Not today*, she thought to herself. *Not on this day. I will not worry today.*

Barnabas Starbuck was considered the black sheep of the Starbuck line—oddly enough, because of sheep. Her father had continued to raise sheep for profit, providing a very modest income at best, despite the fact that all his kinsmen were deeply enmeshed in the whaling industry and growing wealthy for it. The gap between Barnabas Starbuck and all other Starbucks had widened enormously in the last decade.

Phoebe loved her father, but she was not blind to his short-comings. He was a kind and generous man but lacked the business acumen—shrewdness—common to his relations. Barnabas Starbuck always had a venture brewing. New enterprises, he called them, always, always, always with disastrous results. He would start an enterprise with a big dream, great enthusiasm, and when the idea failed or fizzled, he would move on to something else.

For a brief time Barnabas fancied himself a trader of imports. There were the iron cook pots he had ordered from a smooth-talking Boston land shark, far more pots than there were island housewives, so many that the lean-to still had pots stacked floor to ceiling. Oversupply, he had discovered, was a pitfall. Thus the pots remained unsold and unwanted, rusting away in the moist island air.

And then Barnabas had an idea to start a salt works factory in an empty warehouse on Straight Wharf, but once again he neglected to take into account the high humidity of the island. The drying process needed for salt production was so greatly hindered by the summer's humidity that the salt clumped and caused condensation on all the warehouse windows.

Her father was quite tolerant of his business failures. "Just taking soundings!" he would tell Phoebe with a dismissive wave of the hand. "Part and parcel of the road to success."

What her father refused to accept was that all roads on Nantucket Island led to the harbor. Nearly every islander understood that truth and was involved, to some degree or another, in the making of tools necessary to outfit whaling and fishing vessels. Phoebe had tried to encourage her father to consider investing in sail making, blacksmithing, ironworks, rope manufacturing. Anything that would tie his enterprise to the sea. But he was convinced whaling was a short-term industry, soon to fizzle out.

Phoebe had a dread, and not an unfounded one, that her father would soon be declared Town Poor by the selectman. The Starbuck kin had made it abundantly clear that they had reached the end of their tether to bail Barnabas out of another financial failure.

And what would become of them then? The Town Poor were miserably provided for.

Not today, she reminded herself as she poured herself a cup of tea. *I am not going to worry today. Today is a special day.*

Leaning across the table, her father handed her a brown parcel, tied with twine.

"A gift? I thought we had agreed no gifts this year." And here was another sweet but conflicting characteristic of her father—he was a generous gift giver, despite a steady shortage of disposable income.

"This is an *inheritance*," he said, beaming from ear to ear. "It has been waiting for thee until the time was right."

Carefully, Phoebe untied the knot and unfolded the paper, both items to use again. Inside the package was a weathered book, bound in tan sheepskin. When she opened it, she had to squint to read the faint ink. "What could it be?" She looked up at him curiously.

"What could it be? Why none other than the journal of Great Mary!"

Great Mary? She was Phoebe's great-grandmother, her father's grandmother. Great Mary's father, Tristram Coffin, was one of the first proprietors to settle the island. Mary was his youngest daughter, regarded as a wise and noble woman, a Weighty Friend to all, oft likened to Deborah in the Old Testament. "I thought the existence of Great Mary's journal was naught but rumor."

"Nay! Nay, 'tis truly hers. Passed along to me from my father, William, and given to him by his father, Jethro. 'Tis meant to be passed from generation to generation, to whomever would most benefit from the wisdom of Great Mary. For some reason, my father felt I needed it the most."

Reverently, Phoebe stroked the smooth brown sheepskin covering. "And thee has read it?"

He was silent for some time, staring into his teacup. "Truth be told, I always intended to but never found the time." His smile disappeared and he looked uncharacteristically chagrined. "The script is faint, my eyes are weak . . . Ink is so vulnerable to humid conditions." He put down his fork and wiped his mouth with his napkin. "And then . . . I have been so busy with my enterprises."

Phoebe had to bite on her lip to not point out the irony of this conversation. "I thank thee, Father. I will take good care of it, and when the time is right, I will take care to pass it on to the person who most needs Great Mary's wisdom."

It was only after breakfast, as Phoebe knotted the strings of her black bonnet under her chin, swift and taut, eager to hurry to the harbor and catch glimpse of the *Fortuna*'s captain, that she realized the sharp point of irony was jabbed not only at her father, but also at her. She was the one in this generation, amongst dozens and dozens of Starbuck cousins, to whom the journal of wisdom had been passed.

A fine, fair morning it was, with the air washed fresh by the rain. The countryside was soft, shades of green, hints of yellows and reds with the coming autumn. Matthew Macy tipped his hat to bid goodbye to the constable and left the gaol, tucked away on Vestal Street, heading toward the wharf where his cooperage was located. A second-generation cooper, Matthew was, with the knowledge of barrel making passed down from his late father. Late . . . but not forgotten. Never that.

He filled his lungs with crystalline air, happy to be outside on this lovely morning and out of the wretched gaol, at least for the next ten hours. After that, sadly, he was due to return.

As he strode down Milk Street, he could hear the sharp cracking of horses' hooves on Main Street. When he turned the corner, he paused to stop and look down toward the harbor. It was a view that always affected him. How he loved this little island. Thirty miles away from the mainland, not too far but far enough. The rain last evening had chased away the usual lingering fog, and even cleansed the air of the pervasive stink of rendering whales. At the moment, the sea was calm, shimmering in the morning sun, but it could change in the blink of an eye, with nary much warning, into a deadly tempest. How well he knew.

Main Street was slick from last night's rain. The markets were setting up for the day, and he had to move deftly to avoid the clusters of townspeople, horses and boxcarts, wheelbarrows and wagons. Every corner swarmed with people: seamen and merchants, black-cloaked Quaker matrons holding tightly to their children's hands, somber men in their broad-brimmed hats, rat catchers, and peddlers, all going about their lives: bargaining, gossiping, laughing, shouting, teasing, jostling.

In front of him, he saw a bonneted Quaker maid step right into the path of a fast-moving horse. He veered around two old salts and leaped into the street to swiftly rescue the woman. As he yanked her toward him and away from imminent danger, he heard her gasp.

"Matthew Macy, take thy hands off me!"

Bother. Of all the Quaker girls on the island to rescue, *this* one had to be Phoebe Starbuck. He lifted his hands in the air to show her that he heard and obeyed. "'Tis you, Phoebe? Hard to discern who is under that enormous coal scuttle. But then, that is what the Friends prefers, 'tis not? To wear blinders to life going on around them."

Ignoring him, Phoebe tugged at her bonnet and straightened her skirts and dusted herself off.

"Do I not deserve a thank-you for saving your life?"

She frowned. "Saving my life might be an overstatement." Another horse and cart thundered by, its wheels splashing her skirts, and she thought to add, "But I am . . . grateful for thy quick thinking."

"Had I known it was you—"

She glared at him. "Thee might have let the horse run me down, no doubt."

"I was going to say . . . I might have let the Quaker brethren come to your rescue. But then, they all seem far more interested to hurry and greet the *Fortuna* than to notice a damsel in distress."

As he looked around the street, he realized he had unwittingly spoken truth—a crowd was growing near the harbor—though he had meant only to sting Phoebe. Being around her brought out a streak of malice in Matthew that he could not restrain. He seldom left her company without cutting her, or the Friends, with some small criticisms.

As she recovered her composure, her dark brown eyes started snapping. She glanced up Main Street. "How did thee sleep last night? Was the stiff wooden plank comfortable enough for thee? And was a breakfast of gruel fully satisfying?"

"Happily, I am a man with simple needs. I can sleep anywhere and eat anything."

"How delightful. The Nantucket gaol sounds like a suitable arrangement for thee."

And then her attention was diverted by the sight of someone she spotted and Matthew used the opportunity to excuse himself. As he rounded the corner to Water Street, he turned his head and stopped abruptly. The sun was shining down on Phoebe, lighting her like a beam. Her bonnet brim was turned up and she was smiling as Phineas Foulger, captain of the newly arrived *Fortuna* whale ship, and his abominable daughter Sarah, approached her.

Why was Captain Foulger so soon off the ship? Most captains waited until the ship's cargo was unloaded, anxious to overlook every barrel of precious oil and ensure it was accounted for in the warehouse.

Then he saw the look on Captain Foulger's face as he caught sight of Phoebe.

A sick feeling lurched through Matthew. His mouth went dry, his palms damp.

Why should he let himself be bothered? Many a night in gaol he had reminded himself that apart from his brother and mother, he cared for no one and no thing.

Discussion Questions

1. Prior to reading this novel, how much did you know about colonial Pennsylvania prior to the American Revolution?

2. The Pennsylvania frontier was a clash of swelling numbers of immigrants and dislocated, disenfranchised natives. Influential leaders, like "fighting parson" John Elder (a true figure in history!), fed a culture of terror by promoting fear and hatred of the native Americans. Separate groups like German Lutherans and Presbyterian Scots-Irish (who normally despised each other) galvanized together to try to force the Quaker-influenced provincial government to subdue and contain all Indians. Can you think of other times in history when the same dynamics were at work? The Jews in Nazi Germany comes to mind. What about in our modern era?

3. There is more than one theme running through *The Return*—the dark side of our humanity with prejudice and racism, with jealousy, greed, and selfishness. How many threads of prejudice did you notice? One subtle example: Tessa's description of rumpled Martin as a

Mennonite. A *Mennonite*, she said, as if it were an unpleasant word.

4. Describe one event in the story that shocked or upset you. Here's one instance: when the warrior toyed with the scalp of Betsy's mother right in front of her.

5. *The Return* also includes the triumph of the human spirit, the ability to endure hardship, and the sovereignty of God in all things. What memorable moment spoke to you in this book?

6. After suffering great harm by the warriors, Betsy Zook encounters other Indians who extend kindness to her—Caleb and the two sisters, Nijlon and Numees. What influence do they have on Betsy? Is it a lasting effect?

7. What did you think of the character Caleb, whose name, in the Shawnee's Algonquin language, means "Keeps watch over"?

8. Caleb was alone, but he was not lonely. What did his sense of security rest on?

9. Bairn gave Felix a piece of wise advice: "What life does to you depends on what life finds in you." When have you seen that insight, good *and* bad, to be true in your life?

10. There's an old saying that seems to fit Handsome Hans: "He's good from far but far from good." To be fair, his frustration and anger about Betsy's captivity was understandable. In fact, his feelings seemed reasonable. But Anna noted that Betsy's captivity seemed to do more harm to Hans than to Betsy. How could that be?

11. Hans saw the scar on Betsy's face as disfiguring. Anna hardly noticed it. Who was right? How did you envision her scar to look? What did the scar represent to Betsy? To Hans?

12. Tessa was very critical of Betsy, yet she never mentioned the scar. Why was that?

13. Hans allowed himself to be carried away by revenge. Tessa allowed herself to be carried away by jealousy. What makes these particular emotions so dangerous?

14. "Evil will not have the last word," Bairn said, after the Conestoga Indians had been slaughtered. "It will *not*." Was he referring to using the wagon to bring the innocent back to Indiantown for burial? Or did he mean something more?

15. In the very last chapter, the stallion returns to Stoney Ridge and to Felix's broodmare pasture. Do you think Caleb had set the stallion free? Why or why not?

16. Did this story alter your perception of human history? It seems as if mankind gets snagged in the "same song, different verse" story over and over again; we don't learn from our past mistakes, nor from our ancestors' failings. Thankfully, God's mercies are new every morning. He is sovereign over all things. *All* things.

Author's Note

What is true in this story? Quite a lot, actually.

The facts of the Conestoga Massacre are true and verifiable. There was a leader of the Conestoga whose name was spelled phonetically, different in every account. He was referred to as Captain John, because the Conestoga Indians took on English names and named their children English names. He was a wise old man, an honest man, considered a friend to the English. He was said to be kind, with a benevolent temper, and he had assisted William Penn with the original treaty in the early 1700s. Will Sock was also a true character, also called Billy Sock, or Will Soc. His mother Betty Sock was mentioned in historical documents. Christy was a little boy who played with English children. If you're interested in learning more about the Paxton Boys and the Conestoga Indian massacre, some excellent books are listed in the reference section.

The details of the Conestoga wagon are true, though its ship-like design was created by German Mennonites who lived in Lancaster County, not by our Amish Bairn Bauer.

These wagons were the trucks of early America; they transported all kinds of goods and products—coal, tools, mail, flour, eggs, on and on—from one end of Pennsylvania to the other. Some days as many as three thousand Conestoga wagons traveled between Philadelphia and Lancaster, as well as to other Pennsylvania cities to the west: Harrisburg and Pittsburgh. Today, US Route 30 and the Pennsylvania Turnpike follow these old wagon trails, which in colonial times were more like bone-jarring, teeth-rattling rocky paths.

The story of the wild stallion, an enormous Flemish draft horse, is true. Legend says that it was bound for Penn's stables but escaped on the docks of Philadelphia. It was thought to have sired the breed that pulled the mighty Conestoga wagons. Each horse wore a set of bells hanging from an arch that was attached to its collar. These bells announced to people (and cattle) that the wagon was coming, so get out of the way. The expression "I'll be there with bells on" originated from the Conestoga wagon team.

Sadly, the Conestoga horse breed is now extinct.

Now here's some fun pieces of historical trivia to end on:

The men who drove Conestoga wagons were called teamsters because they drove teams of horses. Today most truck drivers belong to the Teamsters Union, a union formed when men drove teams rather than trucks.

Those teamsters, robust and rugged men, smoked four-for-a-cent cigars. They were first known as *Conestogas* but soon shortened to *stogies*.

Acknowledgments

A big thank-you goes to my trusted first-draft readers, Lindsey and Tad, who gave up movies on a long plane ride to read the manuscript of *The Return*, start to finish, in its messy, still-a-work-in-progress state. Lindsey—you had the idea of Betsy's facial scar, a visible sign of what she had endured as a captive. Tad—a comment you made inspired the use of the Conestoga wagon to transport bodies of the massacred Indians to a burial site. Your suggestions and insights made this a much better book. *So* much better.

A big thumbs-up to my family, for encouragement and tolerance and "space" while I dove into the eighteenth century. I suspect it's a tiny bit challenging to live with someone whom you can't ask a simple question without her responding, "Not now! There's an Indian attack going on in my head!"

My gratitude goes out to Joyce Hart, my faithful and oh-so-supportive agent, head of The Hartline Literary Agency.

Heartfelt thanks to my wonderful editors, Andrea Doering and Barb Barnes, and the entire marketing, publicity, sales, art, and editorial team of Revell. All of them, from start to finish, go above and beyond to connect books to readers. Michele, Karen, Cheryl, Jennifer, on and on. So many eyes, hands . . . and hearts are part of this work, and I am so very grateful to each one of you.

To my readers near and far who have enriched my life in countless ways through encouraging emails, letters, gifts, and prayers. *You* are the reason I write. You bless my life!

There's a Post-it note stuck on my computer: "Draw near to the Divine Artist." That is my prayer, every day, as I sit down to work. I like it for two reasons: First, it reminds me to look to God for inspiration and imagination. Second, with each book I write, my hope is that readers will get to the last page with a longing to draw closer to the Divine Artist.

References

Ammon, Richard. *Conestoga Wagon*. New York: Holiday House, 2000.

Eshleman, H. Frank. *Lancaster County Indians: Annals of the Susquehannocks and other Indian Tribes of the Susquehanna Territory from about the Year 1500 to 1763, the Date of their Extinction*. (Copyrighted by H. Frank Eshleman, Lancaster County: 1909.)

Fisher, Leonard Everett. *The Oregon Trail*. New York: Holiday House, 1990.

"General History of Lancaster," PA-Roots.com, http://www.pa-roots.com/lancaster/books/lancasteranditspeople/chapter1.html.

Grove, Myrna. *The Path to America: From Switzerland to Lancaster County*. Morgantown, PA: Masthof Press, 2009.

Kenny, Kevin. *Peaceable Kingdom Lost: The Paxton Boys and the Destruction of William Penn's Holy Experiment*. New York: Oxford University Press, 2009.

Seaver, James E. *A Narrative of the Life of Mrs. Mary Jemison*. Norman, OK: University of Oklahoma Press, 1992.

Silver, Peter. *Our Savage Neighbors: How Indian War Transformed Early America*. New York: W. W. Norton & Company Inc, 2008.

Tunis, Edwin. *Colonial Craftsmen and the Beginnings of American Industry*. Cleveland, OH: World Publishing Company, 1965.

Tunis, Edwin. *Frontier Living*. Toronto, Canada: Fitzhenry & Whiteside Limited, 1961.

Suzanne Woods Fisher is the bestselling author of *The Letters*, *The Calling*, the LANCASTER COUNTY SECRETS series, and the STONEY RIDGE SEASONS series, as well as nonfiction books about the Amish, including *Amish Peace*. She is also the coauthor of an Amish children's series, THE ADVENTURES OF LILY LAPP. Suzanne is a Carol Award winner for *The Search*, a Carol Award finalist for *The Choice*, and a Christy Award finalist for *The Waiting*. She is also a columnist for *Christian Post* and *Cooking & Such* magazines. She lives in California. Learn more at www.suzannewoodsfisher.com and connect with Suzanne on Twitter @suzannewfisher.

Bestselling author
SUZANNE WOODS FISHER
invites you back to the beginning
of Amish life in America

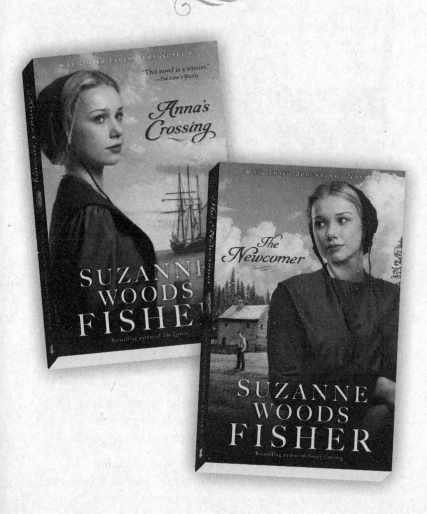

DON'T MISS ANY OF THE BISHOP'S FAMILY

"Suzanne is an authority on the Plain folks. . . .
She always delivers a fantastic story with
interesting characters, all in a tightly woven plot."

—BETH WISEMAN, bestselling author
of the DAUGHTERS OF THE PROMISE and the LAND OF CANAAN series

Revell
a division of Baker Publishing Group
www.RevellBooks.com

Available wherever books and ebooks are sold.

WELCOME TO A PLACE OF UNCONDITIONAL LOVE AND UNEXPECTED BLESSINGS

THE INN at EAGLE HILL

Fisher intrigues and delights with stories that explore the bonds of friendship, family, and true love.

STONEY RIDGE SEASONS